About the author

John served in the Royal Marines for twenty-five years and has travelled the world extensively. He visited Antarctica on several Polar expeditions and was awarded the MBE and Polar medal. He also lived in New Zealand for seven years.

An Expedient Death is the sequel to *In Her Sights*, his first novel published in January 2020. Its main protagonist is a woman who thrives on any challenge and ultimately becomes a cool and calculated killer.

John always felt he wanted to write, and now feels there are many more books to come. His style is open and reactionary, and his creative mindset develops many twists and turns, in multi-faceted plotlines.

John loves outdoor life, enjoys walking, cycling and playing golf, and visiting his fitness gym. He was widowed in 2014 and has two married children and three grandchildren. He lives near Bourne in Lincolnshire with his cat, Bagsy.

AN EXPEDIENT DEATH

John Kimbrey

AN EXPEDIENT DEATH

Vanguard Press

A CIP catalogue record for this title is
available from the British Library.

ISBN 978-1-80016-141-2

*Vanguard Press is an imprint of
Pegasus Elliot MacKenzie Publishers Ltd.*
www.pegasuspublishers.com

First Published in 2021

**Vanguard Press
Sheraton House Castle Park
Cambridge England**

Printed & Bound in Great Britain

Dedication

This for my family…

Acknowledgements

I gain inspiration from many friends, who provide me with
characters that both create and drive my stories forward.
I thank Jude White, who works beyond her brief, my friend Kate
who is always on hand for an opinion and my special thanks to
Bryan O'Callaghan.

PROLOGUE

In Her Sights, a prequel to this book sees a young woman, Edwina (Ed) Mitchell, disguise herself and travel to war-torn France in 1916 to fight in her twin brother's place. She survives twelve months in the trenches but is shot during a sniper mission into No Man's Land, and on an operating table, her secret is discovered. A British general, embarrassed that a woman has been one of his soldiers for a year, falsely accuses Edwina of treason. After a 'one-sided' military investigation, she is charged as a German spy and sentenced to death by firing squad. But through the extraordinary bravery of some British officers, her comrade and friend Frank Smith and her brother, Edward, who travels to France without her knowledge to take her place, she is secretly rescued and returns to England.

The army general responsible for the travesty of justice believes she is dead. This is the extraordinary tale of what comes next.

CHAPTER 1

As the shots rang out in the secluded courtyard of the chateau, Lieutenant Cornelius (Corn) Cavanagh found himself shaking uncontrollably. Private Ed Mitchell dropped to the ground, her body wheezing involuntarily as the air was driven from her lungs. The firing squad were frozen like statues, still on aim, waiting for the order to lower their weapons. As Corn looked across, he could see a tear roll down the cheek of the young private closest to him. It was a bitter moment.

A line of witnesses watched the condemned soldier lying in the dirt before the captain of the guard suddenly reacted. He swallowed hard as he waved the young medic across, then gazed at the six riflemen, the faintest wisps of smoke drifting gently from their rifle barrels. The medic crouched beside the crumpled body, which had, strangely, ended up twisted sideways, the frozen face of the soldier at total peace for all to see. Down on one knee, feeling for a pulse at the neck, he hesitated as he looked down at the soldier's chest. He prayed not to see any rise and fall. This time, there was only blood oozing from the bullet holes high in the chest. He moved his fingers across to another position on her neck, then again, seeking to be absolutely sure the soldier was dead. Only then did he lift his head to the officer in charge.

'Mitchell's dead, sir,' he said solemnly. The officer nodded, briefly, before turning towards the stretcher bearers who were instructed to take the corpse away. He ordered the squad of men to unload, steadying the nerves of those who had taken this young life. They lowered their rifles, cocking them almost in unison, removing the spare rounds and placing them back in their side pouches. The officer calmly dismissed the squad, and they hastily stepped away to a narrow door, only the rear man looking back momentarily. The officer took a deep breath and sighed, thanking

God quietly for not having a repeat of his last execution when he had endured the horrific experience of finding a heartbeat in the soldier stretched out before him. It resulted in the worst of all nightmares, as he had had to use his sidearm.

The padre led the gathered officers and men through the door, one by one. Only then did the young lieutenant walk across to where Mitchell was being lifted onto the blood-stained stretcher. He pulled out his handkerchief and blew his nose, loudly, before speaking quietly to the two men. They laid Ed down, gently, before stepping back.

The compassion Corn felt gripped him with a powerful force. His guilt troubled him as he clearly hadn't done enough to save this fine soldier's life. As he crouched down, he stared at the bullet entry holes in her chest and knew the rounds would have passed right through her tender young body. Suddenly his eyes filled with tears. He removed his leather glove to wipe his eyes before reaching down to touch Ed's right hand, thinking how different she now looked, at peace from the world. He thought back to when they had first met at the firing range a little over a year before. He remembered the immature, small-framed young soldier who had so quickly gained respect from the men she came to fight with, becoming a first-class shot.

With a sad heart, he pushed his knuckles into his own eyes to hold back his tears, but it was futile, and he wept deeply. Behind him, the two soldiers witnessed his distress and wished they were somewhere else. He looked up into the sky and said a silent prayer before his eyes were drawn once again to the fresh-faced sniper he had known so well. He buttoned up the top pocket of her tunic and stood up, looking at the blood now on his fingers. He took one step back and saluted, holding it for several moments. The two young soldiers next to him straightened up in respect, standing to attention. After a brief pause, Corn dropped his arm.

'Where's the grave site?' he asked. The two soldiers looked at each other with worried eyes.

'Don't know, sir,' said one.

'Captain Bridges at HQ has the details, sir,' said the other, nervously. 'Can we go, sir?'

Corn pondered his answer, before nodding his head. 'Yes, yes of course,' he said slowly, and the two men quickly jumped forward to cover Mitchell's body with a dark blue army blanket. They slowly stood upright, lifting her up, before heading away. He reached inside his tunic and pulled out his battered silver cigarette case, looking down at the blood-stained soil that now held his footprint. He placed a cigarette between his lips and held it there for several minutes before squatting down to reach into the soil. He grasped a handful of blood-soaked dirt, shaking his head. General Davis has a lot to answer for, he thought, promising himself to somehow avenge this unnecessary death.

He then heard the sound of distant thunder and looked up to see dark clouds racing in overhead, replacing the blue sky that had been present just minutes before. The gods are angry, he thought, as the rain started to fall, gently at first as if cleansing the earth at his feet. Steadily the light shower turned heavier and then a deluge fell from the dark sky. The noise around him increased, impacting on the silence that had prevailed before. Puddles quickly formed all around the courtyard and the rain soaked his uniform, but he didn't care. He couldn't move; the cigarette drooped as it became sodden and he pulled it from his mouth, discarding it. Water ran from the back of his army cap, trickling down his neck, and he shivered. A pool formed around his boots and he looked skywards once again, the rain hitting his face, masking the tears that flowed down his cheeks. His emotions were raw.

The rain eased, and as quickly as it had arrived, it stopped. He blew droplets from his nose and mouth several times, without real effort. He was alone, his thoughts far away. He knew what he had to do.

As he turned to leave, an empty .303 rifle cylinder caught his eye. He picked it up, looked at it, then put it in his trouser pocket. He walked away and moments later found himself back at the rear of the chateau, standing by the car, not remembering leaving the courtyard. He climbed into the back of his CO's staff car, sinking into the dark leather seat, looking directly ahead with a heavy heart. The driver didn't speak, just gently pulled away, heading for the open road.

Within minutes, the trees by the roadside were flashing by as the sun flickered sporadically through the lower branches, making him squint. He leant against the side window, his breath creating circles on the glass, his mind numb. Time passed slowly.

He avoided the driver's eyes in the rear-view mirror, and within the hour the vehicle had pulled up amongst a city of tents back at HQ. A squeal of brakes forced Corn to stir, the driver careful not to catch the officer's eye. Corn reached for the handle, stepped out and gently pushed the door shut. The car moved off, leaving the lieutenant standing in thick mud by the roadside as he decided his next move. He replaced his cap, took a breath and set off.

Major Hesketh-Pritchard was sitting in his tiny bunker in the rear echelon of brigade headquarters, sucking on an empty pipe, looking around for his tobacco tin. He had only put it down a few minutes ago, but his mind was in turmoil following what had happened earlier that day. As he tapped his tunic pockets for the fifth time, saliva started to hang from the stem of the pipe before falling to the floor in little globules. He pulled the pipe from his lips and sucked his spittle back into his mouth, just as his batman leant into the bunker.

'Sir, Lieutenant Cavanagh for you,' he said.

'Oh, right, show him in, Sinclair.' He stood up and stepped around his small desk. Corn quickly threw up a salute before reaching forward to shake the major's hand. They looked into each other's eyes, holding the handshake firmly for several moments.

'Hello, Corn, take a seat,' the major said, suddenly spotting his tobacco tin in the dim light, tucked behind the photograph of his son on his desk. The young lieutenant sat down and took off his cap. Neither man spoke. The major frowned before stuffing pungent strings of tobacco into his pipe, as the lieutenant looked at him blankly.

The major placed his thumb onto his silver Ronson lighter and stroked it gently, watching Corn in front of him as smoke spilled into the air.

'I am aware the execution was carried out, as ordered by General Davis, and I am desperately sorry. Mitchell was a fine soldier, there is no doubt about that. I am also aware Davis didn't follow correct military protocol. As the divisional commander, and given these rare circumstances, it is clear even to me he should have instructed London to remove Mitchell from France and conduct the court martial in England. I am convinced if this had happened, it would have been a completely different outcome. Having said that, we are now duty-bound, as officers, to accept this outcome or we will feel the full strength of military law ourselves. But be advised, I have been informed that the War Office are after his blood. I say this in the strictest confidence, but his head will roll, I can assure you of that.'

Corn was about to speak but then closed his mouth, and for a few seconds calculated the best way to express himself. The major watched his young officer's agony as his eyes slowly watered and his top lip twitched, before suddenly he leant forward, cupping his hands over his face. He blubbed, once, then heaved upwards in a roar of despair, crying like a baby. The major's heart sank. He wanted to comfort his young friend but simply could not do so. He placed his pipe on his desk and waited. He had seen a great deal of action in the past year and twice had received a mention in dispatches for his leadership in the field. He needed all his strength now.

A moment later, Corn pulled his handkerchief from his pocket, blew his nose and wiped his eyes. He took a deep breath and sat upright, holding his CO's gaze.

'Sir, I apologise. I should not have let myself weep in front of you. I have today witnessed the death of a young soldier, shot by bullets with the general's name on. Mitchell showed the greatest loyalty and professionalism I have ever had the honour to witness and I feel we have let her down terribly. Senior officers of the British army have allowed this to take place and it makes my blood boil. Sir, if you would oblige me, I need to get away from all this. I have several weeks' leave owing and I respectfully request to take some of it with immediate effect,' he said with a firmness the major didn't expect.

'I would not be doing my duty if I did not allow you to grieve, as it is clear you are suffering more than most. This was not your fault, Corn. Mitchell took it upon herself to come here and for her own reasons that we are not privy to. You have not acted incorrectly in any way during these procedures and you must now remain respectful of the military system. You must, above all, act as an officer and a gentleman and show the utmost control in front of the men. I do, however, understand that you feel something should be done, so to support the actions that I know are about to take place in London, I have this morning sent a confidential letter to the War Office with my summation of the events that took place and requesting an urgent enquiry into this matter. I know this is after the event, but it's all I can legally do. So, as far as I am concerned, we as a squadron have done all we can. There is no point in us discussing this further, we have to trust the system,' he said firmly.

Corn nodded, wanting to speak, but his emotions started to build once more, and he was concerned he would embarrass himself again. He coughed several times and took a deep breath.

Major Hesketh-Pritchard reached into his drawer to remove a leave pass.

'I will happily grant you leave but think carefully about what you do next. I will not be able to help you if you follow a path that may bring yourself or the squadron into disrepute.' He paused and looked at his lieutenant to try and gauge his thoughts. 'How much leave do you want?'

'I would like two weeks, sir,' Corn said calmly.

'I will need to speak to the brigadier, as I can only grant you seven days, but under the circumstances, I am confident your request will be approved. Wait here.' He stood up and disappeared.

As Corn sat alone, overcome by his CO's perception, he swallowed several times, trying to clear the guilt building up inside his head. He knew he must give nothing away, to protect not only himself but also this man he so greatly admired. Without warning, the major reappeared behind him, and Corn sat up straight.

'You have been granted ten days plus a travel day, Corn,' he said, and began filling in the form.

'Thank you, I will happily take that, sir,' he said, nodding.

'You will need to sort out duties and rosters with Darcy and the sergeant major, so shall we say from twenty-two hundred hours?'

Corn stared at him, his mind racing, realising all that needed to be done.

'Yes, sir, thank you,' he said, standing and replacing his cap. The CO filled in the various lines on the leave pass before signing it at the bottom. He reached for the squadron crest stamp and breathed on it several times before bashing it hard onto the form, the ink being just soft enough to leave an imprint. The major then stood and Corn reached out to shake his hand, glancing briefly into his eyes.

'Just be advised, Lieutenant, do not venture into anything you will regret. Take your leave and come back refreshed,' the major said, handing the pass over. Corn cast his eyes over it before folding it carefully and pushing it into his tunic top pocket. He saluted, nodded once at his CO, and left.

Corn set off immediately towards a series of communication trenches, heading back to his company lines. He had a great deal to do before he could depart this blessed war for England later that day. He needed to locate two of his men urgently to make a proposition he knew they wouldn't refuse. But first, he had to visit the squadron headquarters. As he trudged forward in ankle-deep mud, many men spoke to him, but he remained in a daze, oblivious to anything other than the courtyard back at the chateau.

He needed to focus on the job in hand and breathed deeply, trying to stop himself being overwhelmed by the immense pressure he was under.

He finally reached his company HQ and offered his leave pass to the sergeant major who entered his details into a large buff-coloured book before returning the pass to the young officer.

'Will there be anything else?' he asked politely.

'Do you know where Lieutenant Darcy might be, Sergeant Major? He will be picking up my duties whilst I am away. Also, can I have two leave passes for Privates Gibbs and Miller? I promised to sign them off before I departed.'

The sergeant major looked up at him, remembering young Mitchell, before reaching into his drawer. He wrote the names on them, then stamped and initialled them in the top corner before handing them over. Corn dated and signed them and wrote 'seven days' in the appropriate box before handing them back.

'I will inform them they are ready to collect from you, Sergeant Major. Thanks for that. And Darcy?' he asked.

'Ah yes,' the sergeant major replied, reaching for his notebook. 'I think he might still be engaged in this morning's recces that have been taking place since zero three thirty. If so, he should still be at the front-line trench, section Bravo Charlie,' he said, closing his notebook. The young lieutenant turned to leave, then thanked him almost as an afterthought.

Corn looked at his watch and saw that he had a little over ten hours to prepare his getaway. Locating Gibbs and his observer Miller was now his priority. He walked north towards the front line, crossing troops on rotation, with long lines of grim-looking chaps heading to the front and hundreds of men smiling as they headed south for a rest. Many offered their respects, but he largely ignored them and just plodded on. At one point, he found he was walking up a down trench, and many soldiers looked at him in annoyance as they had been drilled for many months to stay disciplined, but no one said a word. He felt no guilt, his mind elsewhere, but then as he turned the corner at a cross trench point, he almost knocked Darcy over, coming the other way.

'Darcy, I was just coming to find you,' he said, steadying the man with both hands.

This young lieutenant had only arrived in theatre three months earlier but had quickly become a respected figure amongst his subordinates, even though he stood barely five feet tall. He staggered backwards slightly, greeting Corn enthusiastically with a firm handshake. The gap from a front tooth that he had lost after falling onto an upturned rifle just days before showed clearly as he smiled. He was about to speak but Corn cut him off abruptly, pulling him to one side. He reached for his ops book in his inner pocket and offered it to Darcy.

'I have some urgent leave, Darcy, and you will have to cover my chaps for a week or so. Here's my ops book with everything up to date,' he said quickly. The smaller man held out his hand, accepting it without question. 'I have also signed leave passes for Privates Gibbs and Miller so they will be away for seven days from tonight. Think that's it. Stay safe.'

Darcy hadn't spoken a word and was looking down at the book in his hand while shaking Corn's hand with the other.

'Oh, can you also link up with HQ as there are to be new orders for next week. Thanks.' Corn turned and left him standing, a little stunned. By the time Darcy looked up, Corn was already ten yards away. He shouted something, but Corn was thinking of his next task and never looked back.

He walked quickly away, his mind racing as he collected his thoughts. Many of the young soldiers looked up, smiling in acknowledgement of the officer they recognised, some speaking to him, but he wasn't there for conversation and now sought the one NCO that he had become closest to, Sergeant Worrall.

He was now a trusted friend, and after a brief search, he found him leaning against the entrance to his dugout, writing. You could tell the man a long way off, with a huge bushy moustache, similar to one you might see on a walrus, shielding his face and the gaps in his teeth. He used to joke that he could hide three cigarettes in his 'tache' and you would never know. As Corn approached, a smile ripped across his face and he stood straight to greet him.

'Hello, sir, how ya doing?' he said as he held the butt of a small cigarette in the corner of his mouth. Behind his back, Corn was exercising his right hand, gathering strength to take on Worrall's firm handshake. The sergeant watched with a squinted eye as the officer closed in, then he put his notepad down, and with wide grins, their handshake ritual began. Their right hands snapped forward and their faces grimaced as their two hands locked and tightened their grip in a battle for supremacy. Corn, however, had been fooled on this occasion as Worrall had pulled back slightly at the very last moment, thus gripping the lieutenant's fingers instead of his full hand. Cavanagh instantly knew the cause was lost and winced as the blood was squeezed from his hand. After just a few seconds, he conceded.

'Have you next time,' he said, trying to get the circulation back, as the two men giggled like school children.

'Now, what can I do for you, sir,' said the old hand, regaining his composure.

Corn moved in a little closer before speaking. 'Dick, I am to be away for the next ten days or so. Lieutenant Darcy will be covering for me, so please show him the respect and support you show me and take good care of my chaps, would you?'

'No problem, you know me, sir, I will ensure all is well,' the sergeant said with a grin.

'Can you let me have a bandolier of ammo, no questions asked?' Corn watched Dick's eyes squint, very slightly, before he turned and reached into his shell scrape.

'Here you go, sir,' he said, not asking any questions.

Corn looked at him carefully, knowing full well he could be trusted, and so at this delicate moment decided to open up.

'Look, I need you to know something,' he said, peering round carefully to check no one was in earshot. 'I am taking some leave as I have something urgent to take care of in Blighty.' He paused and took a breath.

'I am heading to General Davis's Yorkshire home, to get revenge for young Mitchell,' he said bluntly. The sergeant didn't flinch; he just stared into the officer's eyes.

'I am going to take Gibbs and Miller with me so will need some rations and other equipment. Can you oblige me?'

Sergeant Worrall continued to stare at him, and Corn's heart thumped heavily in his chest. He suddenly started to worry that he had taken their friendship too far. Dick took a long drag on his cigarette before dropping the stub to the ground. He moved in close to his officer's ear.

'At last, someone is thinking of Mitchell and the regiment,' he said stoutly, reaching for his notebook. 'General Davis is a bastard, and needs hanging for what he has done.' He found a clear page and was ready to jot down his lieutenant's needs.

'Right, sir, what do you need and how long do I have?'

Corn looked at the man he had admired from the first day they had met, who had become a father figure to so many of the lads since they arrived in France, including him. He pulled a small piece of paper from his pocket.

'You won't need that, Dick; it's all written down here,' he said, handing it over. 'Can we collect everything at twenty-one hundred?' he asked, hopefully.

Richard Worrall, a man of honour and well-liked by the men, scanned the piece of paper before nodding. 'No problem, sir.'

Corn thanked his friend and shook his hand, more gently this time, before stepping back into the mass of bodies. Two down, two to go, he thought and headed off to find Gibbs and Miller.

**

Just before twenty-two hundred, he arrived at HQ. Across the road a truck was standing with its engine running, the driver helping to pass kitbags into the rear to smiling soldiers. Corn knew he might never see this land again as he was planning a risky strategy that would test his skills and tenacity. As he reached the rear of the vehicle, he saw Gibbs sitting by the tailgate and passed his officer's holdall up to him. Miller then appeared and between them, they stowed their kit without speaking. Corn looked at Gibbs until he had his full attention. He then mouthed

23

the words 'Have we got everything?' Gibbs nodded once, not wishing to draw attention to himself, and Corn wandered around to the front of the vehicle and clambered up into the passenger seat. He heard the rear tailgate slam shut and in seconds the driver climbed into the cab beside him.

'All set, sir?' said the driver, lighting a cigarette he'd taken from his pocket. Corn nodded as the man selected first gear with an almighty crunch, yelling out of the window to someone below, before pulling away. The driver skilfully pumped the clutch twice each time he changed gear as they sped away.

They were soon clear of the thousands of troops that littered the roadside heading south-west. After twenty minutes, the driver turned right towards the coast and Boulogne. Corn was hopeful they could catch the half-past midnight boat that would arrive in Folkestone around five thirty a.m. With a calm sea and a bit of luck, he could be eating breakfast at his mother's table by eight o'clock. He settled back on the wooden seat, the movement gently easing him into a troubled sleep.

He didn't remember the journey and was suddenly woken by voices, the driver talking out of the window to a man below him. Corn opened his eyes slowly, his neck a little stiff, but he could see lights and ships all along the docks. The driver took back his orders sheet from the sentry before crashing the engine into first gear once again and pulling forward into a long line of military vehicles. He switched off the engine. Corn thanked the lad, seeing his face for the first time, and threw him a pack of cigarettes before dismounting. When he got to the rear of the truck, the twenty or so young soldiers were all jumping down and gathering their gear, in fine spirits. Blighty just thirty-five miles away!

Corn collected his bag and then spotted his two protégés, before heading over to the embarkation line. It was a noticeable change, seeing the young men who had fought so gallantly now cheerful and bright even at this very late hour. The queue shuffled forward slowly towards an MP — military police — checkpoint where they offered their ID cards and leave passes before being allowed through. They walked on for a hundred yards or so, circling around a large building, before arriving outside a single-storey warehouse with the words *Embarkation Point* emblazoned on it in large letters. He walked towards the officers' entrance where his leave papers and pass were inspected again. Once through, he followed other officers towards the canteen and received a mug of tea and a French pastry, the first nourishment he had had since earlier that day.

As the room slowly filled, he saw Gibbs and Miller enter through a door on the far side, but no one would have assumed they were together for their eyes never met. As he looked for a seat, Corn recognised an old friend from Sandhurst, but followed his own rules and stepped away to find a quiet spot near the door, determined not to attract any attention.

At just before midnight, they were called forward to board the boat, officers first. Corn waited almost till last, before rising from his seat and joining the tail end of the queue. They walked up the gangway of the aptly named boat for men going on leave: *The Riviera*. At the top, he was met by an extremely tall MP corporal, with part of his ear missing. His papers were inspected for a third time, but the MP seemed only to check his name before writing something in a book. He then stamped 'Approved' onto the bottom corner and as he handed Corn's papers back, he asked sternly, 'Any weapons, ammunition or explosives in your possession, sir?'

Corn froze for a split second, before regaining his composure. 'No, Corporal, just my penknife.' His first lie of the evening.

'That will be fine, sir. Please go through and up onto 02 deck.'

Corn placed his documents back in his coat pocket and wandered along the starboard rail to watch the crew cast off. A short time later the gangway was dragged back onto shore and the smokestack above him began belching heavy black smoke into the dark sky. He could smell the coal and the sparks flew away like the embers of a bonfire in a strong breeze.

Within minutes the boat was free from its mooring and slowly heading out into a choppy sea. Before he went below, he watched the shoreline slip astern until the only lights he could see were the millions of stars, a sight he had observed a hundred times since his arrival in France. He could feel the engine vibrations beneath his feet, in a steady rhythm, as the bow pushed its way through the dark sea. He dropped down two flights of stairs to the officers' deck, locating a seat on the starboard side amongst officers of all regiments. A major, one eye covered with a medical dressing, kindly offered him a smoke. He reached for a Player's cigarette and dug out his silver lighter, flicking the primer in one go. He lit the officer's cigarette first, then his own and inhaled the strong tobacco before settling back in his seat. The boat now rocked and jerked every few seconds as it fought the waves, but it didn't stop him from resting his tired eyes. A moment later, his boot was kicked by someone and he sat up to see the officer next to him pointing to a young woman with a large tea pot.

'Tea, sir?' she asked. But, before he could answer, a mug was filled and passed over to him. In the gloom of the lanterns that swung in unison with the movement of the ship, he reached forward with both hands to receive the welcome brew, made with real milk! As he drank, the warmth seemed to flood his inner being and he thanked the ladies as they moved away to serve others.

The first hour passed quickly and he spent the time dozing in the gloom, realising he was more fatigued than he had thought. It seemed only a short time before he felt the engine vibrations reduce beneath his feet; the crossing almost complete. People all around him started preparing for disembarkation and he stood to stretch, but the ceiling above was low, causing him to bend his arms. As people moved away, he reached for his kit and steadied himself against a bulkhead until called forward by the deck officer. Men started to gather aft, following the disembarkation arrows, but he realised it would be some time before he stepped on English soil. He stood watching the faint glow of the morning appear slowly before him until they finally arrived in Folkestone at zero four forty. When called, he wandered down towards the gangway, eager to be home for the first time in over a year.

He walked through the MP checkpoint but was not spoken to or searched, so headed out of the port towards the waiting bus queues. He stood back against a wall, running through the orders he had given his men. He smiled to himself as he recalled their reaction when he had spoken to them in the darkness of their shell scrape. It was as he had hoped and he would always remember the loyalty they had shown to their dead friend. That was just eighteen hours ago and here they were, back in England. If they failed in their bid to avenge Ed Mitchell, they would either be dead or locked in a prison cell waiting for a court martial. Only God knew what their destiny might be.

They had agreed to meet at eighteen hundred hours the following day in the nearest pub to the railway station in Pickering, a small Yorkshire town north of the great city of York. That gave them all plenty of time to locate and purchase equipment and provisions for their stay and it allowed the men to grab a night on the town before the long journey. He knew full well the chaps would take this opportunity to find a pub or two, following their request for a few hours to unwind. Who was he to deny them that? He had withdrawn much of his last three months' salary and furnished them with sufficient money to pay for train tickets and buy the items on the kit list, with some to spare. He knew they were the most reliable men he had under his command and soldiers he could trust.

When the bus pulled up, he paid for a single ticket to Canterbury but asked the driver if he would drop him on the roadside next to the Aylesham turn. He nodded and Corn walked to the back of the bus to find a seat.

They reached the outskirts of Canterbury just before seven a.m. and the driver dropped him, as agreed, at the junction. As the bus pulled away, the road was quiet and he crossed over, standing on the corner for a few minutes, hoping a vehicle might come his way. Alas, none did, so he pulled his holdall over his shoulder, took one last look up the road and started walking towards home.

Within the hour, he was striding into the marketplace in the village centre and headed past the post office into Church View.

His mother's cottage appeared, with its bright yellow livery, just as he remembered it. He clipped the latch on the gate, the hinges squealing loudly as he pushed it open, causing the kitchen curtains to twitch. He closed the gate and turned just as the door burst open, his mother still in her dressing gown, standing with her arms outstretched and a smile wider than the dawn. He walked towards her and dropped his kit on the door mat before she reached around him with her tiny arms. She hugged him with all her strength, kissing him on both cheeks before holding his head in her hands.

They stepped into the hall and he closed the door behind them. Upstairs he could hear footsteps and looked up to see Charlotte, his sister, at the top, smiling at him. She hurtled down the stairs two at a time, wearing just her floral nightgown, and jumped at him from the third step up. He caught her, just, before spinning her round as she kissed him repeatedly all over his face. She had grown considerably since he last saw her, clearly almost a young woman who would soon be turning the eyes of the local boys and providing headaches for his mother. They walked into the kitchen as tea was being poured and he finally put her down and undid his tunic. He sat at the table, warming himself in the heat from the range in the corner.

'Now, tell me why didn't you inform me you were coming home, Cornelius? I could have got something in, something special for my war hero,' his mother said.

'Mother, you don't need to go to any trouble and I only knew myself yesterday, so there simply wasn't time. Besides, I can only stay tonight, as I am heading up to London tomorrow morning. I should be back in a week though, when we can have more time.' He reached for the tea in front of him, while his mother looked despondent.

'What, you don't come home for over a year and you can only stay one night?' she said softly.

'Well, I have some army business you see, what can I say?' he said in his defence. 'By the way, is Sebastian still working at the garage?'

'Yes, he is. Starts at eight. Why don't you walk over after breakfast and surprise him?'

'Yes, that's a good idea. I want to ask if I can borrow one of his motorcycles as it will save me time and avoid using the trains.'

His mother reached for the eggs.

'Well, I suppose one night is better than none, which will at least allow me to make a nice dinner for you before you go away again. Ask Sebastian to come over for supper, will you? Now, when will you be back?'

CHAPTER 2

The tall iron gates of Marshall Hall were held open by the 'keeper of the keys', a historical position appointed by successive owners for over two centuries. The black Silver Ghost eased through the narrow entrance, before dropping down the gravel driveway to the railway crossing. Bark, the general's driver, halted at the foot of the hill to check for trains then eased across the tracks before accelerating away towards the general's ancestral home.

General Davis, still wearing his military uniform, remained in shock following his sudden dismissal from the army the previous day. He had reached the rank of lieutenant general and was just months away, he thought, from gaining his well-earned peerage. His command of over ten thousand men, just days before, had been the height of his career. But he had now been cast aside by the ministry he had served loyally since joining the Royal Military Academy, Sandhurst, on the eve of his twenty-first birthday. He was angry at being sacked for doing his duty and now being abandoned by his lord and masters. The rushed enquiry into his actions, where Haig himself was suspiciously absent, had stunned him. His friends too had now distanced themselves from him and no one was taking his calls. He was particularly bitter that men he had trusted and worked alongside for many years now spurned him, several even turning away when he approached them prior to leaving the ministry. He felt alone and dejected and remembered the colonel, whom he had known for twenty years, stopping to tell him to watch his back. Before he could turn to question him, he was gone.

What did this mean? Was his life now at risk? In hindsight, he knew he had acted with a certain degree of belligerence but the risk of being seen as a laughing stock by his peers, when they found out he had had a woman operating as a sniper on the front line would have been too much to bear. He was angry when he had found out all those weeks ago, and wanted someone to pay from the very outset. He stood alone at the entrance to the War Office and realised he faced an uncertain future.

Bark had avoided his master's gaze in the rear-view mirror of the car all the way back from Pickering station. The general's stern look, when he collected him, had discouraged any conversation during the short journey and did not bode well for the rest of the household staff.

As they approached the Hall, Stevens, the butler, was watching from the window and alerted the staff. He had only received the telegram about the general's imminent arrival the previous afternoon, so all the available staff had worked late into the night to get the house ready for his return. He knew all the main rooms were primed and ready, especially the general's private apartment, and the fire was burning brightly in his study.

As the car approached the steps to the main entrance, Stevens was already in position. He leant forward to open the car door and could see his master looked terribly gruff. He took a deep breath.

'Good day, sir, I hope your journey was comfortable and —'

'Yes, yes, enough, Stevens. Are my rooms ready?' the general demanded, getting out and walking past him.

'Yes, sir, of course. I will have your bags brought right up. Will you be wanting tea?' he said, hiding his annoyance, but there was no answer as the man was already halfway up the steps. Stevens, left holding the door handle, looked across at Bark who was unstrapping the suitcases from the rear of the car. He raised his eyebrows.

'It is not a happy day, methinks,' he said quietly.

'No, you're right there, Mr Stevens, he didn't converse all the way back. Whatever has happened?'

Stevens was just about to speak when two footmen arrived to collect the baggage. A voice then rang out loudly from the doorway.

'Stevens!'

'Sounds like I'm about to find out,' he said as he shut the car door and turned to walk quickly back up the steps. He entered the vast hallway and saw the general standing outside his study.

'Refreshments,' he shouted. 'And get me Harper. I need to talk to you both.' He disappeared through the doorway, slamming the door so hard that the chandelier in the hall rattled. Mr Stevens shook his head, knowing it was going to be a difficult day.

He dropped down below stairs to locate Harper, the general's valet, who had been a soldier himself until 1915 when he was shot in the leg. After a long rehabilitation period, he was finally discharged and through sheer luck had obtained his position in this vast house.

When Stevens arrived in the kitchen, Harper was sitting at the servants' table, drinking tea. He looked up.

'So, what sort of mood is he in, Mr Stevens?' he asked, placing his teacup back on the saucer.

'Not the best and he wants to see us, sharpish. So, button up your jacket and make yourself presentable. We should go up when his tea is ready,' he snapped.

Harper tutted to himself, shaking his head as he watched the butler talking to the cook. He just couldn't understand why Stevens had never truly accepted him following his appointment. Was it jealousy, perhaps, in that he had the master's ear? Whatever his reasons, it didn't make for a good atmosphere downstairs and the rest of the staff were very aware of the friction that existed between them. For now, Harper knew his place and stood up respectfully, attended to his jacket in front of the mirror and straightened his tie. Within a few minutes, the cook had prepared a tray and called for one of the servant girls to carry it upstairs.

Stevens then summoned Harper with a sideways sweep of his head, characteristic of his arrogant manner towards him. They headed up the steep stairs, the maid following on behind, into the long hallway. They walked along the corridor to the study door and as Stevens gripped the handle, he stopped and turned.

'Wait here, Harper,' he said, before opening the door and stepping inside, ushering the girl forward. As Stevens entered, he saw a forlorn figure sitting by the fire, rubbing his hands together, a large whisky already on the side table, the decanter stopper lying by his glass. The general seemed to be in a distant place and didn't acknowledge their presence. The maid placed the tray gently on the table beside him and bobbed quickly before departing. Stevens waited for almost a minute, realising his master was absorbed in his own thoughts. He coughed.

'Yes, yes,' the general said, before finishing his drink in one long swallow.

'Harper is outside, sir. Shall I bring him in?'

Davis, seemingly ignoring him, cast his eyes instead over the tea tray. 'Butter?' he said abruptly. 'Where is the butter?'

Stevens looked down and noticed the butter dish behind the day's post.

'It's behind this morning's mail, sir. Will there be anything else?'

Davis looked up at him and frowned, holding his gaze. 'You have had it easy for a long time, Stevens, and let me say that it all changes today. I am back for good and there will be many changes, so you had better get used to me being around. I don't wish to see anyone for the rest of today, so hold any calls and keep the staff away from me, understand?' he said, reaching for the knife.

'Yes, sir,' said Stevens. 'And Harper, sir?'

But the general was now buttering his tea loaf, oblivious to his question. The butler walked back to open the door and waved Harper in. Together they approached the grim-looking figure, stopping several feet away, with Stevens a single step ahead as befitted his status. They watched their master as he poured himself some tea. He took a sip, then another, before peering up at them.

'Gentlemen, sit.' They looked at each other, astonished, as this had never happened before.

'I have resigned my commission in the army, so life for you all is going to change. We have a great deal to do, so get your notebooks out.' Stevens reached inside his jacket pocket for the small black notebook that never left him. Harper tapped his pockets but realised he didn't have one.

'First, I want you to advertise for some additional staff. I want twelve security guards and one head of security to protect the estate, which you, Harper, with your past military experience, will oversee. You will sift through all the applications and select good reliable men in double quick time. I don't want any rubbish. So, you will need to send a telegram this afternoon to *The Times*, and any other publication you deem suitable, for an advertisement to run for two consecutive days for the guards, one housemaid and one junior footman. The advertisements must be in tomorrow morning's newspapers for I want them in place by the end of the week. I will leave you to organise the new staff accommodation, uniforms and routines, Stevens, but, Harper, you must start arranging to convert the annexe into accommodation for the guards. Order sufficient beds and equipment today, by telephone, and order fifteen Lee Enfield rifles and plenty of ammunition. Use the estate land staff for the conversion. This needs to be completed as quickly as possible. Any questions, gentlemen?'

Harper looked across at Stevens, puzzled, but he was still writing. A moment later, Stevens placed the notebook in his side pocket.

'No questions, sir, we will get on with it right away and I will inform you as things progress.'

The general grunted, picked up the newspaper and started to read. Their time was up. As they walked back towards the door, a gravelly voice broke the silence and they turned.

'The army have treated me very badly, gentlemen, and although I am unable to inform you of all the treachery that has gone on, I will say this: loyalty is the greatest asset a man can have and I expect, no, demand this from you both. I am relying on you to keep the estate and all the staff safe as it is my belief people are coming for me. You will need to be vigilant at all times, and for once, damn it, work together. Do you hear?'

They snapped a look at each other. All the time the general was speaking, he never once took his eyes from the newspaper and then, with a wave of his hand, they were dismissed.

CHAPTER 3

That first morning back in England, Edwina was woken by a familiar sound of copper rings being dragged along a curtain pole. It was as if she had momentarily returned to her childhood when her mother opened the curtains in her bedroom each morning. She stirred from her heavy slumber as a beam of light cut across her pillows, making her squint, and instinctively she rolled over, away from the light. It took a moment to realise someone was talking to her, but under the warm covers, she felt secure and didn't move. The voice continued and suddenly a tiny face appeared above her.

'Good morning, miss, did you sleep well?' asked a young maid. Edwina pushed back the sheet, squinting as the maid fussed over her bedclothes. She sat up fully as the maid continued chatting away, but she wasn't really ready for conversation at this hour. A breakfast tray was then placed across her lap with more food on it than Edwina had seen for many months.

'My goodness, surely that's not all for me?'

'Yes, miss, the master thought you should be spoilt this morning and so you have porridge with homemade honey, poached eggs with bacon, toast and a pot of tea. Will there be anything else, miss?' she said, stepping back from the bed.

Edwina thought she must have died and gone to heaven.

'No, thank you,' she said, rather overwhelmed.

The maid bobbed before turning towards the door. Edwina surveyed the food, wondering where to start, then looked up.

'Oh, one other thing, do you know where Frank, um, Mr Smith might be?' she asked.

'He is in the dining room, miss. Shall I say you asked after him?'

Edwina, with a spoonful of porridge already in her mouth, nodded, then the door closed.

It was easily five minutes later when Edwina heard a gentle knock at the door. She stopped chewing, paused and swallowed the last of the bacon.

'Yes, come in,' she said as the door opened. Frank's head slowly appeared then, with a grin, he stepped into her room with one hand covering his eyes, pretending to be bashful.

'Is it all right to come in, miss?' he said, making Edwina giggle, before walking towards her.

'Why, yes, young man,' she said, pushing the tray down the bed.

'Here, I'll get that for you. Have you finished?' Frank asked.

Edwina puffed out her cheeks and blew from her mouth. 'Yes, thanks, I haven't eaten that much in ages. I'm stuffed.'

Frank smiled and placed the tray back on the table, then went to sit on the end of her bed. Edwina shuffled upwards to face him properly.

'It was a long journey yesterday and even though you slept a great deal of the way here, you were clearly very tired when we finally arrived. I never got the chance to show you the house or even officially welcome you to my home. So, welcome to Hardcastle Hall.'

Edwina suddenly felt rather emotional. She placed her hands on her face and unexpectedly started to sob. Concerned, Frank reached forward, placing his hand on her leg, waiting for her to settle. After a few moments, she gathered herself and wiped her tears away on the sheet.

'Oh, Frank, I'm sorry. I'm not upset with you. It's just hit me that I am free after the most exhausting time of my life. I thought I was going to die yesterday and now, miraculously, I am here in this wonderful house with you, wherever here is,' she said, looking around her room.

'I can't imagine how you feel, but I will say this. Life has taught me a number of things and working with you in France showed me that you meet the most extraordinary people when you least expect it. We are lucky, we have survived a terrible war, Edwina, and your life, if you want it to be, is now here, with me. I can offer you my loyalty and my friendship, but I want more than that as you are the most important person in my life.'

At that moment, she knew she would one day marry Frank, never anticipating all those months ago that their friendship would develop so keenly. 'Thank you, Frank, but where is Hardcastle Hall?'

Frank grinned at her, hoping she had taken in his tender words.

'We are a few miles south of Moreton-in-Marsh, just fifteen or twenty miles, as the crow flies, from your own farm. The Hall has stood for over six hundred years and Lord Hardcastle is the seventeenth Earl. We have one thousand, four hundred acres, four tenant farmers and about twenty cottages. Would you like to know any more, miss?' he asked with a grin.

Edwina laughed and wanted to hug him, but this wasn't the moment.

Frank then jumped up and stood at the end of her bed with his arms outstretched.

'Like it?' he asked.

Edwina smiled and instantly threw back the covers and jumped from her bed, reaching for an ornately embroidered silk dressing gown draped over the foot of the bed.

'Do I like it? It's an amazing room, I can't believe it's all for me,' she said, smiling broadly.

'Come and see the view from your window,' Frank suggested. She almost ran over, and then gasped.

'Oh, my goodness, it's breathtaking. It's like being home again, looking across the fields from my bedroom window.'

Frank started pointing out the folly at the top of the hill, but Edwina wasn't really listening and stared at him.

'You called me Edwina, I like that,' she said, smiling. Frank realised she was too excited to listen now and gave up. There would be time later.

'Yesterday, when you told me what Edward had done for me, I thought my life was at an end. I never knew him for what he was; instead, I had him marked as a coward, a weakling and someone who just didn't care. But I was so wrong as his bravery is above anything I have ever known. I will have many questions, Frank, and trust you will indulge me.'

Frank, leaning against the windowsill, nodded, realising the pain she must be in.

'Coming here was something I didn't expect, and to be honest, it filled me with trepidation. But this morning, I have woken full of energy, knowing a new life awaits me,' she said. Frank was opening his mouth to speak when she suddenly walked towards him. 'I think I would like to live here with you very much,' she said, kissing him quickly on one cheek.

Frank reached out to her, but she smiled and went over to the beautiful dressing table and sat down. She picked up the hairbrush to look at the ornate carving on its back, then picked up a small perfume bottle, spraying some of its contents into the air. She sniffed gently, the fragrance landing on her face and shoulders and she blinked as the fine spray fell into her eyes. She spun round, stood up and walked over to a tall dark wardrobe that must have been eight feet across and opened the doors gingerly. On one side, she saw a row of dresses, lined up with equal gaps between them, and shoes tucked neatly on several shelves beneath. On the other side were hats, scarves and several pairs of differently coloured gloves, all placed neatly in rows.

'Are these all for me?' she asked, smiling.

'My dear girl, for as long as you want it to be,' he said, with his arms outstretched. 'It's all for you, Edwina.'

'Well, you had better let me bathe and get dressed then, sir,' she said, grinning. 'A woman has to look respectable for her gentleman, doesn't she?'

Frank got the message, smiling back, delighted she seemed so happy. He started to walk to the door.

'I will send Alison up. Your lady's maid. She is very nice and used to be in service with the Earl of Derbyshire. She has a little dog called Bella.' He looked at his watch. 'Goodness, it's five past eight; I'd better let you get ready. I will see you in about an hour,' he said, moving towards the door. As he opened it, he stopped and turned, smiling at her, before closing it quietly behind him.

Edwina skipped across to the door with a small brass plaque of a bath screwed to the centre of it. She had been tired when she had arrived the previous evening and had simply undressed and climbed into bed, unaware of her surroundings. As she pushed open the bathroom door, daylight flooded into the room and it shone like a magnificent tomb fit for a queen. The colourful tiles, from floor to ceiling, were vibrant and a huge bath, with large brass taps, was the centrepiece. Several ornate mirrors hung from the walls making the room look much larger than it actually was. It was the most stunning room she had ever seen.

She placed the plug in the bath and turned on the water, before using her lavatory. As the bath filled, she undressed and walked to a mirror, peering closely at the large scar on her chest which looked sore and ugly. She frowned, before realising the bath was rapidly filling and stepped over to tip some sweet-smelling bath salts into the water. She got in and slowly crouched down before dropping below the water. When she rose with a splash, she saw the door opening and a young woman entered.

She wiped the water from her face and hair and sat up as the maid placed some towels on a small chair in the corner.

'You must be Alison,' Edwina said.

'Yes, miss, I am your personal lady's maid. I hope you will be happy here, miss.' And she bobbed very slightly.

Edwina looked at her pretty face and neat well-groomed uniform, waving her across.

'Well, come and sit down and tell me all about the house and the people who work here. But firstly, I would like to know all about you,' she said.

Edwina's bath that morning took half an hour as her new best friend opened up to her. As Alison talked, she bathed her mistress, although Edwina felt this would take some getting used to.

'I hear you have a dog, Alison. What breed is it?'

'Well, miss, she is a spaniel and I was very lucky as I found her by the woods a week ago in a terrible state. I spoke with Charles, the butler, who spoke to His Lordship and he has kindly allowed me to keep her. She is coming on and learning fast, although she has to live in the lower scullery. But I love walking her in my spare time and she has this strange urge to find the largest branches, some almost as big as her, and will carry one throughout our walks. I can introduce her to you if you would like.'

Edwina smiled. 'I would be happy to walk with you on occasions. Now, shall we get on?'

Alison dried her mistress with soft white towels before helping her into her dressing gown again. She then led Edwina to the large wardrobe.

'Now, which dress would you like to wear, miss?'

Edwina stared once again at the clothes hanging in a neat row.

'How did you know my size?' she asked.

'Well, miss, the other day, Master Smith stood members of the house staff in a line, until he was happy he had found someone who was your height. He provided me with your shoe size and then instructed me to visit Cheltenham whilst he and His Lordship travelled to France to collect you. I was told to buy you a selection of dresses and other lady's attire until you could select your own. I hope I have chosen well, miss.'

Edwina brushed her hand gently through the soft materials, choosing a pale blue floral mid-length dress, while Alison selected a pair of white stockings and white boots. Once dressed, Edwina looked in the mirror, thinking back to the last time she had worn something other than a pair of trousers. Then, aghast, she thought of the grubby military uniform, full of lice, that she'd been wearing when she arrived at Boulogne.

She stared at herself in the full-length mirror and was stunned at the transformation, realising she looked like a proper lady. Her feminine side had never developed properly in her younger years and she wondered if this really was her future. Was she meant to be with Frank? A man she so admired and trusted with her life. Could she now trust him with her love too?

'So, what do you think, Alison, will I do?' Edwina asked.

The maid beamed at her new mistress. 'Just one last thing, miss, a little face cream and lipstick perhaps?'

Edwina walked to the dressing table and sat down, a little unsure. Alison began by parting her hair with the large brush and placing a silver hair clip on one side. She then showed her the array of different pots, describing each one in turn before lifting out some face cream on her finger. She offered it to Edwina and she gently massaged it into her skin.

'What is rouge?' Edwina asked, looking at the pot in front of her.

'You apply a little rouge on top of your face cream, making your cheeks appear rosy. Your lipstick should be applied bold and bright. It's how the ladies wear it,' she said. Edwina, having never really worn face creams and lipstick before, followed her instructions carefully and smiled with delight.

'There. Will I do?' she asked.

'I think that's perfect, miss.'

Edwina picked up the perfume she had played with earlier and sprayed some on her neck.

'Can I suggest one last thing, miss?' Edwina nodded and Alison went across to the wardrobe and pulled open a large drawer. She took out a cloche hat and walked back, holding it above Edwina's head. 'What do you think? Would you like to wear a hat instead of the hair clip? It would cover your short hair.'

'No, thank you, I think I will just let it grow out. Now, we should probably go down. Would you show me the way?'

Alison placed the hat on the table and walked towards the door. 'I think His Lordship and Master Smith are waiting for you in the library, miss.'

After a final inspection in the full-length mirror, Edwina followed Alison to the door.

'Just one last thing, Alison, you really don't have to keep calling me miss. Edwina will be fine. You make me sound like an old school mistress,' she said with a grin.

Alison pushed the door shut and spoke quietly. 'I would be happy to, miss, but I can only do so in this room. It would be seen as improper to use your Christian name, especially if I was overheard by the other servants.'

'That will be fine, Alison. Shall we go?'

As they left her suite, they both giggled, like young ladies do, before heading along the main landing to the top of the marble stairs. Edwina turned to get her bearings, so she could locate her room later, before stepping down the stairs. A short distance behind, Alison followed her.

Feeling elegant in her clothes and surroundings, Edwina took in the vast number of paintings covering each wall on all sides down to the large entrance hall below.

At the bottom, she was directed along a wide corridor, to the right, arriving at the open library door. She took a deep breath, smiled at her maid and entered.

What met her gaze made her stop and stare. She did a slow pirouette as she absorbed the wealth in the room. Bookshelves filled the long wall, so high there was actually a ladder on rails to reach the very top. Opposite, three large bay windows overlooked the gardens and through the middle of the room long settees, chairs and various tables with ornate lamps set off the room perfectly. Then she noticed a head protruding around the side of a high-winged leather armchair. It was Frank and he grinned at her before rising to his feet as the clock struck the half hour. It was nine thirty; she was terribly late, but a gentleman never spoke of his lady not being on time.

He walked over to greet her and reached for her hand, leading her further into the room.

'Sir, may I introduce Miss Edwina Mitchell,' he said with a sense of pride, not taking his eyes off her. She stepped forward, thinking he was talking to himself, then Lord Hardcastle rose from his seat beside a screen. She remembered his smile from the previous day in Boulogne, and how he had taken such great care of her throughout their long journey home. She walked forward and was beckoned to a seat to his right as His Lordship pulled on a rope hanging by the fireplace.

'May I say how wonderful you look, Edwina.' Frank smiled; Edwina started to blush.

'Did you sleep well?' Lord Hardcastle asked politely. Edwina laughed suddenly, unaccustomed to such formalities. She was more used to life in the trenches where a morning greeting was mucky jokes and bad language. Frank looked at her in puzzlement for a moment, but then smiled as if he realised what she was thinking.

She thanked His Lordship and said she had slept wonderfully. Her initial feelings of unsettlement started to ease and she felt a growing confidence within her and chatted freely. She didn't notice the two people who had entered the room but stopped talking when she saw an elegant man in a smart black suit followed by the same maid who had brought her breakfast tray earlier. She placed a tea tray on the low table and then left.

'Edwina, this is Charles, my butler. He manages the household staff. Charles, this is Miss Edwina Mitchell.' The butler bowed his head very slightly.

'How do you do, miss. I hope you are comfortable here. If I can be of service, please don't hesitate to speak to me. Welcome to Hardcastle Hall, miss.'

Edwina, pleased everyone was being so nice, instinctively nodded back to him.

'Will that be all, sir?' the butler asked. Lord Hardcastle, busy sifting through the morning post, turned to him.

'Yes, thank you, Charles, but can you have the car ready for a quarter past ten?' Charles nodded before leaving the room. When the door had closed, Frank poured the tea. Edwina looked at him, remembering the last time he had made her a brew, sitting crouched in a slit trench in northern France. She smiled to herself, thinking how her life had changed so dramatically in such a short time. She stood up and began walking around the room, admiring

44

the huge book collection, pulling the odd one from the shelves, before staring at the impressive map of the world on the far wall. It was made from layers of different coloured woods, Britain appearing in a dark teak. She then went to stand in a bay window with large French doors, peering out at the rose garden. When she returned, Lord Hardcastle shuffled in his seat to face her.

'My dear girl. What has happened to you in the past weeks is now, I trust, behind you, although I do appreciate that the loss of your brother must be very painful. He was clearly a very brave man.' He paused politely, just for a moment. 'Frank will explain more fully the details of how this all came about and how you were rescued, but can I just say, truthfully, how I admire you for undertaking to fight for your country against the Germans. Frank has told me a great deal about you and it is an incredible thing you have done. I have no doubt, in the years ahead, your tale will be told by many people as you are indeed someone with a story to tell. You are a very courageous young woman. We would like you to try and move forward with your life now, in your own time of course, and trust you will feel content here at Hardcastle Hall.'

Ed wasn't expecting a speech and noticed Frank was looking at her very attentively. She felt she should respond, but His Lordship continued.

'There is one more thing I wish you to know. Throughout this ordeal, I sought help from several high-powered friends in Whitehall, and to say they assisted us is an understatement as without this help, we would not be sitting here today. I should also like to inform you that General Davis is to be retired from the army with immediate effect.'

Edwina flashed her eyes across to Frank.

'I am told he will move back to his country estate in Yorkshire, probably to wallow in self-pity. The matter, as far as we are concerned, is now closed. However, I have been advised that a full military enquiry will take place at a date yet to be confirmed.'

Ed's heart was pounding following the mention of the general's name, and she felt herself beginning to sweat. She knew at that moment she could not rest until she had found a way to avenge Edward's death. Quite how she would achieve this was unclear, but in the days ahead she would form a plan, although she would clearly need help.

'Your Lordship, I—'

She was halted by his raised hand.

'Look, my dear, if you are going to live here, you must start calling me Michael. I hope this suits you?'

Edwina smiled. 'Yes, of course, Michael, thank you. As I was saying, I am so grateful for what you and Frank have done for me. I thought my life was over and if it wasn't for Frank, and others, it would have been.' Frank grinned at her and she smiled back.

'I could only have dreamed of living in a country estate and you have all been so lovely to me, so yes, I would be delighted to live here, Michael, especially as I have become very fond of Frank.' She picked up her teacup and saucer to take a drink, almost as a confidence boost, before continuing. Frank was beaming.

'I will have to visit my farm at some point as it's being run by David Russell who deserves an explanation and, as yet, probably doesn't know what has happened to Edward. I would also like to get to the bottom of where Reverend Bryan O'Callaghan is, my old parish priest. He was, last time I heard, being held in a military prison.'

Lord Hardcastle nodded. 'Yes, I was coming to that. I have been informed that, once certain formalities have been dealt with, he will be released from the military prison he is being held in, but I should advise you he is rather unwell.' Edwina flinched slightly, hearing that his confinement had resulted in him being taken ill.

'He is a fine man, Michael, who has deserved none of this. When is he due to be released, do you know?'

Lord Hardcastle looked down at his pocket watch and suddenly stood.

'Could we possibly take this up later, Edwina?' he said. 'Frank and I have some estate business to attend to. We should be back for luncheon. Why don't we arrange for Alison to show you around the estate and we will see you at one o'clock in the garden room?'

At that, His Lordship stood and walked towards the door. Frank walked over and leant towards Edwina, his face just inches from hers.

'Don't worry, it will all be fine.' He kissed her on the cheek.

She smiled as he walked towards the door. 'See you later then,' and he was gone.

She suddenly felt rather lonely in the vast room and stood up to walk to the window, searching her soul. She gazed across the great lawn, feeling slightly unsettled, thinking of Edward. A tear ran down her cheek, which she instantly wiped away, not wanting to be seen crying. She turned and saw *The Times* newspaper lying open on the settee and went to retrieve it. Sitting back down, she read with interest of General Davis and noticed her breathing had become involuntarily rapid. When she had finished, she laid the paper down, knowing what she had to do. Standing up, Edwina pulled the bell rope and within a minute Charles appeared.

'Could I borrow Alison, Charles, please? I would like her to show me around the estate.'

Charles smiled. 'Of course, miss, but please remember, she is your personal lady's maid, so you never need to "borrow" her. I will send her up.'

For the next hour, Alison took Edwina on a grand tour of the house before offering to take her around the grounds.

'Could we take Bella please, miss?' she asked. Edwina, keen to meet this little dog, nodded enthusiastically. Alison rushed off to collect her.

She returned with a little black spaniel with white flecks on her chest and front paws who wagged her tail enthusiastically as she approached Edwina. As she reached down to pet her, the dog instantly rolled onto her back and her tummy was then rubbed vigorously.

For the rest of the morning, Edwina was shown the formal gardens, the large pond filled with giant carp and the walled garden where several gardeners tended the vegetables growing in abundance. They walked out into the lower fields before returning for a very late morning tea. Afterwards, she studied books on the estate in the library and, before she knew it, Frank had arrived back from his business. It was almost lunchtime when he rushed in, finding her seated by the window.

'Oh, there you are. Have you had a good morning?'

Edwina closed the book as she turned to greet him.

'Yes, I have,' she said. 'Alison has been most helpful and Charles too. I have learned about the household, visited all the floors, seen the wonderful dining room, ballroom and even the kitchens. I think I have met most of the staff and we walked around the gardens and saw the grand orangery. Is it true the vine in there is over two hundred years old?'

Frank started to grin at her.

'What?' she said with a frown. He then laughed aloud.

'It's just so lovely to see you happy and so interested in the estate. Our life in France seems such a long way off already and you seem very much at home. What is mine, Edwina, is yours, and I just want you to be happy. Now, I have something to show you before lunch, so come with me.' She stood and took the hand on offer as they walked out of the French doors and across the lawn. They headed towards some buildings a few hundred yards away.

'Where are you taking me, young master?' she asked, tucking her arm through his.

'You, madam, will have to wait and see.'

A few moments later, they stepped through a large arch cut through some giant fir trees and came out behind the stable yard. As they turned the corner, she saw a groom standing in the middle of the yard, holding the bridle of a bay horse with a long black mane.

'I have a gift for you, Edwina. Meet Arion Dreamtime.'

Edwina's hands flew to her mouth and she turned to look at Frank. They walked over and Edwina reached out to touch the mare.

'My own horse?' she said. 'She's beautiful, Frank. I can't believe it; you are so kind.' Edwina rubbed the animal's nose with one hand and patted her neck with the other.

'So, this was the estate business you had to attend to this morning?'

Frank was already nodding before she had finished her sentence. 'Well, I have to look after my best friend, don't I?'

Edwina's smile was infectious and all the grooms in the yard grinned. She wanted to fling her arms around Frank, but paused as there were many people looking at her.

'How can I ever thank you?' she said, gently giving him a squeeze around his middle.

'Well, a kiss on the cheek might be a good start,' he said, holding his face slightly forward. She smiled and moved her lips to touch his cheek, but he suddenly swung his head round, her kiss meeting him fully on the lips.

'An old soldiers' trick,' he said, grinning at her. She looked up at him tenderly. 'Now, we must go back for lunch, but perhaps we can ride out this afternoon,' he suggested.

'But I have no riding clothes,' she stated.

'Well, actually, that's not exactly true. They should, by now, be lying on your bed.' And he grinned at her as she hugged him.

After luncheon, Edwina and Frank rode out together.

'I will call her Dream, for short,' she said, smiling, as they trotted down the track from the yard and away up the hill behind.

That afternoon she met tenant farmers and their families, played with their children and visited the lake where Frank had arranged for afternoon tea to be served under a tree. They sat in the sunshine, talking of the past and the future. She felt so happy but knew this couldn't last for long and she would have to be away soon. She hoped Frank would understand.

It was in the library the following morning that an opportunity presented itself. She was flipping through the pages of *The Times*, reading stories from the war when, by chance, she stumbled upon an advertisement in the Situations Vacant section relating to Marshall Hall, the home of General Davis. They were hiring security guards and house staff and she sat back, deep in thought. This was her opportunity to get on the inside.

But how could she organise herself so quickly, without help? She was troubled and knew she simply could not do this without Frank. She knew she had to tell him. But would he understand?

After dinner that night, she took him into the drawing room and sat down, full of trepidation. She then told him what she felt she had to do. Frank was silent, staring at the friend who meant more to him than anyone had before.

'Edwina, I think I know you better than you know yourself as I was expecting this. I have no idea what pain you carry for your brother, but I fully understand his death has to be avenged. I can't do this for you and know you have to go away, so you must trust me like you did before and let me help you.'

Edwina reached for his hand and pulled it to her mouth, kissing his fingers. 'I didn't expect that, Frank. I thought you would try and talk me out of it, but yes, you do know me very well. If I have your support, I will go with confidence. Thank you,' she said, looking at him lovingly. Frank said nothing for a moment.

'What if I came too? I could be there if you needed help. I could live off-site and would be ready whenever you needed me.'

Edwina thought briefly about his suggestion but realised that if she was in a vast house, surrounded by security men, it would be impossible for him to be of any real assistance and how would she contact him?

'I think not, Frank. I have to do this on my own.'

The next morning, Frank sent a telegram to Marshall Hall regarding the housemaid's position, along with a glowing reference.

Over two days they prepared for her departure. Frank catered for her in every way, selecting maids' clothes from below stairs, arranging visits to the optometrist and dentist and gifting her a small handgun that she would use to kill the man she last saw in a military court in northern France. A telegram arrived late the second afternoon confirming her position. All was now in place.

On her final morning, he drove her to Moreton railway station, the mood solemn, as he realised this could be the last time, he would see her alive if things went badly. It was hard to say farewell but she had kissed him softly on the lips in the car before alighting to catch her train. As she stepped up into the carriage, Frank closed the door behind her.

She placed her bag on the rack before pulling down the window. Edwina leant forward, holding out both arms to hug Frank around his shoulders and kissed his ear. Then, with a grin, she whispered,

'I will marry you, Frank Smith.'

He froze and pulled back, meeting her smile. 'I haven't asked you yet, young lady.'

'Well, you'd better hurry up then, before I accept a proposal from someone else.'

At that, he suddenly dropped down onto one knee, in front of many onlookers on the platform. 'Will you marry me, Edwina Mitchell?' he asked, with a huge grin.

'Why, yes, sir, I will,' she said, beaming.

As he regained his feet, the conductor blew his whistle, offering them only a brief moment to hug again and then he kissed her.

The train shuddered forward, twice, before it started to move off. He clung to her hand and started to run alongside until he could keep up no longer. As the distance between them grew, she watched him mouth the words 'I love you.' He was shouting it, over and over, but she could hear nothing. She held her hat, smiling, and waved at him as tears rolled down her cheeks.

CHAPTER 4

In the crowded bar, Dave Gibbs was ordering their fifth pint and was already feeling a little drunk. This exuberance was long overdue, following many months living and breathing death in the trenches. As he was being served, he chatted playfully with the young barmaid whose smile went straight to his heart. It had been a long while since he had held a lady so beautiful in conversation and he was hopeful of an exciting evening.

A large bloke, clearly the worse for wear, who was loitering at the end of the bar suddenly slapped his dinner-plate-sized hand onto the bar top, making everyone jump. He stared across at Dave with haunted eyes. Dave decided he was looking for trouble and sensed he might be seconds away from a pasting, something he knew they could really do without.

Ricky Miller, sitting on the far side of the bar, watched curiously as the chap moved around the bar towards Dave, who then stepped back. Ricky didn't wait, he could see what was coming. As he got to his feet, the small table in front of him fell over, glasses crashing onto the floor. Racing across the bar, his fists clenched, he arrived just as the first windmill punch whizzed over Dave's head. Ricky swung into action, deflecting the chap's second punch just in time as he swung back the other way to connect with Dave's chin. With his body now twisted around, he hit the man with a swift jab to his ribs, then again, same place, in quick succession, causing him to buckle and drop down. He was already blowing from his mouth as he tried to recover, but as he stood up, Ricky jabbed twice more in the same place. The big man knew when he was beaten and dropped to the floor, gasping, holding his hand up.

'That's enough,' shouted the barman, coming around from behind the bar. 'If you can't behave, you can get out, Tom.' The assailant looked up at him in pain. 'He was only talking, nothing more. Now get out and don't come back until you're sober.'

The man slowly stood up, hovered for a moment, clutching his ribs, and stared at Dave Gibbs, who was now searching for his money.

'OK, OK, I'm going,' he finally said, as he shuffled towards the door. He would be sore for a day or two, he knew that and as he pulled on the door handle, he took one last look back, gently wagging his finger, and then he was gone.

'Sorry about that, chaps, as jealous a man as you will ever meet. Sarah, these are on me,' said the barman.

The boys went back to their seats and could see the bloke sitting outside on the wall, watching the pub door.

'Is he waiting for us, do you think?' Dave asked, as he sat supping his beer.

'Yes, I think he is, but don't worry, we can have him anytime. As my old dad used to say, "the bigger they are, the harder they fall". Let him just try it.'

Dave turned from the window and casually peered across at the barmaid, smiling, then looked at his friend.

'Hey, I didn't know you could box, Ricky.'

'Since I was six. My dad used to take me. I was school champion three years in a row from age nine. I left school having never been defeated.'

Dave felt happy to be out with a man who could handle himself.

'You know, I've just realised I've worked alongside you for almost six months and don't know much about you at all. I mean, where are you from?'

Ricky put his pint down.

'Well, I was brought up in Rainham in Essex, just north of London. My dad is a carpenter and my mum works in a laundry. She's Italian, which is where I got my name from.'

Dave looked blankly at him. 'What do you mean, where you got your name?'

'Well, I was baptised Riccardo, and when I went to school my mates started to call me Ricky, and it kind of stuck. I have two younger brothers who are both still at school, but the oldest also boxes and he is much better than I ever was. Anything else, nosey parker?' he said, punching Dave playfully on the arm.

It was after ten o'clock when they left the pub, the light had gone and the streets were deserted. Staying in Folkestone was probably not the best option, but they hadn't wanted to pay London prices for the many beers they were going to consume. They had been told of some boarding houses along the road and set off, slightly the worse for wear, keeping their eyes open for the man from the bar. They walked just a hundred yards before turning right at the end of the street, where they saw several houses with signs offering lodgings. Dave knocked on the first door and a little old lady answered in her dressing gown, peering into the darkness.

'Yes, can I help you?'

'We're looking for lodgings, dear. Do you have any rooms?'

She looked them both up and down and seeing they were men in uniform, opened the door wider. 'Yes, do come in, boys. Home from the war, are you?'

Ricky acknowledged her question as they stepped inside. She was very business-like, telling them the price almost before the door was closed and saying they would have to share a bed.

'That will be fine,' said Dave. 'We have spent many days huddled up together in the trenches, so a warm bed will be bliss in comparison.'

Then just as they all laughed, a man stepped out from a side room into the hallway. It was the chap from the pub. Ricky dropped his bag and readied himself for another fight with this brute of a man, but then their host spoke.

'Oh, do you know my boy, Tom?' she asked, and Tom smiled at them, offering his hand. Ricky kept his eyes on him, wondering what was going to happen next. Dave, not wanting further trouble, shoved his hand forward and said, 'Pleased to meet you, Tom. I'm Dave and this is Ricky. He's a boxer, you know.'

'Yes, I thought as much. Good to meet you, boys, sorry about earlier. How long do you have?' he asked, his speech slurred.

'Oh, we're off tomorrow,' Dave said, as Tom seemed to lose interest and disappeared back into the room he had come from.

The lady showed them upstairs to a small room on the top floor, with a tiny window overlooking the road and no curtains. The bed was squashed in the corner with little room for much else, but quite adequate for their needs. They thanked her and gave her two half-crowns. She offered to get them some change, but Ricky, happy to be spending their boss's money, waved her down.

'Don't worry, you can have the change. Buy something nice for yourself,' he said with the smile that had won many hearts back in Essex. She tilted her head sideways and smiled back.

'How nice, thank you. I will buy a new scarf.' And she left them to it. As the door closed, she called out, 'Breakfast at seven.'

Dave lost the toss and got the side by the wall, and almost as soon as they lay down, they were asleep. In what seemed like just a few minutes, they were awoken by the bright sunlight streaming in through the open window. They threw their clothes on and headed down for breakfast, only to see Sarah, the barmaid from the pub, sitting at the table. The boys couldn't believe it. As they walked in, she smiled.

'I wanted to say sorry about last night. Tom is a nice bloke really, he just gets a bit jealous when I chat too much.'

Dave went around the table to sit next to her.

'After almost six months in France, we just needed to unwind, so don't worry about it. I was probably just as much to blame. Let's forget it. So, do you live here, Sarah?' Dave asked.

'Yes, I do, with Tom and his mum. His dad was lost at sea many years ago and now it's just the three of us.'

Tom then came in carrying a large green teapot.

'Morning, lads.'

'You OK this morning?' asked Ricky.

'Ribs are a bit sore. Must have fallen over or something,' he said, laughing, before lining up three large white mugs on the table, and pouring from one end to the other without lifting the spout. Needless to say, not all the tea reached the mugs and he received a firm slap from Sarah.

They ate a hearty breakfast and by seven thirty they were out of the door and on their way to the railway station. They planned to catch the seven fifty-five train to London Bridge station, and then onward across the city to King's Cross to catch the train to York.

The railway station was full of troops from countries as far away as Australia and New Zealand. The carriages were largely full, but they did find one at the rear with just two chaps in, both already asleep. As the train left the station, it quickly picked up speed, leaving the south-east of England behind. As they wound their way through small villages and open fields, they enjoyed a countryside without the noise of guns pounding the earth. They sat close and chatted through their orders, knowing they had plenty of time to achieve their goal.

Lieutenant Cavanagh had told them to be at the pub at Pickering station by six o'clock the following evening, which was easy enough, but they did have many purchases to make en route, including civilian clothes and enough equipment and food to last seven days.

Previously, in the privacy of their tiny dugout, they had carefully removed the screws to their rifle butts, allowing the weapons to come apart. The rifles had been stowed in their kitbags since, wrapped in a waterproof sleeping sheet to avoid detection by the MPs at the port. They knew what they were doing was a court martial offence and was an almighty risk, but without their sniper rifles, they felt undressed. They were prepared for isolation and hardship to get the revenge they sought and were prepared to give up their lives to kill the man that had executed their friend.

As they chatted, the ticket collector arrived in the corridor, wrenching the sliding door open, waking the two sleepers by the door.

'Tickets,' he said, stepping into the compartment. He gazed at their tickets before clipping them efficiently with a small black machine hanging from his neck on a leather strap. A bead of sweat dropped from his nose as he handed the tickets back, his eyes never meeting theirs, and then withdrew back into the corridor.

'Arriving London at ten twenty-three,' he said, before sliding the door closed with a loud bang. The boys laughed aloud, Dave shaking his head from side to side.

'I don't know, we have put up with daily bombardments for over a year from the Germans, and a sliding door makes us both jump. Do you think we have lost it already?' he said with a grin.

Just over two hours later they arrived into the city of London, passing row upon row of terraced houses with backyards so close to the train line they could count the pegs holding up the washing on the sagging lines. As the train slowed, they saw the Tower of London across the river and through the gaps in the buildings, St Paul's Cathedral, the immense dome dominating the skyline. As they gathered their bags, the train came to a halt. They walked along the cramped corridor and stepped down onto a crowded platform. As they joined the throng of people passing through the ticket point, Ricky looked around and was surprised to see they were the only people in uniform.

***

Across London, Edwina Mitchell had arrived at Euston station and completed the short walk to King's Cross. She stepped into a third-class railway carriage on a train bound for York. In her maid's clothes and disguise, she was now playing a part. Frank had provided all the help she had needed and she was ready. If all went to plan, she would be at her new place of work by sunset.

CHAPTER 5

Brigadier Kenneth Cotton, OBE, MC (retired) had had a distinguished career, joining the British army when Britain was still a world power. When he had resigned his commission almost a decade earlier, his peers were shocked as he had seemed destined to make it to the top. In 1909, the British military had created the Secret Intelligence Service, the SIS, often referred to as the bureau. The offer he had been made, behind closed doors, was something he just couldn't turn down and he was now in charge of what some called the most powerful body in the British Isles.

He was a diligent man and had chosen to retain his military rank to maintain a certain superiority over the many government staff where he plied his trade.

Since then, he had successfully developed a dedicated team of ex-Royal Navy and Army officers and selected men from the ranks too, who, by design, protected *the British Isles* with a quiet dedication to duty. With everyone sworn to secrecy, he ran an efficient department from deep below the War Office in the heart of London. He was now specialising in espionage matters, and only a select group of government ministers knew the department existed.

As Cotton became increasingly entwined in the protection of the realm, his life and his relationship with his wife became decidedly distant. He realised the time had come to find alternative accommodation and investigated the possibility of converting some of the department's offices into his own private quarters. He spoke to the quartermaster and within days they had been transformed into a small private bedroom, a sitting room and a small kitchen, with a toilet just down the hall.

His dedication to duty was second to none and he would often busy himself late into the night, delivering highly secret reports to the War Office. Apart from his daily bath, which he took after swimming twenty lengths in the underground swimming pool at his London club, he hardly ever left the building. He lived mostly on sandwiches and tea with the occasional free lunch thrown in at departmental meetings, except for Sundays when he took lunch at his club, but always sat alone.

He had become a pale man, with few friends, who liked to listen to classical music on his gramophone before he slept. He had, over time, become the true mastermind behind the success of the Service, and people in very senior positions, including the Prime Minister, bent over backwards to assist him whenever he asked. He was totally trusted to manage the secrets of the state and this dedication to duty warranted a direct phone to the PM's desk.

His reading material came to him thick and fast every day, in small brown leather boxes, often directly from the Secretary of State for War. Most of the contents were stamped 'Top Secret' and he dealt with them in order of arrival to avoid missing a single note. One typical Thursday morning, his secretary entered his office at six forty-five with his first box of the day, a cup of tea and two McVitie's biscuits. Miss Jane Ritchie had been with him for over a year and he now trusted her completely. He pulled out his pocket watch by the chain hanging from his waistcoat, but not to check the time. Attached to it was the special key that never left his side. He turned it in the tiny lock of the box and lifted the lid, surprised to see just one file inside.

It was an internal memo from the Secretary of State for War regarding the 'early retirement' of General Davis, following a serious misjudgement of his duties in France. The main text was typed, but at the bottom of the last page, he noticed the recommendation had been written in pencil by the senior minister of the land and initialled by Haig himself.

The full story of what had been named 'the Mitchell affair' was laid out before him and he read the pages carefully to see that the general had hastily convened a court martial and then without London's authority had signed a death warrant. That was bad enough, but then on minimal evidence and in double quick time, the soldier had been executed by firing squad without being given the chance to appeal. What Cotton couldn't understand was why a general of Davis's stature and experience had been in such a dammed rush and had ignored military standard operational procedures (SOPs), especially concerning a soldier with such a superb war record. He continued reading and then it hit him. Private Mitchell was female. As he read the recommendation, a chill went up his spine.

He sat back in his chair, reaching for his now lukewarm cup of tea, in deep thought. He was puzzled by how a woman could possibly have ended up at the front line, in full battle dress, for so long, without being compromised. He read the whole document again, before shouting for Jane. The door opened quickly.

'Yes, sir, what can I get you?' she asked.

'Could you get me Colonel Anderson? I need to speak to him urgently.' She nodded and left the room, leaving the door ajar.

'Door,' he shouted, as her hand appeared pulling it closed.

Just a few minutes later there was a tap on the door and an officer in full uniform stepped in.

'Morning, Kenneth, what is it today?' the colonel asked cheerfully. The brigadier looked up and told him to sit. He leant forward and spoke softly.

'We have a problem, Ian, and I need you on it urgently. You'll have to drop everything else until this matter is dealt with. I need you to pull together a small team, two men should do it, to complete a rather special operation. It will go under the banner of 'Corkscrew'. How long will you need to get the men together?'

The colonel knew this man well and that when he stressed a task was most urgent, nothing would stand in the way of achieving the objective.

'I presume we are talking a UK operation, sir?'

Cotton nodded, just once, and the colonel continued, 'OK, I will be back with you within the hour. I would expect we can have the chaps away by nightfall. Leave it with me, sir.'

As he turned to leave, the brigadier spoke.

'Sorry, old chap, nightfall is not good enough. I need them away in the next few hours. It's a long way to Yorkshire.' Cotton looked at his watch and then stood up. 'I have to leave in a minute for the morning briefing, so can you be here at zero seven thirty? At that time, I will provide you with the full details. Time is of the essence, Ian.'

Without further words, Anderson left the room, closing the door behind him. The brigadier placed the file in his top drawer and locked it, dropping the key into his waistcoat pocket. He reached for a red folder from his tray and left for the conference room, five floors above. It was the normal security briefing, held every morning at seven o'clock. When he returned, Ian Anderson was already waiting in his office.

'Ah, Ian, how did you get on?' he asked, walking around behind his desk.

'I have Dave Thomas, or DT as he is known, and Chris Butler standing by, sir. They are reporting to me at zero nine hundred for their briefing. Now, what's the task and how quickly must it be completed?'

Brigadier Cotton sat motionless, thinking for a few moments, pondering the names Anderson had said. He knew these two men had been with the bureau for several years and were often called for when 'dirty deeds' were needed.

'I know these men, sound selection, Ian,' he said, retrieving the file labelled Operation Corkscrew from his desk drawer and handing it over. Ian read in silence for several minutes, without any noticeable reaction, until he read the final lines. He closed the file and looked up to meet Cotton's eyes.

'So, it's from the very top, then?' he said, as he stood up to leave. 'I will be ready to provide a summary briefing in one hour, sir.' He peered at his watch. 'Will that suit you?'

Cotton looked up at the wall clock opposite his desk, then checked his watch. 'Yes, eight thirty will be fine.'

As the colonel turned to leave, Cotton spoke quietly. 'This has the highest priority, Ian. This matter needs to be tidied up with no loose ends of any kind. No change to SOPs, so let's get this one done and swiftly. I want daily briefings from the men, through normal routes. This man is a loose cannon,' he said sternly.

CHAPTER 6

Ricky followed Dave to view the bus timetables which were pinned to a large wall near the ticket office. After studying the many sheets, they wandered over to catch the number 17 bus which took them across the river and up to King's Cross station.

Within minutes they had arrived at the train station and headed for the left luggage area to secure their kitbags, all for the price of tuppence. They purchased two tickets for the train to York, planning to depart on the four o'clock, arriving at seven thirty. Once done, they walked the mile or so north to Camden Market, passing many street merchants along the way selling everything from oysters to hobnailed boots. For a short time, they embraced the lives of Londoners, who smiled approvingly at them. They were enjoying the moment as they eased their way into city life.

A traditional pub on the corner caught their eye, and as they entered the crowded smoke-filled bar, they felt a sense of belonging amongst normal London people. They pushed their way forward towards the brass beer taps on the bar and bought a meat pie, some oysters and a pint of ale each. They were suddenly in a world away from war, away from death, and it all seemed so wonderfully normal.

On leaving, they walked down the lane where several street girls called them over. They grinned at each other, knowing they had no time for ladies today, and headed on towards a large shop with garments hanging on hooks, high above the doorway. They entered the premises and discovered an Aladdin's cave full of everything they would need. They were greeted by a wise old Cockney with a neatly trimmed grey beard, in a brown suit and with a long gold chain hanging from his waistcoat. His jacket was worn at the cuffs, his white shirt grey with wear and his tie knotted so tightly it seemed to be strangling him. When they had made their many purchases, they paid up and quickly changed into their newly acquired civilian clothing.

Within twenty minutes, their purchases and uniforms now packed into two backpacks and a holdall, they were back out on the street. It was only a short walk back to the station where they retrieved their kitbags and repacked everything, leaving their uniforms in a single bag to collect in a week's time. When they'd finished, they looked up at the large white-faced clock that hung centrally above the station floor. It was half past two. From where they were standing, they could see there was a York train leaving in ten minutes from platform 8.

'Let's go for that one, Ricky, save hanging about.' Ricky nodded. They got to the train with minutes to spare and were soon speeding north through heavy rain. The windows, not what they used to be, leaked and water dribbled down the inside and dripped onto the floor. Dave moved a holdall away with his foot while Ricky was oblivious; his eyes were firmly shut.

'Let me know when we arrive,' he grunted. Dave grinned at his mate who always found time to sleep.

Unremarked by either of them, the train finally approached York station. There was no squeal of brakes, just a steady coasting as the train decreased speed then, suddenly, a crescendo of noise reverberated from below the carriage as the bogie wheels ran over interconnecting railway lines, creating a disorderly clatter. The train rocked and the wheels screeched until finally peace reigned once more. The noise was enough to stir Dave who jumped up as if from a trance, rubbing his eyes. He kicked Ricky's foot.

'Ricky, wake up,' he said.

Startled, Ricky opened his eyes to see Dave peering out of the window shielding his eyes with his hands against the glass.

'What's up?' he asked, stretching his arms forward.

'We're here, mate,' Dave said, looking outside at the distant cathedral towers. 'Looks like we are bang on time.' He checked his watch. 'It's just after seventeen fifty; we've made good time.'

Neither of them had been to York before and as they stepped from the train, laden with the heavy bags, their eyes were drawn to the great arches of the old Victorian station building. It was a mighty structure with glass going up sixty, seventy feet, so neither was looking where they were going and didn't see a suitcase right in their path. Dave tripped headlong onto the concrete platform, yelling in pain as he landed. A young lady, alerted by his cries, ran across from a chocolate machine, looking rather flustered.

'I am so sorry,' she said, with a red face. 'I was just getting something to eat and didn't see you. Please forgive me. Are you OK?'

Dave brushed dust from his knees and then looked up at a stunningly beautiful woman with brown hair and lips to die for. How could he possibly be angry, he thought?

'Oh, that's all right, miss. Nothing damaged. Is your suitcase OK or does it need a bandage?' he asked jovially.

His clever wit brought an instant smile to her face, before she laughed aloud, her eyes warm and bright. Ricky had, by this time, retrieved the bags that had fallen away to the side and stood the lady's suitcase upright.

'Have you got time for a cup of tea?' she asked. 'It's the least I can do after almost breaking your neck.'

Ricky, forever the punctual one, looked at his watch, but Dave spoke for them both, quickly interjecting, 'Well, yes, we would like that,' before Ricky could respond. He slung his two bags over his shoulder and reached down to pick up her suitcase. 'Where shall we go?' he asked.

'The station tea shop is right outside, by platform 1,' she said, pointing across the way.

'Well, if you insist,' he said with a smile, and the three of them walked off like old friends.

Some twenty minutes later, after swapping stories of their lives, Dave, now fully swooning over this new love in his life, asked if he could write to her. She paused for a moment before taking a small green notebook from her handbag, tearing out a page and carefully writing her name and address in bold print followed by a single kiss. She folded it in half and handed it to him. Ricky, fully aware of Dave's love of all things in a skirt, knew that this was probably not a good idea and was just another one of his many short-lived attachments. He smiled though and suggested to Dave that they needed to be heading off. Dave looked down at his watch and then at the girl.

'Look, we are heading back at some point, can I come and see you?' he asked eagerly.

'Yes, I would like that,' she said, beaming at him. 'I work at the London City and Midland Bank on Church Street if you come back during the day. If not, well, you have my address. When are you visiting again, did you say?'

Ricky kicked Dave's foot under the table without looking at him.

'Not sure, but I will make every effort to see you again, and soon. Must go now. Bye, Nancy.'

She sat looking up at him, wondering if she had said something wrong, as they picked up their bags and headed off. As soon as they were far enough away from the tea room, Ricky opened his mouth, about to lambast him, but Dave beat him to it.

'Yes, I know. I can't believe how quickly she turned my head.'

'Anything in a skirt turns your head, Dave, everyone knows that,' he said, laughing.

As they headed towards the ticket office, Dave took a quick look back to where she was sitting to see if she was watching. She was; he smiled.

They now had a little over twenty-four hours to purchase the remaining items on the kit list their lieutenant had provided, catch the train to Pickering and find their way to Marshall Hall. It was crucial to locate a secluded hide as a base for the five days and that had to be done under the cover of darkness. They bought two tickets and once again stored the kitbags in the left luggage before heading into town.

York was a bustling place and the old wall around the city was a remarkable spectacle. They crossed the river and wandered up towards the great cathedral of York Minster. As they approached, they saw the huge windows over the entrance and couldn't resist taking a few moments to step inside one of Britain's iconic buildings. As they entered, their jaws dropped, seeing for the first time the immense Gothic nave that seemed to go on forever. The stained-glass windows ran the whole length on both sides towards the central tower and high altar and the Minster's huge organ. Beyond, a magnificent roof arched over the altar and the presbytery stretched up five storeys or more. They both sat down for a moment, bowing their heads in silent prayer. They were greatly moved by their surroundings and as they left, they dropped a few coins into the receptacle by the door.

They still had to complete the purchases on their kit list before catching the train to Pickering. Ricky checked his watch.

'First, a pub,' he said. 'We need to eat.'

Dave nodded enthusiastically and they headed away from the Minster towards town. Ten minutes later they walked through an old brick gateway, which had probably stood for hundreds of years, into the welcoming Lamb and Flag pub. It was warm and comfortable and full of people, with hardly a free table anywhere. They walked to the bar and ordered some mutton stew and two pints of dark ale. As they turned, two gentlemen dressed in fine clothes stood up from a table by the window and Dave moved over swiftly to secure it. They supped almost half of their beer in one swallow before Ricky pulled a map from his pocket and spread it across the table. Unobserved by anyone, they chatted about their next move, eyeing their destination. They plotted the distances they had to travel, before studying the access routes and surrounding land.

'There is a wood there on the north side of the boundary wall; we should target that,' Dave suggested. Ricky checked the distance from the track and realised they would have to cross a railway line to get there. He was about to mark the map with his pencil when a maid arrived with their meal and he quickly folded the map and tucked it inside his coat.

Half an hour later they left the pub to make their final purchases of cheese, cold meats, bread and fruit cakes before heading back to the station.

When they arrived, the train was already at the platform and they walked through several carriages, searching for an empty compartment so they could talk and repack their kit. Alas, the only seats available were with an old gentleman who sat by the door and smelt of moth balls and a lady with a small white dog that yapped incessantly. Ricky flung his bags on the rack above the seats and sat by the window, and Dave sat opposite the old man, one seat down. Within minutes, the train jumped forward and the platform started to move past the window as the train gained speed. It quickly left the lights of the city far behind, the view outside suddenly gone, as if they had entered a tunnel.

It took a little under thirty minutes to reach Pickering, and without a word spoken between them, they stood to gather their belongings as the train slowed. Ricky stood up and slid the compartment door open, and they walked along the corridor and stepped down from the train.

The platform was quiet with only two other passengers. Ricky went to sit on a bench, taking the map from his pocket, as he waited for Dave to walk over the footbridge. The train guard slammed the final door shut and blew his whistle. By the time the train had departed, Dave was heading for the exit. When all was quiet, Ricky stood up and slung his rucksack and large kitbag over his shoulder before heading up the footbridge steps too.

He left the station five minutes after Dave, just as a man ran out of the Station Hotel opposite and was violently sick in the gutter. He was too drunk to notice him, he thought, and looking first to the right then to the left, he headed up the gentle rise to the north.

It was a star-studded night with a new moon which allowed him just enough light to see Dave a couple of hundred yards ahead turning the corner. He set off at a brisk pace, and although heavily laden, he quickly closed the gap until he was upon him. Dave stepped off the road to the left and sat down against the hedge, Ricky dropping in beside him. Without speaking, they stripped off their outer clothing, tucking their jackets under the flaps of their rucksacks.

'OK, we have several miles ahead, let's make a move,' Dave said softly. As they stood, they could both see the outline of an old castle high on a hill above them. It was in ruins now, but, as soldiers, they could both appreciate the tactical advantage of its placement all those years before with all-round views of the surrounding land.

They knew the tab would take a couple of hours and they set off up the gentle rise and away into the night.

They stayed vigilant and every time a vehicle approached, or they heard voices, they would drop down and lie flat beside the road until all was clear. Being compromised now would be extremely unprofessional.

Happily, they saw very little traffic through the first hour and a half and none at all as they approached eleven o'clock. A little further on, they stopped at a bend in the road to take a short break. Quietly they reached for their flasks to have a drink and eat some bread and cheese, carefully monitoring the road in both directions. It was a very still night, with only a gentle breeze as company. Dave pulled out his torch with its red lens and crouched carefully against the hedge to view the map, Ricky closing in tight.

'We have another mile to go before the turning. Are you OK?' Dave asked quietly. Ricky didn't speak, simply tapped him on his shoulder before rising to set off on the last leg.

They had adopted the old army method of distance against time, using three miles for each hour as their guide. Knowing their own pace, the turning appeared almost exactly twenty minutes later. They paused at the corner to check the map once more and settled in behind a wall. They heard voices ahead, but this didn't concern them as they were now turning off the road. As they were about to move off, there was sudden movement to their right, stopping them in their tracks. Their sniper training immediately kicked in and they slowly sank back to the ground, eyes wide, their hearts pounding. They fixed their eyes on the disturbance and saw several small bodies scurrying away in the semi-darkness, one bleating as it went.

They walked in single file, keeping about five yards apart, their eyes peeled for any sign of activity. As they crept over the rise, they could see ahead a dim light outside a cottage on the corner and a large barn next to the road. They approached with caution. They paused in the hedge to the left, keeping their heads below the skyline.

'Water,' Ricky whispered, and he went across into the yard next to the barn, searching for a tap. He was back almost immediately. 'Just to the left past the gate is a small outside tap. Let's fill our flasks now.'

Five minutes later, their flasks full, they were on their way again, skirting around the corner into a narrow lane. If their map reading was correct, it would bring them to their final destination.

It was now almost midnight, and as they cleared the tree line to their right, which had been screening the valley below, the lights of a vast house came into view in the distance. Ahead, some two hundred yards away, a small lodge appeared out of the darkness, and as they closed in, they saw the entrance gate. They dropped to the ground and waited a few moments, but the cottage was quiet. Dave stepped up to see a single bolt holding the gate shut and waved Ricky forward. By the time he had walked over, Dave had slipped the bolt back and the gate swung open. They passed through it and he pushed the bolt back into position. They headed down the slope to the valley below.

At the bottom, they crossed the railway track quickly, before tucking themselves under the high wall. They could now see another pair of gates ahead, but the wall ran both ways, north and south. Ricky pulled Dave in close.

'I suggest we head north and follow it round to the east towards that wood we saw on the map. What do you think?' he said in a faint whisper. Dave walked up to the gates and looked through the bars, studying the land that led up to Marshall Hall. Within a minute, he came back and leant his arm on his oppo's shoulder.

'Agreed. It's less distance, and the wood is key.'

Ricky moved off, following the wall parallel with the rail tracks on their left for several hundred yards. After about ten minutes, the wall turned ninety degrees and headed east and they followed it carefully, avoiding the many tree stumps along the way.

Soon they were walking through a tree line. It was dense in places, offering good protection. After a further ten minutes, Dave observed a small structure of some kind off to his left and headed over towards it. The flat-topped shelter, with just three sides and a tin roof, was clearly meant for sheep. Ricky shook it gently, and finding it sturdy enough, dropped his pack from his weary shoulders. He crouched down and crawled in, seeing it was long enough to lie down full length. From the entrance, Dave looked back over his shoulder and noticed he could actually see the lights from the Hall over a section of the wall that appeared to have partially collapsed. This would prove to be a real asset.

They agreed the shelter was suitable as a temporary hide and sat down to sort out their gear. Ricky pulled some food from his pack, offering it to his best mate before taking several slugs of water. They rearranged their gear but unpacked very little in case they were compromised. As they rested, Ricky yawned. He hadn't realised how tired he was. Dave, forever the considerate soldier, offered to do the first watch and Ricky nodded before settling back and slipping quickly to sleep. Dave stood twenty yards away, munching some dried meat, peering through his binoculars at the house over the low point in the wall. Over the next six hours, they took turns to grab some sleep an hour about until, just before dawn, clouds appeared overhead. They ate some fruit cake for breakfast, had some water from their flasks and checked their watches.

'Right, one of us has to be back outside Pickering station at eighteen hundred. So, do you want to toss for it?' Dave asked. He didn't have a coin so put a stone in one of his hands behind his back, asking Ricky to choose. He lost, much to his annoyance.

For the rest of the morning, they cleaned and rebuilt their rifles, oiled and loaded the Webley pistols, sorted and repacked their kit and studied the map.

They tried to judge the distances between the Hall and various parts of the estate, studying the house for movement whenever they could, all the while keeping a strict lookout along the line of the wall. Ricky volunteered to do the recce, while Dave rested up as he had the long walk back to town.

'I'll circle round to the east, following the wall to the far side, and probably circle back along the railway line. I will take my small pack with me along with some provisions and the Webley. If I am not back when you go, I will see you both here around twenty hundred. OK?'

Dave was satisfied and handed his friend some food and a flask of water. Ricky tucked the Webley pistol in the holster under his arm.

'I'll hide both rifles away from the hide,' Dave said, looking around. 'There, over by that pile of branches. I'll camouflage the gear in the back of the hide. If someone finds our kit while we are gone, we will at least still have our weapons and ammunition.'

Ricky nodded.

'Good luck, mate, keep your head down,' said Dave.

Ricky smiled before pulling his cap down over his eyes and setting off along the wall to the north.

CHAPTER 7

The gallant young lieutenant who had spent almost two years at the front was now feeling wet and rather miserable following three hours on the back of his brother's Norton motorcycle. Water had penetrated through all his outer layers and now at intervals irritatingly trickled down his neck. He gathered his thoughts of those worse off than him and even tried to focus on Charlotte, his sister, and his mother to avoid being distracted. His time at home had been special for them all and his visit to the War Office had proved very useful, with his old school friend, now a civil servant, providing vital information. His secret was safe, he was sure of that.

As he peered through his steamed-up goggles, he saw a petrol station ahead and hoped it had somewhere he might get a hot meal. As he pulled in, he parked his bike close to the door, flicking the stand with his foot and pulling the bike backwards until it clicked into position. He could see the place was largely empty, but to his pleasure, there was a small tea room to the side. The petrol attendant was pulling on his coat as he stepped from the door of a tiny office, but Corn waved him back, shaking his head, imitating drinking tea with his hand. The man smiled and went back into the dry. Corn stretched his back before walking over to the tea room.

He left his bundle on the rear rack but took the small satchel and the holdall containing his weapons and ammo. The warmth immediately struck him as he stepped through the door. He shook his coat in the foyer before dropping his kit by a small table near the window. As he did so, a man at a table opposite spoke to him.

'Is that a Big 4 Norton, 600 cc?' he asked, looking at the bike through the steamed-up window.

Corn didn't answer straightaway but began to pull off the wet leather helmet and long woollen scarf that his mother had insisted he wear, placing them both on the chair. He looked across at the man, who was thickset with a few days' beard growth, probably mid-thirties and supping a large mug of tea.

'Yes, it is. Do you know motorbikes then?' he asked.

The man struggled to his feet and started walking over to Corn's table.

'I used to have several of my own until the war came. Lost a leg in the second battle of Ypres in 1915. Never ridden one since,' he said. 'What speed do you get? I used to get sixty from mine.'

Corn was now free of his wet clothes and walked over to the counter to order some tea and something hot. When he looked round, the man had perched on the table next to his gear. Corn paid the lady and walked back to his table. As he pushed his change into his trouser pocket, the man sat down on a chair at the next table.

'I get just under sixty, about fifty-eight I think, which is pretty good considering it's the 1910 model,' he said, smiling. 'I do find the start-up procedure a bit of a faff though, what with the fuel switch and tickle value, before fiddling with the retard switch, but it does always seem to start first kick. Not a good day to be on a motorcycle today though.'

'Army man, are you?' said the chap.

'Yes, I have some leave for a few days, up visiting a lady, you know.' He nodded his head sideways at the man.

'Oh yes, indeed I do. Does she live far?'

Corn sat down and rubbed his hands together, not wanting to get too involved with the stranger. 'Oh, some way to go yet. What about you, where are you heading?' he asked, deliberately trying to deflect his questions.

'Oh, I got wind of some work on a large estate north of here, a retired general no less, heard about it on the old boys' network. He needs some security for his house or something, not sure really, but hopefully, he can use an old soldier.'

Corn felt an instant tingle run up his back as the man spoke, making him shudder. He paused for a moment, thinking of the odds of meeting someone heading to the same estate as him, but for quite different reasons. He needed more information and decided to engage him in some general chatter, realising he could well be speaking to a prospective foe.

'Oh yes, which estate is that then?' he asked nonchalantly.

The man reached inside his coat pocket and pulled out a notebook. He turned a few pages. 'Here it is. It's called Marshall Hall, near a town called Pickering. I have to report to a man called Harper. Do you know it?' he said, putting the notebook back. Corn hesitated as he didn't wish to show his interest, only make polite conversation.

'No, no I don't,' he said. 'Does he need any more help, do you know? I have a friend who badly needs a job, he's ex-army too. Where could he find out, do you think?'

The man sat down opposite him, his false leg protruding out into the aisle. 'Well, there were jobs, but don't know how many might be left. Why don't you telegram your friend to contact a Mr Harper at the Hall? I will mention it to him if you like?'

Corn was determined to take full advantage of the gift he had been presented with, as getting someone on the inside was an opportunity not to be missed.

'Would it be all right to mention your name, old chap?' Corn asked.

'Why, sure, no problem. I'm Pete Kemp. And you?'

Corn had to act quickly so as not to give anything away.

'Lieutenant Richard Darcy of the Oxford and Bucks regiment. Pleased to meet you, Pete, and sorry about your leg.'

The man shook his head rapidly. 'Oh, that's OK, quite used to it now. Bloody Jerries,' he said, sipping his tea. 'I thought you were an officer. How long do you have?'

Corn waited, as his meal arrived, with a large mug of tea. 'I have five days. Have to be back in France by Saturday.' Then he lifted his mug and took a long drink.

'Well, good luck, sir. I have to go now, my bus is due any minute. All the best and I hope you and your young lady have a nice time,' he said, winking at him. Corn stood to shake the hand of his new enemy, something the chap would hopefully never know.

Kemp pulled his collar up around his ears and placed his cap on his head before limping out into the rain. Within minutes, a green bus pulled up. Corn wiped the steamed-up window with his fist so he could see the sign on the front of the bus: York. The chap got on and the bus quickly pulled away.

He ate his meal quickly as his mind wandered, knowing the benefits of getting Miller or Gibbs on the inside. He hadn't really had a proper plan, but now their way in had been handed to them on a plate. He felt reinvigorated and was keen to get on. Ten minutes later he wiped the last of the gravy around his plate with a piece of bread. He stood up and reached for his damp scarf, winding it back around his neck, before putting on his long oilskin coat, buttoning it all the way up to his neck. As he placed the leather helmet back on his head, it squelched as water ran down his neck. He bent down to reach for his satchel and holdall before heading outside.

Within minutes he was once again thundering north on the open road, but at last, the rain was easing. After fifteen minutes, he saw the green bus and passed it at speed, not looking up.

CHAPTER 8

At five o'clock, Harper and Stevens entered the drawing room. General Davis was sitting with papers all over the small table in front of his armchair and looked up as they entered.

'Ah, gentlemen, please sit,' he said, pointing to two dining chairs by the refectory table. They sat down quickly, pulling the chairs to face him. He cast his eyes across at them, in turn, as if reading their every thought.

'I have thought long and hard about how much I should tell you, but if I don't divulge certain details, you won't be able to do your duties. So, listen carefully.' The general paused, sipping his glass of sherry several times.

'Right, as you know, I left the army just two days ago and I will be in full residence here for the foreseeable future. I expect you have been wondering what has been going on with all the new security arrangements. Well, before I left London, a friend in the War Office told me I should keep one eye looking over my shoulder, following certain incidences that happened in France. My life, gentlemen, I believe is at risk,' he said forcefully.

'Now, following the sudden retirement of Mr Lockhart, who has been with me on the estate for twenty years, and not having time to search for a replacement, I have decided to promote you, Harper, to the position of estate manager.' Stevens was shocked. He felt aggrieved and wanted to look across at Harper, but refrained from doing so, to avoid seeing the wry smile that was already spreading across his face.

'Harper, you will not only be running the security for the Hall and the estate, but now will take on the management of all the staff cottages, the three farm tenancies, the gatekeeper's lodge, plus all future shooting parties.'

Harper looked across at Stevens with a sly grin, but he retained his poise and didn't look at him.

'Stevens, I need you to get used to the idea quickly, as I cannot have you two embroiled in any sort of power struggle. You will remain in charge of all household staff and duties, of course; however, there will be areas that cross both roles. I ask that between you it is managed in an orderly way. Is that clear?' he said, filling his glass once more.

Stevens could hold his inquisitive thoughts no longer and looked across at Harper, a man he had never warmed to, before looking back.

'May I ask who is in overall charge, sir? As it will get mighty confusing for the staff if matters are not done in accordance with house procedures. And—'

The general held up his hand to stop the man's questioning.

'I am,' he said sternly. 'All staff and household matters will go through you, as usual, but do not let them mix with the Hall security team. Inside the house, it's your responsibility; outside, Harper, you take charge. Is that clear?' he said firmly.

Stevens looked pensive. 'Yes, sir, I understand.' Harper didn't speak but was joyous that he might get the upper hand in this arrangement.

'New faces will be arriving shortly with two house staff already on their way here; one housemaid and a junior footman. The security team will be interviewed and then hired as they arrive, but this is your call, Harper. Don't let me down,' the general said, staring at him.

'Once you have selected your team, I want to see your security plan. As estate manager, I will now expect you to join me each day to discuss routine matters of the estate. We can arrange a time that suits us both.' Harper smiled to himself, feeling Stevens' eyes on him.

'So, brief the house staff accordingly tonight after hours. I ask that you do not, under any circumstances, mention to anyone, what I have told you regarding the threat to my life. If asked, just say we are simply beefing up security due to a series of thefts in the area following advice from the police. For this all to work, you will both need to get along, as have no doubts, I will not hesitate to get rid of one or both of you if you cannot work together. Finally, I realise you have not received salary increases since before the war, Stevens. So, I have decided you will receive an extra twenty pounds a year, from the start of the month. Is that satisfactory?'

Stevens raised his head and smiled. 'Yes, sir, thank you, sir,' he said, casting a glance at Harper.

'OK, you may go.'

They both stood and the butler nodded his head slightly before turning for the door.

'Not you, Harper,' said the general, and he sat back down.

When the door was closed, Davis opened his folder and read for a few moments before looking up.

'I am aware it's only been twenty-four hours, but how are the building alterations coming along? Are you on top of everything?' he asked.

Harper reached for his notebook and for almost ten minutes ran through the progress he had made. General Davis didn't speak throughout but, surprisingly, offered his congratulations when he had finished.

'Sounds like you have things in hand. I will leave you to it then, but let's agree to meet daily at five o'clock. You will also be pleased to learn that you too will receive an addition to your pay. I have taken advice from my solicitor and I will double your current wage from today in line with your new status. I will also provide you with fifteen pounds to purchase suitable clothing, which you can do in your own time. Estate manager is a big responsibility; I hope I have not misjudged you. Now be off with you.'

Harper went straight down to locate Stevens, finding him in his tiny office below stairs.

'Albert, do you have five minutes?' he asked, and sat down in the chair across from the desk. Stevens folded his arms and frowned.

'A lot is at stake here. So, what do you say we meet here, in your office, at four o'clock each day, prior to the general's briefing? We can clear up anything that has occurred and deal with it without delay. I want this to work, as I am sure you do, so please let us get along,' Harper said.

Stevens looked at him, affronted. 'Firstly, I have not given you permission to call me by my Christian name, so please don't. Second, if you think for one minute, I am going to make this easy for you, you have another think coming. I have been at this house for over twenty years and will not stand by and watch you try and take over. Finally, keep your hands off my staff. I am senior here, and you will respect me as butler at all times. If you need something done, you will need to come to me. If you wish to change something, you come to me. Do not try and cross me, Harper, as I will make life extremely difficult for you if you try.' At that, he lifted his chin, tucked his folder under his arm and walked out, leaving Harper sitting forlorn, shaking his head.

***

The next day, Harper started work before six o'clock and visited Lockhart's estate office. He had clearly not been an efficient man as it was in a terrible state. He had so much to learn, what with taking on the running of the estate and now increasing the house staff twofold over the coming week. Organising the accommodation for the men in itself had been a challenge; however, placing an early call to their suppliers in York meant all the new beds and equipment would be delivered later that day.

The new security team would be billeted in the old annexe which, although it was conveniently positioned directly to the rear of the house, would not prove to be the most comfortable of places. Work was already underway to build washing and toilet facilities by converting two small storerooms at the rear that were fed by cold water taps. A high wall built across the width of the building separated the sleeping quarters from the new rest area, which was being filled with old furniture that had been in storage for many years. With a fireplace in the middle of one wall and a good stock of logs, it would provide reasonable comfort. Harper was content with progress in just one day and, although the men would not be best comfortable, they were to be paid well for their work.

He had begun developing the security plan which would cover the house and grounds on a twenty-four-hour basis. He would place two men on the roof each night, covering the front and rear entrances, while other men would share general patrols. There would be one stationary guard post outside the general's quarters. The men would eat in the servants' pantry at a second sitting and those having duties within the Hall would have access to all rooms on the lower floors according to their individual responsibilities. Over the coming days, he hoped to have a team of capable ex-soldiers ready to defend the estate and his master's honour.

As he wrote out his orders, and his actions policy, he stopped to wonder what had brought on this massive change. What had happened in France, he wondered? It was clearly very serious as he had been relieved of his normal duties. After a further hour's work, he sat back, content, deciding the telegrams were his next priority.

He donned his coat and hat, locking the papers in the top drawer of his desk and pulled the door closed. The walk to the village gave him time to clear his head and he felt pleased with his progress. When he arrived at the telegraph office, he took three blank forms and stood in the corner to write them out. First, he drafted one to an old regimental sergeant major he had remained in touch with, who now worked within the War Office. He wanted to quiz him on the general's retirement. The second was to a friend in London to publish the estate jobs through regimental associations. The final one was a private message sent to his old friend, Sergeant Dick Worrall, who was serving with the Glosters at the front. He and Dick had grown up together but had not been in touch for some time. If he knew anything, he would pass it on, he was sure of that.

Throughout that day, the plumbers put the finishing touches to the ablutions and the old furniture was set in position in the rest area. The sleeping quarters would be filled with four sets of bunkbeds and four single beds placed down both sides of the room with enough old boot boxes under the beds for everyone. There would be little privacy, but it was dry and warm.

After dinner, Stevens brought all the house staff together and everyone quietened down as the house butler stood in front of them. Harper watched from the back of the room waiting to deliver his new message as estate manager.

'I won't keep you long, but there are to be some major changes at the Hall which some of you have noticed already. But first I want to welcome Edna and James to the staff. You will find us all hard-working and friendly but learn quickly, as there is always much to do. The housekeeper will show you your duties, Edna. James, you will work under me. OK, the general has decided to employ some security guards, who will start arriving tomorrow, to protect the estate and all of us from the upsurge in theft and pillage. Mr Harper will take charge of the men who will be accommodated in the annexe to the rear. They are staff members; however, they will only enter the house for duties and meals. You are not to fraternise with them, but I ask you to be civil. Mrs Tate, can you arrange for them to eat after the main house staff, in a second sitting, please. I will leave you to liaise with Mr Harper about timings and your weekly allowance will be increased pro rata. We will obviously have to introduce some new procedures over the coming days and weeks, so, for now, just follow your normal duties until told otherwise. I will brief you each evening as things change. Are there any questions?' he said, believing he had covered every detail. The kitchen assistant sitting at the back then raised her hand.

'Well, Mr Stevens, I was just wondering if we are in danger. I have to leave the house in darkness early each morning to go down to the farm to gather eggs and collect the milk which takes me about thirty minutes. I am all alone and away from the house.'

Stevens smiled. 'Morag, we are not in danger. The security men will protect us from any hostile intruders if they come knocking.' He looked across at Harper. 'Perhaps it can be arranged for you to be escorted each day to put your mind at rest. Anything else? No, OK, that's all then.'

Before he could finish his words, Harper cut in quickly. 'Just a minute, everyone, we have not quite finished,' he said, flashing a glance across the room towards Stevens. 'I just need two minutes of your time. You should know that I have been promoted to estate manager. Parsons, the under butler, will assume my old duties as valet with immediate effect. We are employing twelve men, many of whom will be army veterans having served in the war. They will be experienced at what they do and will be armed. Some will have access to the upper floors in this house, but not your quarters on the top floor. These will be out of bounds as will their accommodation to all of you. Any indiscretions will result in immediate loss of employment. Finally, some changes will occur to daily routines, so learn them quickly and listen carefully when these nightly briefings occur. Within a week, it will be running smoothly. That will be all, thank you.'

Stevens looked across the room at Harper, who was already rushing over to him, with eyes of an eagle. As the staff dispersed, he asked to speak to him in his office. Stevens casually looked up and nodded to him, in a condescending way. 'Come this way,' he said, and led him across the hallway into his tiny room. Harper shut the door and turned to face him.

'It serves us both poorly if we, in the eyes of the staff, are battling against each other. You knew full well I had some details to announce regarding security issues and yet you dismissed them deliberately. The unprofessionalism is just not helpful. I will say nothing to the general on this occasion, but be warned, Mr Stevens, you make this difficult for me and I will inform him of your conduct and unproductive attitude which will look very badly on you. Take heed.' He turned and left, leaving the door wide open.

Stevens pondered his next action, thinking that Harper had to go.

***

Bark arrived at Pickering station a little early. He was to collect the first arrivals in the small estate truck and while he waited, he opened his small flask of tea that Mrs Tate had prepared for him. He was her favourite and she always looked after him. He hoped one day they might become closer and was daydreaming about their future together when a whistle sounded as the train approached the station, killing his thoughts. He headed for the platform and met five burly chaps, the first instalment of the new security staff members.

CHAPTER 9

Sergeant Dick Worrall was engaged in demonstrating the technique for stripping a Lee Enfield rifle, blindfold, a regular undertaking for all the new boys who joined from training. Many thought the practice a little unusual, but he was of the old school where a soldier must be able to do anything, day or night, to the same standard. It was extremely important that these young soldiers could strip and clean their weapons in any conditions and without losing or dropping the moving parts in the mud. Too many rifles had been rendered useless due to cold fingers and failed practices. So, on this damp morning, he had a small group of four who had arrived the previous afternoon, horrified at the conditions, looking cold and hungry. He was determined to cover details not touched during training and he knew they would thank him for it one day.

One of each pair now had a scarf wrapped around their head covering their eyes, the other watching carefully for any mistakes. He had tried over the many months to make it light-hearted and awarded cigarettes to the best of the bunch. On this occasion, a young private who stood barely five feet three tall and probably weighing less than eight stones became the butt of all the jibes from his comrades. He struggled to assemble his rifle, even though his partner handed him the pieces when the sergeant's back was turned. Worrall struck a match to light the cigarette hanging from his lips, shaking his head as he exhaled the first drag. He persevered for some time and each man did well, all apart from one.

'OK, that will do. Digby, you are to report to me each morning to repeat this exercise until you have grasped it. The rest of you have passed, well done. You can go,' he said. The young soldier received a ribbing from his chums but accepted his extra duties.

'Yes, sergeant, what time?' he asked.

'Zero eight thirty each day until I am satisfied. Now bugger off.'

As Worrall sat down to make a brew, one of the young squaddies slapped Digby gently around his head and nudged him forward.

Lance Corporal Adams, of the Royal Engineer's postal section, was a favourite visitor amongst the men as he brought the mail down from HQ on Tuesday and Thursday mornings. He was known to the men of the company as 'Smoky' due to the fag-end that never left his lips. The lads always stopped what they were doing or woke from their slumber when they heard his morning shout of 'posty'.

As he wandered down the line handing bundles of mail to each platoon sergeant, men would gather expectantly, hoping to receive a letter or parcel from a loved one. It was always the highlight of any man's day, but the disappointment was hard to hide if you went without.

Sergeant Worrall was just pouring hot water into his mug when he heard the sounds of joviality off to his right. The Germans, just three hundred yards to the north, must have wondered what on earth was going on as the men circled and cheered in fine spirits. Dick stood on an ammo box with the rather large stack of letters that had been given to him in a small brown sack. Apart from those on watch, the men gathered around him as he pulled a handful out and watched the happy faces around him as he read out the names. Reaching over the heads of others, men would be desperate to grab their personal letter before stepping away. Dick took great joy in this twice-weekly task, sometimes teasing the men when letters smelt of perfume. He would sometimes call out a name and then say, 'Sorry, none for you today!' in typical military humour.

It wasn't always good news of course. On this day, in particular, Private Franklin received two letters but his joy was quickly spoilt as he realised his efforts to stay smitten with two girlfriends at the same time had been rumbled. He gathered some of the lads in his section around him and read out the story of his error. It seemed he had put their respective letters in the wrong envelopes, resulting in some rather curt replies!

Dick wasn't expecting anything himself and was surprised to pull out a telegram with his name on it. He stuffed it inside his tunic until he had finished. 'That's it, lads, away you go. There is always Thursday,' he said as many men walked away with empty hands.

He pulled out the telegram and looked at it with interest, wondering who on earth was sending him a telegram. He broke the seal and opened it up to see the usual post office telegram heading wrapped around the crown of His Majesty the King.

Sergeant R Worrall, 2/5th Royal Gloucestershire Regt
Working for General Davis in Yorkshire.
Appreciate details if known, of his sudden retirement.
Best.
Bill Harper, Estate Manager
Marshall Hall, Pickering. Yorkshire.

He had not heard from Bill since he left the trenches well over a year before. This old school friend, a man he had sat next to all through school and who had shared his family table until they were fourteen, was now working for the man who had masterminded and implemented the arrest and death warrant of his young friend, Private Ed Mitchell. He hated Davis more than the Bosch he fought on a daily basis. To compound the problem, he knew Lieutenant Cavanagh was heading to his location to spoil the party. What was he to do?

He certainly couldn't send a signal from the trenches and the sensors would pick holes in any letter relating to Davis directly. No, he must leave well alone. He screwed up the telegram and placed it in the burner under his metal pan of water, the flames quickly taking hold.

CHAPTER 10

At a little before six, Dave Gibbs was sitting in the hotel bar opposite the railway station, pleased he had made such good time on his long walk back to Pickering. He had met very little traffic en route, stepping away from the road every time he heard the sound of a vehicle approaching. Although an active soldier, his feet ached after limited marching over recent months and he was glad to reach the hotel.

At the bar, he asked for a brew of tea, some mutton soup and bread. As he waited, he was forced to shift from foot to foot to reduce the stinging sensation in his soles. When his food arrived, he headed for a table near the window that offered him good vision across the street. After quickly devouring his meal, he sat and waited.

As the bar clock chimed a quarter to seven, his ears pricked up as he heard the sound of a motorbike. Peering outside, he saw a motorbike pull up, not recognising his lieutenant at first. As the bike was silenced, he tapped on the window and Corn's eyes flashed towards him. Seeing Dave through the discoloured pane, he nodded before unstrapping some of his kit from the bike and walking towards the door. Dave headed back over to the bar.

'Can I have two pints of ale please and another bowl of soup?' he asked with a smile. The girl nodded and asked for one shilling and threepence which he duly handed over. By the time he had turned back to the table with the beer, Lieutenant Cavanagh had entered the bar, looking cold and pale. He dropped his holdall on the floor by the table, observing the people in the room. He climbed out of his heavy overcoat, removed his helmet and then sat down with a sigh. Dave Gibbs stood beside him, offering his hand as if greeting an old friend. Corn shook it warmly, turning his chair to face him and shivered.

'You look frozen, boss.'

'It has been a cold testing drive, I can tell you, but it served a purpose as I now know how we are going to attack this problem.'

Dave pushed a pint towards him, rather intrigued.

'But, how was your journey? Did you get everything?' Corn asked, just as the serving girl arrived from the kitchen, placing the hot soup in front of him. After she left, Corn thanked Gibbs, picked up the spoon and started to sate his rampant hunger. As he ate, Dave briefed his lieutenant on all that had occurred. The soup was gone in a flash and Corn turned around to call across the room to the barmaid.

'Can I have two more soups, please?' he asked.

Dave sipped his pint then informed his lieutenant that Miller had been starting a full recce of the estate just as he left and would meet them at the hide. The officer seemed content with progress but pressed him for information about the layout of the estate. Dave, about to offer further details, was halted once again as the girl arrived with more food. Dave delved into his pocket once more and paid her a shilling, telling her to keep the change.

'There is an estate lodge by the outer gate, about half a mile from the house. That in itself is not a problem; however, getting the motorbike past without being noticed is practically impossible. But there is a small lane that turns right from the road about five hundred yards away from the lodge, and we might find a spot there under the trees and collect it when we need to. We have also found a water point, but we can only use it at night as it's near a small cottage. So, we are all good. How did you get on?' he asked.

'Well, I had a real break on my way here, bumping into an old soldier, injured at Ypres, by the name of Pete Kemp. He was invalided out of the army two years ago and is on his way up here right now in an effort to get employment on the estate. They are looking for security staff. It takes little imagination to realise the advantage of having a man on the inside as it will make our task a great deal easier. It's very risky, but I want you to be that man, Gibbs. Are you happy to go undercover?'

Dave was a big man, well over six feet tall, and was always the first to volunteer for any mission at the front, so nodded eagerly, thinking of the honour it would bestow on him to avenge his old friend Ed Mitchell.

'Great. Tomorrow, you will turn up at the house with a cover story to avert suspicion. We will confirm all the plans tonight when we meet up with Miller.'

They finished their soup and drank the ale rapidly before gathering up their belongings and departing the hotel. It was half past seven.

As they reached the motorbike, a small truck pulled up and parked fifty feet or so up the road. As the lieutenant prepped the Norton, then kick-started it, the late train from York was just pulling into the station. The Norton suddenly roared into life and he throttled it back several times. Gibbs swung his long leg over the rear saddle, carrying the rifle case and holding onto the officer's holdall. Cavanagh put the bike into gear and twisted the throttle, pulling away up the slight rise. Dave peered over his shoulder as they left to see several men walking down the steps from the station, where a man with an open book greeted them. Corn powered on the throttle and sped off into the night, the old Norton not seeming to mind the heavy load.

Gibbs, having never ridden on a motorcycle before, hung on for dear life. He leant slightly sideways to see past the lieutenant's shoulder at the road ahead, but the wind was too strong and he lost all vision. Slowly, his eyes became accustomed to it and before long he was grinning to himself as he opened his mouth, making it billow like a sail. He moved his head slightly from side to side and his cheeks vibrated as the air was forced inside. He laughed aloud, finding the whole experience rather thrilling.

After a short time, Gibbs tapped Corn on the shoulder and shouted in his ear to take the next right turn. They wobbled a bit as they slowed, Corn struggling with the excess weight behind him before pulling on the throttle once again. A little further on, they approached the small cottage on the right and Dave told him to stop. Corn turned off the engine, coasting around the corner until they pulled up on the grass. They got off and Corn pushed the bike quietly along the road for a hundred yards, to a small copse on the left. They sat for a full five minutes, hidden from view, hands on the pistol grips of their Webleys, listening. A few minutes later, a vehicle pulled round the bend, turning left. They stepped from cover and watched a small truck turn into an entrance and disappear down a hill.

'That must be the truck we saw at the station,' Dave said. 'It's just pulled into the lodge entrance. That's our entry point.' They sat for a further few minutes, and once satisfied no one had seen them, they covered the bike with branches and set off on foot towards the lodge.

As they approached, the lights of the building shone brightly and instinctively they moved into the tree line. As they watched, a man came out and stood in the porch, sucking on his pipe, staring into the night sky. Ten minutes later he disappeared back inside, and as the door slammed shut, the small porch light was switched off.

'Follow me,' Gibbs whispered, stepping towards the large iron gates and easing the bolt back before slipping through. Corn closed in behind him and they quickly secured the bolt before dropping down the hill and crossing the railway track. The lights from the Hall appeared ahead of them and Corn stopped and peered through the gates.

'So, that's our target, is it?' he said quietly. They stood watching for several minutes.

'We should go, boss,' Dave said, and they headed north along the outside of the wall before turning east. After fifteen minutes, they arrived at the primitive shelter where Miller was crouched to one side under a tree. He walked over and greeted his lieutenant with a handshake, saying he had heard them coming several minutes ago. Dave smiled, knowing he was always an excellent scout and seemed to have the hearing of a bat. They dropped their gear and were about to clamber undercover when Corn stopped as he caught sight of lights away to his right.

'So, we can see the Hall from here?' he asked.

'Yes, sir,' Ricky said. 'It's just lucky the perimeter wall is partly down on this side which provides a good line of sight. I have done a full recce. Do you want me to brief you now?'

After nine hours sitting on a motorbike, Corn was tired and his backside ached. He wished he'd caught the train.

'Right, listen in. I want to bring you up to date first, Miller, following some luck I had earlier today.' For the next ten minutes, Corn told them about his opportunistic meeting with the ex-soldier with a limp. He explained how this offered them a significant advantage and he had decided that Gibbs would be at the front gate in the morning to try and gain employment. Miller looked at him with some envy, as his involvement would now be key to their success.

'Have you eaten?' Ricky asked.

'Yes, we ate in the pub,' Dave said. Corn pulled out his hipflask containing his favoured Dalwhinnie whisky and handed it round. Gibbs coughed, Ricky laughed and Corn shook his head.

'OK, what of the estate, Miller?' Corn asked eagerly. Ricky put his memory head back on and took out the map he had drawn. He switched on his low-light torch and began explaining the layout and areas of concern.

'The estate is completely surrounded by an eight-foot wall that has crumbled in some places, allowing for easy access which I've marked here and here,' he said, pointing. 'It's approximately two miles in length and has two small access doors which were both locked. There is also one double gate, central, on the eastern side, but there is no track that I could see. At various points, trees overhang the wall and gaining access would be easy enough, but although I did climb up to look, there are no obvious ways that I could see to get back over the wall from the inside. I saw no one in the grounds, just plenty of sheep, and the nearest point the house sits to the wall is about five hundred yards. The grounds do have lots of trees, shrubs and gardens so there is cover if needed. I have located several possible escape routes which I can show you tomorrow. Most importantly, I have found another shelter that is well hidden in the trees not three hundred yards from here. I doubt many people even know of its existence as it seems undisturbed. It's opposite another damaged section of wall with a large overhanging tree. I think it's ideal and believe we should move there tonight.'

Corn thought for a second before answering. 'Well done, Miller. I think that might be wise. Can we carry all our gear in one lift?'

'I think so, sir, and it would be good for Dave to see its precise location in case he needs to leave quickly.'

The officer nodded. 'OK, let's get moving now.'

Gibbs interrupted them. 'Did you collect the rifles, Ricky?'

Corn looked confused.

'It's OK, boss, we hid them as we were both away from the hide this afternoon. But yes, I've got them,' said Ricky.

'What about the motorcycle, sir?' asked Dave.

'It's quite safe where it is and tomorrow it won't be here anyway as you will need it to drive up to the house.'

An anxious look appeared on Dave's face. He was about to speak when the lieutenant crawled out of the shelter, ready to leave.

As they gathered everything up, they took great care to feel around on the ground, not wishing to leave anything behind. Miller used the wall as his guide, and after a hundred paces, he reached a boulder he had placed next to a tree stump. He told them to stop, turned left and set off again at ninety degrees to the original direction.

'It's this way, boss,' he said quietly, and they followed him closely. Less than a minute later, they came upon a thicket of gorse and crawled through a gap low to the ground, before a small timber structure, some eight feet square and four feet high, appeared. They were not sure what it was used for, but it would suit them well. They placed their gear in three corners, only unpacking what they needed, ready for withdrawal at any time. When settled, Gibbs spoke.

'Sir, there is something I need to tell you. I had never been on a motorcycle before until tonight. I can't ride!'

'OK, don't worry, I will teach you in the morning. You'll be all right.'

Dave, always keen to do any job well, shrugged his shoulders and settled down to rest.

'You have done well, chaps. Heads down now for a few hours and we will talk more at first light. There is one thing, no more surnames or rank. From now on its first names only, as if we are ever overheard, people will know we are military. Clear?'

'What should we call you?' asked Ricky, nervously.

'My name is Cornelius but Corn for short. Ricky, you take first watch, one hour about, we rise at dawn.' As they settled down into their well-practised routine, sleep came quickly.

The night passed in a flash and dawn was quickly upon them, bringing with it a fine drizzle. It was just after six o'clock and still dark when Corn walked back to the track with Dave. In the dim light, he pushed the bike back to the main road and set off for a mile or so, turning left before they came to the village. They stopped in a narrow gate entrance half a mile down the road and Corn began describing the basics of the bike, beginning with the 600cc engine and the four gears. He showed him the fuel switch, the tickle button and the retard switch, checking that Dave understood at each stage.

'This is the choke, but she doesn't generally need it, then you find the compression point on the kick-start, pull in the valve under here and twist the throttle back slightly. Once done, give a kick.' He then asked Dave to repeat all he had just learned, but he struggled to remember the order. Running through it all again, Dave slowly started to grasp the procedure.

'OK, any questions?' Corn asked. Dave stood looking at the beast of a machine before him.

'It's like riding a bicycle,' Corn said, smiling at him. Little did he know that Dave had never learned that either.

'On you get,' Corn said, and Dave straddled the bike, feeling the full weight for the first time. He was nervous, but it had to be done. He ran through the starting procedure, methodically, before kick-starting the bike, a grin instantly appearing across his face when it started. He twisted the throttle and it revved up loudly as if there was no tomorrow. Corn grabbed his hand quickly and he released his grip.

'Gently, old boy, treat it like a lady,' he said with a smile, and showed him again. Dave moved the throttle gently back and forwards, slowly getting to grips with this new skill.

'OK, clutch in, select gear and throttle up, gently.' But as Dave did what Corn said, the bike suddenly jolted forward and stalled. Dave persevered for five minutes more but just couldn't get the hang of it. When he did finally get it going, he pulled too hard on the throttle and the bike charged off down the road, out of control, ending up in a hedge. Corn ran after him and arrived as Dave was clambering back to his feet, the rear wheel of the bike still going round.

'This isn't going to work, is it?' he said. Corn frowned, admitting defeat.

'No problem, I will take you to the house and drop you. No one will be any the wiser and I won't hang about. If anyone asks, tell them your brother dropped you.'

They drove back to the hideaway just as the sun was up and hid the bike as before. They were back at their new hide position in fifteen minutes and together they ate a cold breakfast of bread and some beef. Corn then announced the change of plan.

At seven thirty, Dave carefully selected the items he would need and stuffed them into his pack. He was about to leave his weapon behind when Corn suggested he took it with him.

'Why not, they don't need to know you have it and anyway, if they do find it, you were using your initiative. What can they say?'

Dave placed the pistol into his shoulder strap and completed his packing.

'OK, chaps, this is what we are going to do.' The two snipers listened intently as they had done dozens of times before in the trenches in France. Their lieutenant ran through their orders, paying particular attention to escape routes and rendezvous points (RVs). He told Dave he had to find a way to provide daily updates on his progress and gave him an old tobacco tin to put notes in to then toss over the wall by the giant tree. They would sit tight every day at zero seven hundred for three hours. Once they'd read the update, they would drop the tin back over for the next day. If all else failed, he was to go to the northern perimeter door and they could chat through it. If he missed the meeting, they would simply try again the following day.

'OK, any questions?' the officer asked.

'Just one,' said Dave. 'What cover should I use?'

There was a pause before Corn answered. 'I have been thinking about that and feel it's best if you stick to your own name so you don't get caught out. Also, stick to your time served to avoid any contention but tell them you were invalided out. It's your call in what you say, but for Christ's sake, stay consistent. This way, nothing is new to you and you have a suitable and reliable reason for leaving the army.'

Dave nodded and grabbed his bag.

'Good luck, mate,' Ricky said, reaching forward to shake his friend's hand. Corn and Dave set off back towards the lodge and twenty minutes later, Ricky heard the throb of a motorcycle and waited for them to come into view.

Corn swung up to the lodge gate, gently revving the engine. An older man with a large wiry moustache stepped outside and walked over, looking them up and down.

'Yes?' he said.

Corn left the bike idling and stood up, leaning the weight of the bike on his legs. 'Here for the security job. Shall we go straight up?'

'What, both of you?' he asked.

'No, just dropping my brother off at the Hall, if that's OK?'

'Oh yes, that will be fine. When you arrive, go around to the right, and ask at the servants' entrance for Mr Harper, the estate manager.'

Corn waited for him to open one of the gates, then smoothly manoeuvred through it before dropping down the hill and across the railway tracks. As he crossed the valley floor, he could sense

Ricky watching their every move but wasn't tempted to look across. He drove slowly, observing everything he could as he knew the knowledge he might gain now could come in handy later. He followed the road around to the rear of the Hall, into a courtyard, pulling up away from the main house. Dave climbed off and tapped Corn on the shoulder. He took a good look round before doing a wide circle and disappearing back down the drive.

Dave was standing looking up at the large building when a young girl, with dark hair and glasses, appeared from the very door he was heading for.

'Hello, miss, is Mr Harper available?' he asked politely. The maid appeared rather shy and dropped her head forward slightly.

'He is in the pantry, sir. Come this way,' she said, but as he took his scarf from over his mouth, she suddenly flinched, before scurrying towards the door. He followed her into a dark hallway lined with wood panelling, a stone floor underfoot, with doors on both sides all the way down the passageway. He had hoped to talk to her, but she kept ahead at a quick pace before stopping outside the pantry and pointing to a man seated at the far end of a table. She didn't speak and then quickly crept away.

Dave thought her actions a little odd, but then looked at the chap he was there to see, wearing a dark suit, roughly his own age, reading a newspaper.

'Mr Harper,' he said confidently.

'Yes, can I help you?'

'I was told to report to you about a job. I have driven all the way up from the south overnight as a mate said you were forming a security team.'

Harper smiled politely as, for once, someone other than a veteran in his forties was applying for work. This chap looked tall, strong and capable. They shook hands and Dave made sure Harper felt the full force of his strength.

'What experience do you have?' Harper asked.

'Spent two years in the army, invalided out two months ago, nothing hugely serious, but a back issue, which has healed pretty well, and I feel almost back to full strength.'

'Who did you serve with?'

Dave paused for a moment before answering. 'I was a sniper,' he said, giving nothing more than was absolutely necessary. His comment brought a smile to Harper's face.

'Well, that will do nicely,' he said, nodding slowly. 'I was with the Royal Warwickshire's. Caught some shrapnel one night at Passchendaele and came home. Still have some in me, too, which causes me pain from time to time, but hey, I'm alive.'

Dave nodded and smiled.

Harper looked at his wristwatch before telling him to see Cook and get some breakfast.

'Report to me in the rear annexe, that's the building directly across the courtyard, at ten o'clock. Mrs Tate, the cook, will tell you where it is. I have to see the general in a few minutes so we will have to chat later.' He supped the remainder of his tea, folded the newspaper neatly, placing it on the sideboard behind him, and stood up.

'Welcome to Marshall Hall. I have a special role in mind for you.'

As he headed for the door, Dave asked, 'Is it OK to take a walk around the grounds later to familiarise myself with the estate? I'm a bit stiff from sitting on the bike all night.'

'No problem. Stow your gear in the annexe. I will see you at ten.' He then left.

Dave turned around and saw the kitchen across the hall. Well, that was easy, he thought, and made his way across the corridor just as the young maid who had shown him in earlier returned down the spiral staircase. She looked a little pale and her dark hair and wire-rimmed spectacles seemed to hide something. An unhappy past, perhaps? When she saw him, she paused, then turned around and went straight back upstairs.

Mrs Tate, dressed in white, stood by the giant range in the kitchen, stirring a large saucepan. 'Edna has work to do, young man. What can I do for you?' she asked sternly.

'Oh,' he said, disappointed. 'Sorry, Mr Harper said I could get some breakfast. I'm to be employed as part of the security team. My name is Gibbs, Dave Gibbs.'

'Well, Mr Gibbs, please don't bother the house staff. If you go through to the staff dining room, I will have something sent through.' Dave felt a little uneasy after his encounter but politely thanked her.

When he had finished his meal, he asked the cook for directions to the annexe. She turned around and looked at him inquisitively.

'Army, were you?'

Dave put the tray down on the side and walked across to her. She was in her fifties, smartly turned out, her dark hair tucked neatly under a white cap. She was trim and quite tall.

'Yes, I am, as it happens. Got invalided out a couple of months ago due to injury. I did serve two years at the front though,' he said proudly.

'My nephew was killed just last month, shot by a German sniper, the only son to my dear sister.'

Dave stood solemnly for a moment, not wishing to say the wrong thing, then said, 'I was a sniper,' which seemed to startle her.

'A sniper, eh, so did you kill many Germans?'

Dave paused again, aware he must give little away. 'Yes, Mrs Tate, I made some kills but it's a torrid business and I'm glad to be out of it, quite frankly.'

She stood up and offered her hand. 'Less formality, young man. Please call me Rosemary, not in front of anyone else though; there are standards, you know. If you ever need anything, come and find me.' She smiled as she gave him directions to the annexe.

The building was just across the courtyard, and as he approached, several men were standing around outside, smoking. He introduced himself and for the next ten minutes, they chatted freely, swapping war stories and making jokes. At five minutes to ten, Dave went into the annexe and through the sitting area to the bunkroom at the rear. He dropped his kit on a bunk at the far end, returning outside just as Mr Harper stepped out from the rear door of the Hall.

'OK, chaps, inside if you will,' he said. Dave followed the men through the arched doorway and into the large sitting room with just enough chairs for each man. Harper took up a position at the front, by the small fireplace. Ten sets of eyes now watched his every move.

'I am Mr Harper, the estate manager, and I welcome you all to Marshall Hall. I have taken you all on and I will get you to sign a contract after this briefing. I had expected more than we have but hope to increase your number in the coming days. Your role is house security to protect the family and all staff within the estate. Duties will be wide and various and I will allocate you roles to suit your particular skills. Rosters will be pinned up on the notice board, including patrols of the grounds and, for some, personal protection duties for the general. I will brief those of you selected later. It will be necessary for you to be armed at all times as there is a direct threat to life. Did anyone bring their own weapons?' he asked, looking at the face of each man in turn. Several chaps raised their hands into the air. Dave didn't.

'OK, you can leave them in your accommodation or take them with you on duty, but each man will be given a Webley pistol and Lee Enfield rifles will be housed in the gun cabinet in my office. These will be issued only if there is a direct threat, apart from Dave Gibbs, who will keep one with him at all times. Gibbs was an army sniper and will be positioned to provide top cover from the roof.' Dave had wondered what he had meant about a 'special job' and now he knew.

'I am the only key holder to the rifle cabinet, but we will sort out a batting order for covering each other in due course. You will mostly work in pairs on a six-day rota. Each shift will be twelve hours long commencing at zero nine and twenty-one hundred, with a ten-minute handover. Now I realise we are currently down on numbers for the next day or so but hope to make this up very soon. We are also expecting Sergeant Major Howie, who has recently retired from the army, who will be my 2ic. He will be responsible for daily routines and discipline and will run all training.'

The rest of the briefing was suddenly a blur in Dave's mind. Howie was a broad Scot who was attached to the Glorious Glosters and Dave had seen him many times. He remembered that Howie left the trenches after his heroic action to save the life of a soldier that had become a piece of folklore in their quadrant. The sergeant major, without any thought for his own safety, climbed up to free a soldier who was caught on some wire just forward of the leading trench. It was memorable as even when the stretcher took him away, carrying a fresh bullet hole, Howie was still barking orders to all and sundry. Dave then heard his name being called over and over.

'Dave, are you with us, Dave?' Harper said loudly. He suddenly flashed back to life and focussed once again on Harper's briefing.

'Yes, sorry.'

'After each four-week cycle, you will receive two days off. Your salary for this work will be significantly more than any pay you would have received in the army at five shillings per day. This will rise every quarter by two shillings, and at the end of the first year, you will receive a bonus of five pounds. I trust that is satisfactory, men?' he said with a smile.

Each man looked impressed as this was a great deal of money and with lodgings thrown in too! Dave tried also to look suitably impressed but knew he would never receive a single penny.

'You will receive your pay every Sunday afternoon. You will be called into my office to sign a pay-book. If you wish, you can receive only part of your wages and bank the remainder until you leave our employment. The balance will remain in my safe if you so desire.' He looked down at his single sheet of paper, reading quickly. 'OK, finally, you are not to fraternise with the house staff under any circumstances. There are many young ladies here and so, apart from work contact, keep yourselves to yourselves and let them be. Meals will be eaten after the house staff at a second sitting. Mrs Tate, the cook, will provide for all your needs. Any questions?' he asked as he scanned the men before him.

'Yes, I have a question,' said a short stout man with long sideburns. 'Who are we up against and what are our actions?'

Harper realised that he had forgotten the most important part of the briefing: Actions.

'Yes, I was coming to that,' he said, trying to hide his error. 'Actions will be put up on the noticeboard alongside the rota by the end of today. Read them carefully and if questions arise, we will discuss them together with the sergeant major during daily briefings. We will commence operations at nine o'clock tonight. Mealtimes will be promulgated on the notice board. Finally, make yourself familiar with the house and grounds and each other. Your life may depend upon it. OK, to the cellar then.'

At that, they all moved to the basement under the main house and collected their Webley pistols and twenty rounds of ammunition. Dave also signed for a Lee Enfield rifle. He realised it would not be a match for his own, but he doubted it would be used in anger anyway. He had been paired with Kemp, and following their visit to the roof, he deliberately lost him and set off to familiarise himself with the estate.

The time was now eleven o'clock. Dave was keen to drop a note over the wall to provide an update so slipped back to the annexe to retrieve his notebook and the tobacco tin. He loaded his Webley handgun, slipping it into his waist belt; he left his own in its holster under his arm. He loaded his rifle and fitted the sling before stepping out across the forecourt. As he looked up, he saw a face at the window and smiled. It was Edna. She turned and disappeared from view.

Dave headed out across the field towards the wall, counting his paces as he went. As he walked across the land, little did he know that he was being observed by a pair of trained eyes through a set of military binoculars.

When he was well away from the house, he turned in a slow circle as if assessing the land, before sitting beneath a giant oak tree, facing the house. He pulled out his notepad and pencil and began sketching the layout of the estate and the distances he had measured before writing a brief note to his partners just over the wall. He was careful as he did so, as he clearly didn't wish to spook anyone looking from the house.

Boss.

10 men signed up, mostly old soldiers. Rising to 12 in the days ahead.

12-hour watches in pairs through the day, with only 3 on night shift, myself plus one on the roof, the other stationed in the corridor outside the general's room. Protection of target acute, all fully armed. Estate manager ex-army, limited experience. Team billet is the old annexe to rear of house. Ex CSM Howie's arrival imminent as head of team!

Dave

He looked around again, casting his eyes to every corner of the house and saw several of the chaps some distance away, looking around the grounds, but they were not going to disturb him. Without looking down, he carefully pulled the tin from his pocket and slipped the note inside. He then realised the tin was very light and so picked up a flat stone and placed it inside. Dave then continued adding to the primitive drawing of the house, the main tree line and the wall and wrote various distances down. He sat for a moment before moving off towards the perimeter wall some one hundred yards to the north. On several occasions, he dropped to one knee and raised his rifle to his shoulder as if taking aim before moving further west along the wall, counting each step. He finally came to the overhanging tree and crept in behind it and in a single action, without stopping, tossed the tobacco tin through a gap in the branches. Seconds later, he heard a faint noise. He turned east and walked all the way up to the corner of the wall, counting paces again as he went before writing the distance in his notepad. He then headed back to the house.

As he arrived, he stopped and wrote the final distances on the map, just as Harper came out from the side door. He called him over and Dave meandered across, looking at his watch. It was almost time for lunch. When they met, Harper looked at him suspiciously.

'What were you doing, Gibbs? I saw you writing things in a book, over by the wall. What's going on?'

Dave was pleased Harper had seen him, as it provided him with an opportunity to prove his worth and to nip this man's suspicions in the bud. He paused for just a tantalising moment.

'You sound suspicious of me, Mr Harper. I was simply pacing out distances from various points around the estate. If I am to be the man covering from the roof, it's good to know how far a target might be.' As he spoke, he slung his weapon and withdrew the notebook from his pocket. 'Take a look,' he said, holding the page open. Harper looked at the primitive drawing of the house and grounds.

'You see, it's five hundred yards from the rear door to the wall, two hundred and twenty up to the corner, one hundred and ninety across to the large oak and —'

Dave stopped speaking as Harper put up his hand to stop him. He realised this man was a professional and he should not have questioned him.

'It's OK, Dave, I understand what you are doing now. I like what I see and apologise for being suspicious. Come on, let's eat. You don't want to miss Cook's pie! It's one of her specials. See me afterwards and I will take you to meet General Davis.'

He turned suddenly, leaving Dave standing alone. As he put away his notepad, he smiled to himself, pleased how quickly he had gained Harper's trust. Now he just had to hold it together when he met the general.

At just before two o'clock, Dave stood at the bottom of the grand staircase, waiting as instructed for Mr Harper. The hallway was spacious with panelled walls of dark timber. A huge window overlooking the stairs illuminated it and many portraits of people from a bygone age stared down. A polished slate floor completed this rather dull entrance with its sparse furniture and a tall grandfather clock that ticked laboriously just across from where he stood. As the clock whirred and struck twice, the door opened and Harper emerged from the room behind it.

'Come with me, Gibbs,' he said and set off down the hallway, stopping outside a panelled door.

'Wait here,' Harper said, before knocking once and entering. With the door slightly ajar, Gibbs could hear Harper talking to someone, but the voices were muffled. Suddenly the door swung open, startling him.

'Come in, Gibbs,' said Harper. Dave straightened up and stepped into a vast room with a high ceiling, full of light. He followed Harper for some thirty or forty feet into the room. He could see the head of a man sitting in a tall armchair by the fire. As he turned, Dave saw the man responsible for his friend's death. The man he had come to kill.

***

On the top floor, Ed was sitting on her bed, sweating from the exertion of running all the way up from below stairs. She felt tense and her eyes were glazed as she stared at the bookcase across the small room. She wondered how it could be that Dave Gibbs was here in Yorkshire! She felt her heart pounding and was worried she had been recognised. Thank goodness Frank had insisted that she wear a disguise. As her breathing settled, she realised she must stay well clear of him but, crucially, it was time she began to explore how she could get access to the general's room. Her task, however, had just got rather more difficult.

CHAPTER 11

Ricky had been sitting near the gap in the perimeter wall for over an hour before he finally saw a figure closing in towards his position. He knew by his gait that it was Dave and sat very still, watching him approach.

There was no one else anywhere in sight as Dave moved behind the large tree in front of Ricky, then seconds later Ricky saw something spinning in the air, landing just twenty feet away. This was a totally unrehearsed practice that they hoped to refine; if he was seen their ability to communicate would be severely hampered.

Ricky went and retrieved the small tobacco tin before scurrying back to the hide. His lieutenant, studying the map of the estate drawn the previous day, looked up.

'Anything?' he asked. Ricky handed the tin to his officer who looked inside and found a small note under a stone. He read it once before reading it aloud to Miller. They let the details settle before Corn formed his plan.

'OK, Dave has been trusted with the night shift which may play out well. He is clearly not alone, but I am sure he will be able to slip away if needed, creating any diversion that is necessary. Let's drop a note back and suggest this for tomorrow night.' He looked at the hand-drawn map once again and noticed a small brick shed just fifty feet or so from the north-east corner of the house. He reached for his notebook, turned to a blank page and started to write.

RV, 17/0100/CGM, Brick shed NE corner of house.
Require details of security team and firepower
Use Howie to your advantage.

'Can you think of anything to add?' he asked. Ricky read the note quickly, looking rather puzzled. He shook his head.

'Boss, have we not got this the wrong way around? If I have this right, it's more important that we receive messages from him and not the other way around. He has to be able to make his own plan according to his situation and restrictions. We can ask lots of things, but he may well not be able to deliver them which might compromise us all. It might also put him under more pressure to try and achieve something he simply can't do. We don't know the lie of the land, only he can do that. So, surely, we should let him run this and provide back-up for his withdrawal? He's on his own.'

Corn considered what Ricky had said and reached for the tin.

'Your perception is bang on. It's not practical to swap notes on a daily basis.' He ripped up the message and looked at his young subordinate.

'I think we should go in under the cover of darkness tonight and do a full recce ourselves, so we have a good idea of the layout in case his withdrawal gets complicated. We can select good locations to cover him if the shit hits the fan or, if all goes well, plan an alternative route out if compromised.'

Ricky was nodding his approval. 'Now you're talking, boss. We could also locate an emergency drop point near to the sheds if needed.'

Corn stared into space as he churned this change of plan around in his head.

'Assuming he comes back on one of his walks again tomorrow, let's just communicate verbally over the wall. He could stand having a fag and we can chat freely, swapping details as necessary. No one will know. Surely that's much easier?'

Ricky agreed. 'So, a recce tonight then. What time should we leave?'

'We will set off at midnight and cross over at the break in the wall by the large tree. We will go in light order, carrying handguns only, normal camouflage with water flasks. If Dave is on watch, and we can realistically expect him to be, he will no doubt see us, but crucially can create a diversion for his opposite number if necessary. OK, let's get some food and some rest. There is little we can do now until tonight. I'll do the first watch.'

Ricky nodded in the gloom and reached for a food sack, taking out some fruit cake and tearing a large chunk of cheese from a block. He passed some to Corn and they ate in silence as they prepared for their first sortie

At twenty-three thirty, Ricky shook his lieutenant awake. They stowed all the kit not in use and prepared for their first visit into their very own No Man's Land. At just after midnight, they set off towards the wall, Ricky leading. The night was dark, with low cloud and no moon. When they reached the wall, he pulled out his binos and set them on top of the bricks, peering into the darkness. He scanned the house for almost a full minute before pushing them inside his jacket.

'It's all quiet, let's go,' he whispered. They climbed carefully onto the wall and slid down into soft mud on the other side. Ricky stepped four paces away and lay down silently, watching and listening. Corn didn't make a sound as he crossed over and tapped Ricky on the leg. They walked east along the line of the wall, towards some trees which Ricky hoped would give them cover all the way to the outbuildings by the gardens. It didn't take them long to reach them, even with their well-practised routine of going to ground every one hundred paces when they would watch and listen. It was during one of these pauses that they heard someone yell from the direction of the house, then it came again and they stayed put for several minutes until they were sure they hadn't been rumbled. Finally, when all was quiet once more, Ricky sucked on his tongue twice, making the noise of an insect, and moved off, Corn following him, stepping softly on the wet earth.

After ten minutes they reached the tree line where they once again went to ground. Ricky pulled Corn to him and whispered carefully in his ear that this was RV1. Corn instinctively tapped him on the shoulder. They had no real view from their position, so stepped inside the tree line and continued walking south towards the house, keeping a separation of two trees between them. After a few minutes, they finally came to the end of the line of trees and saw a light in one of the ground-floor rooms. They closed in together again and Ricky whispered, 'RV2.' Corn tapped his shoulder again before cupping his hand next to Ricky's ear and whispering his plan.

'Let's move towards those two small buildings by that lone tree and find some shelter,' he said very quietly. 'We can assess things from there.'

Ricky didn't need asking twice and walked forward, crouched, placing each foot slowly before easing his full weight onto the ball of the foot. The main house was now just one hundred yards away. They stopped behind the first of the small brick sheds, with a door at the south side. They sat down, back-to-back, fully observant, beside the side wall. Ricky reached for his flask, taking a swig before handing it to Corn. Just as Corn put his lips to the flask, he stopped dead as a clock chimed somewhere ahead of them.

'We need to identify a drop point close enough to allow us to reach it easily and for Dave to visit it without suspicion,' Corn whispered, handing the flask back. 'We should then circle round the east side of the house and identify access points, but I want us back here by zero three hundred.'

Ricky nodded in the darkness and rose to start looking around the side of the shed for somewhere to stow the tin. He reached up with his hand and followed the line of the roof. In the corner, tucked up under the metal guttering, he found a loose brick. Gripping it carefully, he moved it from side to side, tugging gently. In the darkness, dust fell onto his face, which he didn't notice, and he inadvertently inhaled. He bent down, desperately trying to stop himself from coughing, but it was no good, the automatic response of his body took over, and he felt his chest suddenly heave. He dived for the floor, burying his face into the crook of his arm, his lungs reacting to the intrusion. Corn, aware something was amiss, peered down into the darkness, as Ricky coughed several times, muffling it as best he could. Corn felt for Ricky's head and leant down to whisper in his ear, 'RV2, now.'

Corn was up and already running softly along the tree line. Ricky struggled to gather himself, desperately fighting off the cough, before following him.

It took them less than a minute to get back to the RV, where they lay down on opposite arcs, facing the house. They waited for the follow-up that was surely going to come, their weapons drawn, listening for footsteps. But none came. Ricky took the small flask from his hip pocket and took a long drink. They stayed absolutely still for a full half hour, peering into the darkness, watching their arcs.

Corn then crawled over to Ricky and got in close. 'You OK, old man?' he said. 'What happened?'

Ricky, unsure whether talking would start the coughing fit again, swallowed hard before gently clearing his throat with another swig. 'Brick dust went straight into my lungs. I'm fine now, but I did find a suitable location for our drop point,' he said.

'OK, let's go back and check it out, we still have lots of time.' They moved forward with increased caution, taking a slightly different route just in case they had been seen. They stopped next to the small shed once again and Ricky showed Corn the hole in the wall.

After careful inspection, he agreed it was a sound position and told Ricky to place the brick back in position, leaving a narrow gap big enough to hide the tin. Once done, Corn reached for Ricky's shoulder and pulled him in tightly.

'I am going to circle round to the east for twenty minutes and then turn back. You cover me and if I am compromised, you will hear me before you see me. We will then meet up back at RV2.'

Corn studied the ground in front of him for a few moments as he slipped a pair of socks over his boots to reduce the noise on the stone flags. He walked low across the gap along a line of bushes to the side of the house, Ricky straining his eyes until he could see him no more. He sat leaning against the corner of the shed, awaiting his return. Little did he know they were being watched.

CHAPTER 12

Dave had managed to get the corner bunk, right next to the rear door of the annexe, offering him an easy exit if he ever needed to run for it. He observed his newfound colleagues and thought several of them particularly brutish and loud. They reminded him of the many cocky young soldiers who would arrive at the front, having finished their training, thinking they knew everything. He decided to keep himself to himself and leave them to it.

His opposite number was the chap with a wooden leg who Corn had met on his journey north. Harper clearly saw him as the best fit, knowing he would find it difficult to patrol the grounds. He seemed decent enough, was a little older than Dave, but had only limited army experience. They were chatting freely in the rest area, drinking tea, when Harper stuck his head around the door, indicating with his head that he wanted to see Dave outside. He quickly got to his feet and gave his excuses.

Outside, Harper chatted to him amicably. 'Look, for now, I want you to be my 2ic, how do you feel about that?' Dave was immensely flattered, knowing this to be a huge advantage to aid them in their quest.

'No problems, Mr Harper, I would be happy to. Do you still want to give me the key to the gun locker?'

'Ah, yes, I do, Gibbs, we'll do that now.' They walked across the yard and into the rear door of the Hall, and as they entered Dave saw Edna and smiled, but she once again passed him by. He frowned and turned to look at her, but Harper noticed.

'It's not worth her job, Dave,' he said looking at him. 'If she fraternises with you, she could be out of here quicker than you can cock your weapon. I am sure you don't wish for that. She is a nice young lady, please don't pursue her.' Dave finally accepted his attempts at flirtation were futile.

Harper switched on the single light that hung low in the centre of his tiny office under the stairs. Dave peered in and saw a large metal cabinet against the back wall. Harper placed the key that hung on his waistcoat chain into the lock and released the door catch to show the small arsenal of Lee Enfield .303 rifles in two neat rows. Dave knew them well, of course, and saw how pristine they were.

'OK, as you can see there are fourteen rifles, plus the one I gave you and enough ammunition for each man to have fifty rounds. Here is the second key which will only be used if I am unavailable. If the shit hits the fan, I expect you to make your own decisions. Keep it with you at all times and find a safe place to carry it. Now, we must sit down later and prepare further action plans and you may need to find time to provide some refresher training on the .303 as some have not fired one in anger for some time. OK, any questions?' he said as he locked the cabinet.

'Yes, just one thing, Mr Harper. What are the rules of engagement? Is this legal and are we immune from prosecution if we shoot anyone?'

Harper realised he actually had no idea what would happen if anyone from the security team shot and killed an intruder, but he needed to bluff Gibbs until he had spoken to the general.

'Do you honestly think the general would have arranged all this security and not looked into the legal situation? Don't you worry about that. If you shoot a trespasser, whether he is armed or not, you will have the full backing of me and General Davis. He holds a lot of weight in this area, especially with the chief constable.'

At that, Dave backed out of the broom cupboard office and headed back to the billet. Harper watched him go, thinking he was glad to have him along. He locked the door and headed back to the lower floor.

Just after a quarter to nine, Dave was putting on his warm jacket as Kemp, his mate, walked over, his limp quite pronounced. Dave stood up and buttoned up his coat, looking the man up and down as he reached for his hat. 'All set?' he asked.

'Yes, I'm ready to go and have my hip flask with me too so we can have a nip later. Am I to have a rifle tonight, Dave?' Kemp asked, as Dave slipped the working parts of his own rifle backwards and forwards several times before loading.

'No, not tonight, Pete. Harper wants everyone to have some refresher training first, which we will do tomorrow. OK, let's go or we will be late.' And they left the annexe for the main house and headed for the side stairs that would take them up to the roof.

It was four floors up and the stairs wound round several times until they came to a small wooden door. Dave pulled back the large bolt with a heavy clunk and pushed the door open, the cool wind gripping them as they stepped out into the night air. Dave put his woollen hat on but kept his ears free. Once the door was closed, they familiarised themselves with the roof layout, spending time at each corner of the building, paying particular attention to the arcs of fire. Dave placed Pete looking west, overlooking the driveway down to the main gate almost a thousand yards away. He sold this to him as the most important position of the various arcs they had to cover and Pete seemed content to sit leaning against a row of brick chimneys, out of the wind. Dave could now concentrate on the northern view as he expected Corn and Ricky to do a recce at some point that evening. He found a gap in the corner by the rear chimney that afforded him a view right across the land to the north and the large tree in the distance. It also had the added advantage of being a warm spot, from the fires in the rooms below.

The first few hours seemed to go very quickly with no sound from anyone below or across the vast estate. Dave stood up and stretched his back before wandering over to where he had left Pete, but as he approached his position, he heard him breathing heavily, snorting at intervals. As he turned the corner, Pete's head was back against the wall, his mouth open. He was sound asleep. This, to Dave, was as unprofessional as it got. No soldier worth his salt would ever sleep on duty, but here they were only a few hours into their first watch and already sleep had taken Pete. He knew he now had him over a barrel and was going to capitalise on the situation as much as possible. He squatted down in front of him, pulled his Webley from his holster and placed the barrel under Pete's chin. The sleeping warrior quickly woke and felt the barrel jammed against his skin.

'Bang,' Dave said. 'Not a good start, my friend. What would Harper do if he knew?'

Pete, realising he had been rumbled, felt very embarrassed, speaking quickly in response. 'Look, old man, please don't report me, I need this job. I need the money and I will make sure it doesn't happen again. I will do anything for you, Dave, anything, just ask. Just let this go, will you?'

In the darkness, Dave smiled, knowing he had got Pete right where he wanted him. He didn't answer straight away, deliberately building on his agony, before he pulled his weapon from his neck.

'You can have this one on me, but you owe me, Pete, big time.' As he turned to head back across the roof to his position, he stopped. 'Why don't you nip down and get two mugs of tea from the kitchen, Pete? I'll stay here and keep watch. See if there are any pastries or something, too; it's going to be a long night.'

Pete walked past him like a child who had been caught with his hand in the biscuit barrel and headed for the door. Dave smiled as he left and took a deep breath before heading back across the roof to his position. He pulled out his binos and set them towards the big tree where he had earlier thrown the tin over the wall. It was dark, but there was still just enough light to see by. He strained his eyes for several minutes, panning right, but saw nothing. Just as he was tucking the glasses back into his coat, a faint scream went up at the rear of the house. He ran across and leant over the edge of the roof, peering down into the rear courtyard. He stared into the darkness and then it came again. The noise was coming from the annexe where he and his new comrades were billeted. Seemed one of them was having a nightmare or having his throat cut.

He went over to the roof doorway and stuck his head inside, looking down the narrow stairs, wondering where on earth Pete had got to. He must have been gone twenty minutes and still no sign of him. Parched for a brew, Dave walked around the perimeter of the roof line before dropping back to his position. As he waited, the image of the beautiful face of the girl at York station filled his head. He wondered if he might have time to visit her when this was all over. Oh, the wonders of love at first sight.

His reverie was interrupted by a noise filtering up from the garden below. He stared down into the darkness. Then he heard a faint cough, and another, before it went quiet. He pulled out his binoculars and studied the area, looking through the tree line and across to the small potting sheds. After a few moments, he spotted two shapes scurrying away, about fifty yards from the house. He followed their line, before losing them amongst the trees, just as he felt a presence beside him.

'What's up, Dave? Is there something there?' asked Pete in the darkness.

'No, it's nothing. An animal, I think. Now, where's that brew?' he said, to distract him.

'Here. I found some buns in the pantry too,' he said, offering one from his pocket. They sat quietly in the cool of the early morning, the tea warming their chilled bodies right through. Dave decided Pete wasn't all bad and did have his uses.

'You should get back across to your position now, Pete, and I need a leak,' Dave said, as he stepped away.

The logbook would show no mention of a sleeping sentry or the figures in the darkness, simply a routine watch report that filled just a few lines. Dave wasn't going to bed yet, but he needed an excuse to get to the wall.

***

Following Dave's efforts to hold Ed in a conversation by the rear door, she went straight upstairs to finish her cleaning. As she walked along the landing, she noticed the sentry's chair by the general's apartment door which, to her surprise, had been left open. She wandered past, just peering inside, but her curiosity got the better of her. She stopped a few feet past, looked around, and realised she was quite alone. She had to take this chance.

She walked back and pushed the door open and quickly stepped inside, closing the door behind her. If anyone came, she would simply make out she was confused about which rooms she had to clean. Time was of the essence.

Ed could only chance it for a minute or two, so with a cleaning cloth in her hand, ready to begin dusting the moment she heard the door open, she quickly walked around the room, assessing the layout. She peered into the bathroom, saw how the furniture was placed and realised the only other way out seemed to be through the bathroom window. But as she turned to leave, she saw a tall bookcase that was positioned away from the wall. She thought this odd, and looking behind it, noticed a narrow doorway.

CHAPTER 13

Corn quickly covered the distance to the main house, instinctively holding his breath as he moved. When he finally cleared the space, he dropped down onto his heels, leaning up against the wall, pausing for a moment, to look over his shoulder. He could see nothing of Ricky, who had simply blended into the night. All was quiet and he crept along the north side of the Hall, dropping below each window as he approached, before moving on. There were no lights on in the house and the moon was shrouded by a thin veil of cloud, creating a ghostly halo.

Moving stealthily towards the north-eastern corner, he almost walked straight into a large flowerpot which, although almost waist height, was completely invisible in the deep shadow. When he got to the corner, he peered round into the courtyard where he had dropped Dave. The long single-storey building was directly ahead of him with an open door at one end and several small windows along its length, all set above head height. As he sat watching, loud snores reverberated from within and he realised this must be the accommodation for the security team. But he saw no patrols and the night was still.

His attention was drawn to the far end of the Hall, off to his right, where a small light over the rear porch had been left on. He carefully made his way along the east side, avoiding various shrubberies en route, until he came to double width stone steps with ornate balustrades which were significantly wider at the bottom where they dropped to ground level. He paused again and looked up, wondering if Dave might be watching from the roof. After scanning the area carefully, he nipped past the steps into the darkness on the far side and nestled into a corner. Nothing stirred, but his discipline told him to stop and observe and he stayed put for several minutes, watching and listening. He checked his watch and saw he had been gone for thirty-two minutes. There was nothing further to be gained, so, if he was going to stick to their plan and be back over the wall by zero three thirty, he had to leave. Just as he was rising to turn, a door opened just thirty feet from his position. A man came out and stopped under the rear light for a few seconds, studying a sheet of paper. Totally unaware he was being watched, he lifted his head and strode across the courtyard, his feet crunching on the stones, the noise disturbing the silence of just moments before. Corn stayed in his position, sitting back on his heels, safe in the darkness.

Ten minutes passed, then he heard an inner door close and the man reappeared and headed back across the courtyard. Corn had his weapon ready, watching the face of the chap whose eyes stayed fixed on the door in front of him. He had no reason to suspect an intruder and walked straight in through the porch door, then the light went out.

Corn sat still for a few minutes waiting for his eyes to readjust to the darkness. Quickly he retraced his steps and turned the corner, but just as he got to the first window, the room lit up like a beacon, blinding him for an instant. He dropped down to the flagstones, rolling tight under the window. It was a full fifteen minutes before the light went out and he was able to head back across to the small sheds which he had left over an hour before.

Ricky had been observing him since the light came on and was ready for his arrival. Corn crouched down beside him, fully alert.

'RV2, now,' he said in a whisper, before getting back to his feet and heading north towards the tree line. At the RV, Corn sat down, leaning against a tree, as Ricky closed in, taking up a kneeling position where he could keep a defensive arc towards the Hall.

'OK, the route round the house is littered with large garden pots and small shrubberies that spring up on you. Central at the rear of the building is a long stairway, which is five paces wide at ground level, leading up to the floor above. At the far end, there is a porch, with a rear door opening into the courtyard. There are six windows all overlooking the courtyard and what appears to be the bunkhouse, housing the security team. It's about fifty paces from the house. The rear area is part stone and part gravel.'

Ricky had listened carefully but thought they gained little from staying where they were.

'Boss, I get that, but we are vulnerable here and we should go,' he said. 'You can fill me in when we are safely over the wall.'

Corn sniffed, realising he was being taught the basics of patrolling by a man he had himself trained. But, on this occasion, he was right.

They reached the wall and headed west, staying fully alert until they were safely back at the hide. It was zero three forty. They sat down and chatted quietly before Corn once again offered to do the first watch. Ricky, never missing a chance to grab some kip, wrapped himself up in his jacket, pulled his hat over his face and within minutes was sound asleep.

By eight thirty, although fatigued from the night's excursion, Corn and Ricky were in position, leaning against the wall under the large tree. For thirty-minute intervals, one stood by the wall, watching, the other covered the track, weapon drawn, observing both directions. Ricky drank from his flask of water, placing it by his feet to use his binos. Just after nine o'clock, they heard voices to the east and looked at each other, startled. Almost in unison, they scuttled over to the thicket where the hide was, dropping down into the undergrowth. They lay still, eyes peeled, their Webleys drawn.

The voices slowly grew louder, then two men came into view, wandering along, chatting, heading from left to right in front of them. At first, they thought they were farm workers, or some lads out shooting rabbits; however, as they got closer, they could see one was playing with a handgun and they knew instantly these were two of the guards from the Hall. They looked quite disinterested and ambled along noisily, paying little attention to their surroundings. They were not patrolling with any professionalism and one even had his hands in his pockets, looking at the ground.

Ricky suddenly touched Corn's arm. He turned to look at him as he pointed to the wall.

'The flask,' he said in a whisper. Corn looked and saw a black water flask leaning against a rock, where Ricky had been sitting. It was too late now, and they could only watch, hoping it wouldn't be discovered. To their surprise, even though the men walked within several feet of it, neither saw it.

With the panic over, they moved forward again and Ricky resumed his position at the wall and drank from his flask.

Fifteen minutes or so later, the men appeared in the distance, walking up the driveway towards the main house. As Ricky cast his eyes across the open land to his front, he saw a lone figure running from the Hall, and he knew instantly that it was Dave Gibbs.

He alerted Corn who walked over to join him, raising himself up just enough to see his young subordinate trotting through the tree line and down towards the wall. Dave then turned left and ran steadily west until he came up to the large tree. Ricky saw a wide smile as he approached that was instantly infectious. Dave leant back against the tree, facing the Hall, and pulled his cigarette tin from his pocket. He casually stared into the distance, not reacting when he heard a familiar voice.

'How's it all going, Dave?' Ricky asked, just loud enough for his voice to carry.

'Hello, mate, pretty good thanks. I have a key job on the roof which allows me time each night to poke around a little. I am concerned about the sergeant major's arrival though, as he knows me well. I was there when he rescued that soldier, so we may have to move fast.'

Corn looked back at Ricky.

'Look, if he knows you, then he will recognise a professional which surely will give him confidence. We have just witnessed the quality of the men you are working with and judge them pretty poor, to say the least. So, I suggest you don't rush in, but take a couple of days to get to know Howie again, assess the situation each day and gain his trust. From what we have seen, he will be delighted to have you on the team.'

As Dave rolled his cigarette, he considered Corn's words.

'Roger that, boss, but don't be surprised if I just turn up one night unannounced, job done!' he said, lighting his fag.

'We will remain ready to evacuate at short notice, don't worry about that. What are your watch duties?' Corn asked.

'Twelve-hour shifts starting at twenty-one hundred. I have been given the key position to see across to this location and have the chap you met working with me. He will be no trouble as I have one on him, so he will do as I say. I think I can gain access to the floor where the general's bedroom is from the back stairs. Will check it out tonight. But I don't want to charge in and murder the man without any form of escape route. I would probably end up killing innocent men and that's not what we came here for.'

There was silence as they all thought of a way to overcome this difficulty.

'What's the security situation with General Davis at night? Is he easy to get to?' Corn asked.

'He has a guard with him on a daily basis, outside his study and on the landing by his bedroom door. I can render any sentry unconscious before making my move quite easily, but my concern is whether Mr Howie will change my duties which will fuck up any plan we may have. I think you are right, boss, we must hold fire for a couple of days until I have completed my recce on the landing and found my escape route. If nothing changes, I should be ready to take him in two or three days,' he said, stubbing out his cigarette.

All this time, Corn had been staring at Ricky, listening intently and thinking. He then turned as if talking to an invisible man through the wall.

'What time do you do your rounds and how long can you be away from your post?' he asked.

'I can easily sneak away for twenty minutes. Kemp, the chap I mentioned, owes me a big favour after sleeping on duty. I will work something out so he doesn't suspect anything.'

Corn had been scribbling a few notes on his pad and delayed answering.

'By the way, how's the cough?'

Ricky frowned at Corn with an embarrassed look.

'It happens, but glad it was you on the roof. OK, let's work with that,' Corn said. 'But remember, Howie is a formidable man. He got a mention in dispatches for his action in saving the private and I think he even received a glass of whisky from the colonel. Not many people get that honour. He won't know you are still serving and will probably be glad to have you aboard. You may also be able to use him as an ally due to your serving together. And if he doesn't remember you, then you are home free.'

There was silence over the wall and, for a moment, Corn thought Dave had gone. Then his voice piped up again.

'Right, boss, I will have to leg it. Is there anything else?'

Corn read his notes. 'Yes, one more thing. We found a position closer to home for you, at the potting shed, to leave messages. Top right corner on the north side, there is a loose brick, but it would be easier to exchange details verbally, here. Can you get down here every morning?'

Dave thought for a moment. 'Yes, no problem. See you tomorrow.' When Corn spoke again, there was no answer: Dave was gone.

***

The general, who had returned to his bedroom, saw a figure in the distance leaning against a tree to the north of the Hall. He took his old army binoculars from his bedside table drawer trying to identify who it was, then walked over to pull the bell rope by his bed. Within a few moments, his door opened and his valet walked in. He opened his mouth to speak but was cut short as the general told him to get Mr Harper immediately. He nodded as he closed his mouth again, returning downstairs.

He found Harper in his office, busy scribbling notes in a large book.

'Mr Harper, I—' He was stopped in his tracks by Harper's left hand. For a full minute, Harper carried on writing. Parsons started to fidget and looked keenly at the clock on the wall, then decided to speak again. 'Mr Harper—'

'Parsons, I told you to wait, now give me a minute,' Harper snapped. But Parsons wasn't about to receive a bollocking from his master again, so talked over him.

'The general wants you immediately.'

By the time Harper had lifted his head, Parsons was already turning back into the corridor. In haste, Harper attempted to place his pen back into the inkwell tray as he stood up, but wasn't looking properly and missed, tipping ink across his desk. He gasped in annoyance and, shaking his head, reached for his large blotter.

He was out of breath when he arrived at the general's room. He gently tapped on the door, pushing it open simultaneously.

'Yes, sir, what can I do for you?'

'Where have you been, man? I sent for you nearly five minutes ago. Now get over here and take a look at this,' the general said abruptly.

Harper walked quickly across the room to the window, unsure what was going on. The general offered him the binos and pointed to the north but didn't look at him.

'There, running back from the wall. Who is that, what's he doing?'

Harper looked over the line of the glasses first, before placing them to his eyes. He peered into the distance and studied the figure who was now halfway back. He realised it was Dave Gibbs and dropped the glasses to speak.

'Ah, that's Gibbs, sir, the sniper. You met him the other day if you remember. What seems to be the problem?'

'Well, what is he doing, Harper. He was leaning against the tree for several minutes, smoking. Why would he be all the way over there by the wall? What's his game?'

Mr Harper took one last look through the binos before handing them back.

'Sir, without being prompted, Gibbs took it upon himself to make a map of the estate with distances marked across from different points. He does the night shift from the roof, sir.'

The general looked at Harper, frowning. 'Can he be trusted?' he asked.

'He only left the army recently, but he is clearly one step ahead of the rest of the men. I have asked him to be my 2ic until the sergeant major arrives, but yes, I think we can trust him.'

The general pursed his lips and nodded to himself. 'OK, Harper, that will be all.'

Harper turned and made his way out and back down to the ground floor. He headed towards the rear door to the courtyard, to meet Gibbs on his return. He shouted, 'Gibbs, have you got a minute?'

Dave swung his head round sharply and focussed on the man approaching him.

'Yes, Mr Harper, what's up?'

'The old man saw you at the wall. More measuring, was it?'

Dave stayed calm and didn't take his eyes from his face.

'Mr Harper, are you going to check on me every time I leave the house? Are you going to sit up all night maybe to ensure I perform my sentry duties to your satisfaction, or are you going to let me do my job?'

Harper was rather stunned at his outburst, but realised immediately he was dealing with a pro who knew far more about soldiering than he ever would. His approach must have appeared rather clumsy to a professional soldier and he pulled back a little from his stance.

'Sorry, Dave, more interested really, as the general saw you and, although I explained our conversation of the other day, he insisted I check up what you were doing. That's absolutely fine. I know I can trust you.' He turned quickly to leave but stopped short and turned back. 'Oh, and Mr Howie is arriving tonight.'

Dave was about to snigger for getting the better of him but, instead, felt his heart race as he knew that changes could well be afoot.

***

Corn and Ricky were back in their small hide, taking some sustenance, talking quietly. It was day four of their jaunt and, all being well, they would be on the overnight boat from Folkestone on Sunday.

The map Ricky had drawn previously was lying open by their feet and they studied it with care.

'So, how do you want to play the extraction, sir?' asked Ricky. Corn looked up but didn't answer immediately. He seemed strangely lost in his thoughts. 'Corn!' Ricky said, and he lifted his head again.

'Sorry, Ricky, miles away. OK, let's assume Dave fulfils his objective and takes out the target in two days' time. Now, our extraction plan must be simple and run like clockwork. We can't leave anything behind and, as the motorbike is registered to my brother, we can't leave that either. Extraction from here with just one vehicle and a pile of gear won't be easy, but it will enable us to move quickly and put some miles between us and the Hall. We will therefore have to find a home for some of our equipment.'

Ricky was poised to speak when Corn went into one of his frozen mind states again, staring down at the map. He suddenly lifted his head and looked at him.

'It's imperative that you and Dave are on the first train out of Pickering once the job is done. I will ferry you one at a time to the outskirts of the town with all the gear. Once you're on the train, I will drive to meet you at York station, where we will all catch a train, including the bike, and get back to London as fast as we can. I have no doubts the shit will hit the fan rapidly after we have gone, so our withdrawal must be decisive. Any thoughts?' he asked.

Ricky shook his head. 'No, boss, nothing from me.'

They sat in silence for several minutes, the young lieutenant thinking deeply about the reasons they had travelled all the way to Yorkshire, knowing if they got caught, they were for the gallows. He closed his eyes and pictured the firing squad where Ed Mitchell lay prone, her eyes open, blood spilling from her chest. Revenge would be sweet.

CHAPTER 14

The rain suddenly lashed against the windows as the train left the protection of the high Victorian roof of York station. It was pouring from the heavens and ex-Sergeant Major Bill Howie thought of the many soakings he had endured in the trenches of northern France. He smiled to himself, happy for once to be in the dry.

He struggled for balance as he took off his old army greatcoat, fighting the train that rocked as they picked up speed. He was alone in the compartment and shook the coat several times before hanging it on a peg by the door. He reached into the inside pocket, took out his notebook and settled down to read the description of the job he had accepted over the phone. As the train sped north towards the small town of Pickering, he thought back to all that had taken him away from the war.

He had been honourably discharged just two weeks previously due to injuries sustained at the front, with part of a German bullet still in his lower back. He had been shot almost three months ago and had convalesced in a military hospital in Sussex. The memory of that day never quite left his mind for long. He didn't blame anyone, as it was his own stupid fault, but he remembered the lad who had desperately hung on to life, panicking and screaming for help as bullets flew overhead. His gaiter had stuck fast on some friendly wire just ten feet from safety. No one wanted to risk their own lives, but he hadn't hesitated and had climbed up the ladder, knowing full well he would be at great risk. His officer shouted for him to step back down before he realised his orders had fallen on deaf ears and shouted for smoke. He could still taste the acrid smoke that had clung to his lips and stung his lungs, but although there was an imaginary safety net around when smoke masked your position, it didn't deflect the enemy fire and that was his downfall. With the best intentions, it all seemed to happen in slow motion as he crawled over to the stricken man, far too young to die. He had reached him quickly and, if he closed his eyes, he could remember the cracks above his head as bullets passed just inches away. Some hit the earth in front of him and the boy near him screamed louder and louder, driving him on. When he finally reached the young private, he simply undid the gaiter, leaving it attached to the wire, something the boy could have done had he not been stricken by fear. Once released, he quickly shoved the boy headlong into the trench below. As he got up onto one knee to launch himself in the same direction, he suddenly felt the burn of hot lead in his rear end which tumbled him over the lip of the trench, landing heavily on top of his unsuspecting officer below.

***

Twelve weeks on and following his discharge, he was now heading to a new job on General Davis's private estate in Yorkshire. He didn't know the reasons for the general's retirement from the army but had served under him for almost two years. He always thought him a hard but fair man, who recognised a good soldier at a hundred paces. He would face the man later that day and hoped for a trusting relationship.

Pickering wasn't far away and, before long, the train slowed as they approached the small town. He saw the word 'Pickering' on several boards along the platform and quickly stood to climb back into his greatcoat before grabbing his kit.

The station was empty when he stepped down from the train, apart from two guards and several old gentlemen who were gathered together by a bench, drinking tea. He climbed up over the footbridge and back down to the other platform, heading towards the exit. Handing his ticket to the collector, he wished him a good day and walked down the steps to the roadside. He looked up the street, to see a man waving his hand at him from the window of a car. As he walked over, a stout man jumped out to greet him.

'Mr Howie, is that you, sir?' asked the driver.

'Yes, I am Howie, and you are?' he said, holding out his hand.

'I am the driver from the Hall, sir, the name is Bark. How do you do?' he said with a smile.

'I am very well, Bark. Is it far?'

Bark opened the boot of the car and placed Howie's leather-bound case in it before they climbed aboard. When both doors were shut, Bark quickly put the car into gear and they sped off to the north. 'It's just a few miles, sir. Won't take too long.'

'Look, Bark, my name is Bill, please don't keep calling me sir.'

Bark smiled as they sped north, thinking he was going to like this chap.

In less than ten minutes they turned through the large iron gates and dropped down the hill to the railway tracks before speeding through the grounds towards the main house. Bark pulled the vehicle around to the rear, stopping in the courtyard next to a green door. Bill stepped out to view his new home, reaching for his holdall and small leather bag while Bark retrieved his case from the boot. When he looked up again, a man had appeared from a door in the corner and was walking up to meet him.

'Mr Howie, I am Harper, the estate manager. Welcome to Marshall Hall,' he said, offering his hand. 'I want to brief you as soon as you are settled, so if you follow me, I will take you to your room.'

Bill swung round to thank Bark, before picking up his case to follow Harper. They climbed three flights of stairs in silence before heading along a short corridor to a door at the end.

'Please make yourself comfortable and I will see you in the kitchen in, say, fifteen minutes,' Harper said, checking his watch. 'Key is on the inside of the door; the lavatory is two doors down on your right and the bathroom is next to it. When you are unpacked, just go back down the stairs and at the bottom turn left. The passage will lead you to another flight of stairs to take you down below stairs. I will see you there.'

Harper left Bill Howie to open the door to a large room that surprised him. This is better than the trenches, he thought, and dropped his case by the wardrobe before walking over to the window. He saw it overlooked the courtyard at the rear and various outbuildings. He could see for several miles over the boundary wall, half a mile or so away, and beyond moorland stretched as far as the eye could see. Below him, some fifty yards away, two men were smoking cigarettes beside a single-storey building. He assumed they were part of the security team and this was their billet. He was just about to turn around when a man appeared from the building, a face he recognised.

He decided to unpack later and hung up his coat, straightened his tie and combed his hair to look presentable. Pulling his notebook from his pocket, he locked his door and followed the directions given to him, arriving a few minutes later to a room full of faces.

'Can I help you?' said the cook, her hands buried in a large lump of dough.

'Ah yes, my name is Howie, Bill Howie. Mr Harper asked me to meet him in the staff dining room,' he said with a smile.

'Oh yes, dear, he's in his office. Just park yourself through there,' she said, pointing with a white floury finger. 'I am Mrs Tate, the cook. How do you do,' she said.

Bill wandered through and took a seat at the far end of the table, looking around the room. While he waited, he read some notes he had made earlier, then Harper's head suddenly appeared round the doorway.

'That was quick. Unpacked already?' he asked.

'No, no, I thought I would get to it later. I wanted to get started and begin my new role. When do I meet General Davis?' he asked. 'I would like to get reacquainted.'

Harper was alarmed. The general was an ardent fan of former soldiers with a history, especially one as knowledgeable as Howie. He must ensure he kept an upper hand.

'Indeed. Before we commence, can we first sort out a tiny matter of house etiquette? The two seats either end of the staff dining table are reserved for Mr Stevens, the butler, and myself. Please refrain from sitting in them at all times. You may use any other seat you choose.'

Bill, after years of service in the army, understood rank structure; however, he wasn't about to accept this pompous attitude of who sat where below stairs. He leant back, folded his arms and frowned.

'I have no intention of playing games of who sits where, Harper. If this seat is free when I enter, I will sit in it if I so desire. I assume I am a senior house member as head of security, so please grant me a little latitude. Now, can we begin?'

Harper didn't quite know how to react to this outburst and stood nervously staring at him. He then took a seat further down the table and opened his writing case. Howie remained seated.

'Before we start, I thought I saw a man I knew earlier, from my window, over by the building to the rear of the courtyard. I think we served together at the front. Have you employed anyone who recently left the army?' he asked.

Harper thought for a moment and smiled. 'Yes, many of the chaps are ex-soldiers, but I expect you mean Dave Gibbs. He was a sniper and I think served with the Glosters.'

'Is he a tall lad, early twenties?'

'Why, yes, that's him. I will reacquaint you with him when I take you on a short tour of the estate. For your notes, the general has asked to see you at ten o'clock tomorrow morning.' Bill nodded and opened his notebook.

Bill Howie listened intently to Harper for almost an hour but found it necessary to constantly interrupt him because much of what he said was rubbish. Harper's operational procedures were very outdated and he knew they would have to be changed. He wrote copious notes to reorganise things and towards the end was only half listening. As Harper's 2ic he had a job to do, but he realised he had to instigate changes, and soon.

The small room had become rather stuffy and Harper suggested they pause for tea. Bill closed his notebook before rising to look around the room and inspect the photos hanging on the walls.

'So, how was your war, Bill? What, if I may ask, happened to you?' Bill was in no mood to discuss his valour or indeed his time in the trenches. He was a man of dignity and kept his cards close to his chest, like all good soldiers do.

'My war was like everyone else's, Mr Harper, nothing dramatic, just the normal horrors of trench warfare. Let's just leave it at that, shall we,' he said, sitting down and reaching for the newspaper.

'Why, of course, I wasn't meaning to pry. Would it be OK to ask when you actually left the front?'

Bill looked at him with distaste. 'Did you order tea?' he asked abruptly.

Harper didn't answer, realising Bill had avoided the question. A moment later, Edna appeared with a large tea tray. She had recognised the ex-sergeant major and walked in from Howie's rear, deliberately shielding her face. Now she had two soldiers from her past to deal with. As she put the tray down, the crockery slid sideways, a spoon falling to the floor. Harper shook his head. Bill simply picked it up and smiled at the young girl, who turned away quickly.

'She's the new girl, still learning the ropes,' Harper said. Bill Howie ignored his comment and really didn't care; it was only a teaspoon.

CHAPTER 15

The pub menu blackboard displayed just fish pie or sausages. While Chris sipped his beer, quietly trying to decide what to have, he was distracted by the reflection in the mirror behind the spirit optics of an older man staring at him from across the bar. He picked up his change from the wet bar mat and looked at his watch. It was nearly seven o'clock and he was getting ravenous. He would not order, however, until his colleague and friend DT returned from making the all-important telephone call to London.

He glanced once more at the old chap, who was now leaning forward, staring at the brass binoculars on the stool beside him. Chris didn't wish to appear overly suspicious but turned to look around the room before catching the man's eye.

'Want to see?' he asked, offering them up.

'Nice binoculars,' the man said, picking up his beer glass and walking across. 'Can I?' he asked. 'Always did want a pair of quality field glasses. Always handy, you know. What do you use them for?'

Chris was about to answer when his friend arrived back.

'Want another?' Chris asked the old gentleman.

'I don't mind if I do. A pint of mild, if you please,' and he quickly finished the dregs in his glass and placed it on the bar.

'Making friends?' DT asked as he sat next to him.

Chris grinned. 'Everything all right?'

'Yeh, tell you later. Now, what's for dinner? I'm starving.'

The old man lifted the glasses to his eyes and turned his head towards the far end of the room. 'God, they're powerful, ain't they? I could see a flea on a dog's backside from a hundred yards with these. So, what do you use them for?' he asked again.

'Oh, we are ornithologists, we study birds, for the British Museum.'

DT cringed. Bird watchers, he thought. Yes, that would just about sum Chris up.

'Museum, eh, what for?'

DT waved at the barman and he walked across from the other bar.

'Yes, gentlemen, what'll you have?'

Chris looked at the blackboard one more time and went for the fish. 'I'll have the sausages and mash, I think,' DT said, 'Can you put it on our tab?'

The barman nodded before walking off towards the kitchen hatch. 'Mabel, one sausage and one fish. Room six.'

'Expensive, were they?' the old chap continued, fiddling with the focus.

Chris turned back to him and smiled. 'Well, yes, they were actually, so please be careful,' and just as he said it, the old man started coughing and as he reached into his pocket for his handkerchief, the binos slipped from his grasp, falling onto the stone floor. When DT lifted them to his eyes, one of the lenses had been dislodged inside. He said nothing. Chris knew by DT's face that he was furious. They were the only pair they had. His eyes said it all and Chris knew he had made an error of judgement. The old man picked up his pint and sipped it twice before walking slowly back to his chair. He didn't seem the least bit bothered by what he had done.

'Nice one, Chris,' said DT, before picking up his beer and heading for a table in the corner. Chris followed, just as a young girl arrived from the kitchen with two steaming plates of food. She put them down and almost before she had left, they were digging into their meals with gusto.

'Message left, OK?' asked Chris.

DT flicked his eyes around the bar and saw no one was interested in them.

'I tried two telephone boxes and each time I couldn't get through. Then found one on the platform. All done but they want regular updates, at least one per day. But quite how we are going to manage that once we are in position, I don't know. He did emphasise no loose ends whatsoever,' he said, pondering his own words.

'Yeh, I've been thinking about that since he briefed us. As all the staff will know of us, does he mean all of them? That's a bit of a tall order if he wants them all killed.'

DT considered Chris's comments.

'Look, there is no way he would want us to create a major bloodbath up here in this small community, leaving a dozen or so bodies to be cleared up. It goes against all our training, so let's assume he means the primary target only or if we are compromised,' he said.

'What are we going to do with the car?' Chris asked.

'According to the map, there's a small lane not far from the main entrance to the house where we can stash it for a few days. So, tomorrow we should leave here at zero five hundred and, by the time we have found somewhere under cover for the car, we should get to the house around six. We then sign up as security staff and plan our attack.'

When they had finished, Chris went up to their room, while DT settled their bill, telling the barman they were leaving very early the next morning, before breakfast. He arrived in the room just five minutes after Chris, who, as was his usual habit, was already in bed with the light out. DT staggered over to the window, drawing the curtains back to let some light in from the street, and as he did so he noticed a motorbike pull up opposite. The rider remained seated and stared up at him for several moments before climbing off and pulling the motorcycle onto its centre stand. He glanced up again before walking off towards the station. DT stepped back so he couldn't be seen, quickly assessing their situation, wondering if they had already been compromised. He woke Chris.

'Time to go. I think we've been rumbled.'

Chris, suddenly fully awake, reached for the light, but DT said no, finish up in the dark. He was up in a flash, climbing into his trousers.

'What's happened?' he asked, grabbing all his gear and stuffing it into his holdall.

'There is a chap on a motorbike taking rather a keen interest in us from the street. Something's up, we have to go.'

They slipped down the rear stairwell and out of the back door, walking at a lope back to the car, checking their tail all the while. It was just after ten fifteen and the town was dead. They stood in the shadows opposite their vehicle for several minutes but saw no one, before crossing and throwing their kit into the back seat. DT quickly started the car up and pulled around the corner towards the railway station. It was quiet, but as they drove past, they saw a chap standing next to a motorbike, fastening his helmet.

CHAPTER 16

Howie was sitting in his room writing new operating procedures. He had gathered together his notes from the meeting with Harper and details from his estate walk earlier that day. He was fully aware he had been seen by many of the house staff, striding around the grounds, which was just as he had wanted. There was just one place he had yet to visit and at ten thirty that evening, he climbed up the steep stairs to a narrow door that led to the roof.

He would have to leave the visual inspection until the morning, but he was keen to get reacquainted with young Gibbs, a man he knew from front line action in France. As he approached him from the doorway, Dave was looking through a pair of binoculars, his rifle lying beside him. He heard footsteps behind him and turned, smiling at the figure of a man he recognised. He quickly jumped to attention.

'We're not in the army now, Gibbs, relax please,' Howie said, shaking the hand of a fellow professional soldier. 'Thank goodness there is someone who knows his stuff. The last time I saw you, I think, was when you were heading out on a night patrol into No Man's Land many months ago.' He took out his tobacco tin. 'So, what happened to you?'

Dave knew his cover story wouldn't hold water if checked, but why would he do so? He swallowed hard, determined to make it convincing.

'It's my back, sir, I fell from a truck onto some ammo boxes, did some damage to my spine and was paralysed for a time. I was sent back to England, but the doctors thought it a risk for me to return to the front. I was discharged about a month ago.' Eager to change the subject, he quickly continued, 'Didn't you get shot helping that sapper, sir?'

'Yes, my friend, you have a good memory. I was shot as I tried to untangle him from some wire, not ten feet from our own lines. Part of the bullet is still in my back, too close to my spine to remove it, apparently. But it's not too bad and I have many good days now. But enough of our old injuries. We have an important job to do here and I am pleased to have you aboard. Tomorrow, I am going to start some formal training as I sense the standards are pretty poor. I would be glad to have you assist me if you fancy some extra pay,' he said, lighting up his rolled cigarette.

Dave smiled. 'Always good for a few extra bob,' he said. 'You do know, sir, some of these men have forgotten an awful lot and one or two really shouldn't be here at all. I had to show one chap how to load the Lee Enfield rifle yesterday. It made me cringe, sir, to be honest.'

Bill shook his head, sighed, and said, 'Let's drop the sir, shall we? It's Bill from now on.' Dave smiled to himself and was glad his new relationship with this battle-hardened man had begun well.

'I am sure between us it can all be fixed, Bill, and although some won't enjoy the training, it's time for a shake-up. I should remind you though, I don't finish until zero nine hundred,' Dave said. 'Kemp needs a refresher though.'

Howie walked to the edge of the roof and peered down, then out across the fields.

'Chilly spot. Anything happening?' he asked.

Dave, feeling quite relaxed, responded, 'No, Bill, quiet night and haven't seen anything since I started three nights ago.'

Bill Howie looked out towards the tree line and shivered. He knew having a professional soldier amongst a bag of rough diamonds would be very useful.

'So, what is your brief up here?' he asked as Kemp appeared out of the darkness behind them.

Dave looked at the man.

'I thought I heard voices,' Kemp said as he approached.

'Oh, this is Pete Kemp, Bill, he is on watch with me. We cover two arcs; one down towards the main entrance to the west and south and the other to the north and east.'

Bill looked at the chap who had limped over, assessing him with a cold stare.

'Kemp, is it?' he said. 'So, what is your history and how familiar are you with that rifle?' His manner unsettled Kemp.

'Well, sir, I lost a leg at Ypres in 1915, but manage pretty well. I haven't fired a .303 in ages but was always a pretty good shot,' he said, rubbing his hands together nervously.

'Well, we will soon put that right as training begins in the morning at zero six thirty. Kemp, I know you will still be on watch, but I want you to head down at zero six hundred and wake everyone in the billet and then grab a brew, and one for Dave, before joining in. When you have finished, you will come back up to complete your duty. Understand?' Kemp nodded.

'OK, time for me to go, chaps. See you tomorrow,' and he was gone.

The men didn't realise what had hit them the next morning when, to their surprise, Pete charged through the annexe just before six, making such a noise that only the devil himself could have slept through it. He made sure several of them were out of bed before diving into the kitchen for a brew. He took a mug of tea up to the roof for a very grateful Dave before heading to the training area in the courtyard.

Howie arrived five minutes before the training commenced, looking at his watch. It was clear some of the men would be late. As the Hall clock finished its last chime for six thirty, he lifted his head and bellowed, making everyone jump.

'I am waiting,' he shouted, and within seconds the last two men came running from the annexe, still tucking their shirts into their trousers. Everyone realised the holiday was over.

Howie began with a brief introduction followed by a firm reminder of what he expected of them. He warned them that the next time anyone was late for training or a duty of any kind, they would be docked a day's pay. He then looked at every man, briefly studying each face in turn and asked them to give a summary of their military service. He had the men's full attention.

Harper was watching this spectacle from an upper floor and knew his decision to employ this man had been sound.

Howie then unveiled a blackboard with a large sketch of the house and grounds to demonstrate the size of their task. He had an ability to hold attention and the men never once lost their focus. On a table to one side, covered by a sheet, lay a stripped-down Lee Enfield rifle which each man would practise on later in the morning's training. Harper had come down for the last part of Howie's talk and stood leaning against the wall behind the men.

A little after seven thirty, the training was complete for the day and everyone was dismissed, disappearing into the kitchen for breakfast. Kemp went back to the roof and Harper walked over to Howie, who frowned at him.

'I have no problem with you coming down to listen to the briefings, Harper, but don't let me catch you leaning against a wall again in my company. I am trying to instil discipline into this slovenly bunch and you taking the weight off in such a manner really doesn't help. Now, what can I do for you?' he said, taking the board from its easel.

'I was purely interested in how it went, Bill,' Harper said.

Howie, a man from a long-standing Scottish military family that had served three generations in the Black Watch, had been taught to deal with conflict by his father. He remembered the Black Watch motto: *No one provokes me with impunity.* Referring to these words had allowed him to resolve many troubled times in his life and deal with difficult situations. Harper was to be no exception, no matter what his position.

'You really have taken on some crap, Harper, what were you thinking? Some have hardly any experience at all and the others can barely remember basic drills. We have a lot of work to do, so I would like to speak to you in your office at ten hundred,' he said, challenging his authority. Harper thought better than to argue and nodded, almost too frightened to speak.

'We will need to extend training, too, certainly for the first week anyway, as it is clear we have a great deal to do.' With that, he shouted to two men to take the table and the blackboard and easel into the annexe. They duly ran to obey his instructions and Bill walked off, leaving Harper standing rather forlornly gazing after him.

***

During morning tea, when the general was in his study and all the staff were below stairs, Ed sneaked back up to the first floor. She took a breath and opened the main door to the general's apartment, walking straight over to behind the bookcase. Below the shelf to the left two small keys were hanging on a hook. She quickly tried them both before placing one in her pocket. She was back downstairs before anyone had missed her.

CHAPTER 17

Ricky was envious of his sniper partner as, although he was his greatest friend and at huge risk, he had the best part of this operation. He didn't dwell on it and wanted his friend back safely above all else, but he would have loved to have been offered this role by their lieutenant.

He had never shared with an officer before, but even though Corn showed him the greatest respect, he was often distant. He did, however, always take his share of the jobs, made brews, had dug the shit pit behind the tree and always took the first watch.

Ricky pulled his small notebook from his pocket and realised the days had passed quickly. He was actually looking forward to getting back to France but knew he could never speak of this little excursion to anyone. What they were undertaking would have to remain a closely guarded secret for life.

Corn decided they should bury any items they now didn't require, so, for the rest of the day, they sifted through their gear and reduced it wherever they could. As Dave could arrive at any time and they might need to move quickly, they trimmed down to the bare essentials.

They dug a hole, some two feet deep, next to the basher, dropping all spare kit into it, scattering the spare soil around the area.

The equipment they'd need, along with several days' rations, their weapons and ammunition and some outer clothing was all that remained. They wore pretty well everything else and felt ready for a fast withdrawal when needed. All their kit would have to be carried in one lift to the motor bike to make their escape. As dusk descended, Corn called Ricky over.

'I've been thinking. We need to be in a position to cover Dave at any point during his extraction in case he is compromised. So, assuming he moves as planned, we will leave here, packed and ready to go, at twenty-three thirty and move into a forward observation position halfway between the wall and the potting sheds. If we get into position just after midnight, we can do a watch rotation until he makes his escape. We are then a team again and can operate as such. We will return here, collect all the remaining gear and head directly back to collect the bike. All good?'

Having listened carefully, his subordinate thought through the scenario and asked just one question.

'Yes, all clear, boss, but in what order are you ferrying us to Pickering or is it possible we could do it in one move?'

Corn puzzled over this problem.

'I think without any gear it would just be possible, but we will have several packs and rifles, so think I should ferry you one at a time. It shouldn't take too long. It's only five or six miles. Plus, if I take you first and drop you at the level crossing down in the trees about half a mile short of Pickering, Dave can run down the road and await my return. Once I have dropped you, I will set off and meet you in York.'

Ricky then thought of something else.

'So, when do we get our tickets? Is it something we could do in advance, tomorrow maybe? We can just get straight on then.'

Corn realised that was something he had quite forgotten. 'Yes, good thinking. It's probably best if I get them tonight; one less job to do. I will leave at nine thirty and be back well before eleven. Anything else?' he asked.

Ricky, satisfied this change to their plan made good sense, nodded. 'Can you top the water flasks up too?' he asked

At nine fifteen, Corn woke Ricky and told him he was just leaving. Ricky clambered out of the hide and sat on the step, watching him go. Corn took his handgun and four flasks packed into the small rucksack and twenty minutes later Ricky heard the faint but distinctive sound of a motorcycle.

It took little time for Corn to reach Pickering and he parked up outside the station. As he pulled the Norton onto its stand, he noticed a chap looking down at him from a window on the upper floor of the hotel. He glanced up for a few seconds before switching the engine off and walking towards the station ticket office. There was no one about and he tapped on the counter and leaned through the hatchway where he saw a man listening to a radio. He tapped the counter again and finally he was seen by a stern old chap who was coughing into his handkerchief.

'Two singles to York, please,' Corn said and pulled a ten-bob note from his pocket.

'That will be two and fourpence,' the man said as he walked over. He exchanged the money for two tickets, counting out Corn's change from piles of neatly stacked coins. Then he frowned at him.

'Are you travelling today, sir?' he asked.

Corn, not wanting to get involved in a conversation, just shook his head.

'Probably early Sunday morning,' he said, starting to turn.

The man tutted. 'There will be some disruptions over the coming days due to works to the track. If you travel before seven a.m., you should be fine.'

Corn nodded before walking away, down the steps and back into the dark street. He stowed the tickets in his inside pocket along with his change before walking back to the bike. As he swung his leg over the seat and pulled the Norton from its stand, a car swung around the corner. Two men passed him in the car, the passenger taking particular interest in him. He stopped for a moment, thinking it strange that at that late hour he was of interest to anyone. But he couldn't dwell on it as he had to get back. He set the starter and, with a single kick, the engine fired first time. He put the bike into gear and powered away up the hill.

As he approached the turning, he noticed a car some way ahead, turning right. What were the odds at that time of day of a car taking exactly the same route as him? Instinctively, he switched off the lights on the bike, using the moon as his guide, and slowed down, driving now in first gear. He turned right and switched off the engine, cruising to a stop. He pushed the bike in behind a wall and walked the rest of the way to the corner but could see nothing. He then ran up the road until he saw the farmhouse on the right-hand side, and as he approached, he could hear voices. He dropped quickly down into the ditch as two figures suddenly appeared from the bushes opposite and walked right past him. They headed down the track towards the main entrance of the estate. He watched with interest until they merged into the darkness, following at a safe distance until they reappeared at the gatehouse. The glow from the porch light illuminated them as they knocked on the door. It took a moment or two, but eventually, a man opened it. Words were spoken before they were sent towards the side gate. As the men turned, Corn was sure one of them was the same chap he had seen watching him from the car.

He trotted back down to the junction and eased the bike from its stand before pushing it up the road, turning right at the cottage on the corner. It was hard going on the grass, but he wanted to avoid the noise of the engine and laboured on, finally locating the previous hiding place. As he was just ducking under the outer branches, he noticed some fresh tyre tracks underfoot into the same small wooded area. As he moved forward, he could see the rear end of a car. He turned around and went back to the track and headed further up it until he found another thicket, dense enough to hide the bike safely. He withdrew his penknife and cut the lower branches halfway through, bending them down over the bike. They would now provide sufficient cover, but crucially wouldn't die and give the position away. He then walked back down to the location of the car.

Something was amiss. Why would two chaps heading to the hall hide their car and not proceed up the drive unless they were up to no good. If his hunch was correct, he needed to ensure the car couldn't be driven, so decided to leave them a little surprise.

Several minutes later, he went into the small farm to fill the flasks before stealthily making his way back past the gatehouse and dropping down the bank to the railway line. Within fifteen minutes, he was safely back at the hide. Ricky, forever alert, heard him coming a good way off. Corn plonked himself down beside him.

'All OK, boss, any problems?' he asked.

Corn felt a little uneasy as he pulled a flask from his pack. He then ran through the story of the two men in the car at the station and then seeing them entering the estate, before finding their car hidden in the wood. Ricky was confused.

'Hang on, so these men hide their car and then enter on foot? What do you think it means?' he asked.

Corn was by now eating what was left of the cold meat, the tough beef sticking to his teeth. He chewed for over a minute before he could swallow.

'I have the strangest feeling about this, Ricky. I think they may be doing something rather covert, as we are.'

Ricky's face froze.

'I think we might have some agents in our midst. Why else act so suspiciously? We need to alert Dave. What time is he due?'

'Around nine tomorrow. Is he in danger, do you think?' he asked.

'I believe we are all in danger and so we must be ready to move at a moment's notice.'

At just after nine twenty the next morning, they saw Dave running out from behind the main house heading down the hill towards the main gate. Halfway down, he stopped and did some exercises before running through a large flock of sheep, scattering them to the four winds, and then heading over to the tree. They readied themselves for his arrival as once again he stopped and did some exercises, just under the main canopy of the huge pine.

'Dave, we may have a problem. We think the two men who arrived last night may be British agents. I want you to observe them and report back to me tomorrow.'

Dave, still doing his twisting exercises, took in this new order without flinching.

'Yes, we saw them arrive last night from the roof. Bill Howie showed them into the annexe around ten forty-five. I then saw them attending the morning training. Haven't met them yet though, but do know Mr Howie didn't take to them much. He confided in me not fifteen minutes ago.' Dave then lay down and started doing some sit-ups.

'I won't fill you in completely now; however, the vehicle they have hidden near to where we stash the bike now has four flat tyres, so they won't be on our tail when we slip away. Same time tomorrow, then?'

Dave stood up and pushed against the tree, stretching his calf muscles.

'Just one last thing, boss,' he said, grunting with the exertion. 'There is a guard posted outside the general's apartment all night, but I have found a side door in the next corridor. So, I have my way in. I'm set for Saturday night,' he said, standing up. Corn looked across to Ricky who gave him a thumbs up.

'OK, Dave, keep your head down and watch out for those two chaps. We will watch out for you tomorrow as normal, but don't feel pressured to come unless you're able. Otherwise, see you late Saturday night.'

Dave didn't respond, just took off east up towards the far corner of the estate before turning and appearing again in the rear courtyard. As he ran in, the two new men were sitting talking together, cleaning their weapons, and gave only a casual glance his way. Dave made a point of going over and introducing himself.

At all meals that day, he watched them avoid mingling with the other men, returning instead to the billet at every opportunity. He started to believe the boss could well be right.

CHAPTER 18

With the team now largely at full strength, further training lasting a full ninety minutes took place on the Saturday morning. With a marked improvement showing in the professionalism of the whole group, the training was clearly having an effect.

Bill Howie had changed the billet around and opened a small room at the far end for the night team, so they could be out of earshot of the others.

Dave rose around five thirty each afternoon, eating dinner at seven before his evening watch began. This timetable was working well for him to keep daily contact with Corn and Ricky, his morning run also providing an opportunity to stretch out his stiff body. After breakfast each day he headed for his bunk.

Dave's night duties offered him suitable opportunities to recce areas of the house and he told Kemp he had additional duties of patrolling the upper landings. Kemp would not question this following the recent mishap of sleeping on duty, but to overcome any resentment, Dave would promise to bring him a brew on his return.

Dave found out the routine for guarding the general by having a casual chat with the sentry during the long nights. They were, in fact, glad to have the chance of a brief chat at three in the morning when the mind starts to dip and the urge to sleep is hard to resist. It was easy to glean information from the sentry and it was clear the general didn't go anywhere unaccompanied, apart from eating his meals. He also took a nap mid-afternoon while Harper worked in his office right across the corridor. He would sit with his door open and a handgun on his desk, just in case. Dave now knew his approach line and how to take out the guard, but he could only pull it off safely at night.

As the routines for the household and security team settled down, he felt certain he could finish the task in the early hours of the next morning.

After his shift the next day, he stripped off his shirt, rolled up the sleeves on his undershirt and set off as usual on his morning run. The freedom was bliss as he ran down the main entrance road, cutting north on a bend in the road, scattering sheep as he ran. He stopped at his usual spot to perform his exercises and then noticed someone looking at him from the roof. He thought it was Howie but took little notice as he pushed his body hard, working out the stiffness from standing for ten hours.

Once north of the Hall, he cut across the land until he closed in on the wall where Corn and Ricky were probably watching him. As he approached, he slowed until he reached the large tree where, as before, he started stretching his arms and back. As he did so, Ricky, who had been following his route for twenty minutes, crept up as close as he dared to a position about thirty feet away.

'Can you hear me, chaps?' Dave said. Corn and Ricky crouched together, listening. Dave explained the changes that Howie had made, but that happily he had been retained as king of the roof. He told them he was making his move that night.

'If you judge that to be the best time, we will go with that, providing you are sure,' Corn said.

Dave, always ready for a challenge, stopped exercising and took out his tobacco tin and leant against the tree. He began rolling a ciggy, staring across to the house. He was careful not to make any gestures, and when he spoke, he dropped his head down.

'Corn, it has to be done tonight as I suspect Mr Howie has different plans for me. Plus, I want to get out of here.'

Corn nodded to Ricky, who wanted to leave too.

'OK, taking our plan in reverse order, we need to get you and Ricky on the early morning milk train to York, which leaves Pickering at zero three thirty. Assuming I can ferry you both to the station with your kit in thirty minutes, and the extraction from the house takes another twenty, I think you need to make your move sometime around zero one thirty. That allows for a little fat on our timings to cover any unforeseen problems. Will that work for you?' he asked.

Dave, as he usually did, remained totally confident in his boss, who always seemed to think of everything.

'Yes, that's all good, but don't be alarmed if I run a little late. I have no way of knowing what might get in my way. So, are we set, sir?' he said, rather formally.

'Yes, Dave, I think we are. I have decided we will meet you in the line of trees between the potting sheds and the wall. That way, if you are compromised, you have instant back-up.'

Dave, thankful for this support, finished his fag and flicked the dog end into the undergrowth.

'Right, until tomorrow then,' he said, and set off once again, running east along the line of the wall in reverse of his planned escape route. When he arrived back in the courtyard, several of the chaps were drinking tea outside the annexe. He grabbed one from the pot, just as Howie walked from the rear door of the Hall.

'Good run, Dave?' he asked. Dave nodded.

'Yes, Bill, I find running helps my back immensely, and it's nice out on your own sometimes. Happy for you to join me if you like, same time tomorrow.'

Bill frowned, wondering how Dave could run so quickly with a back injury that caused him to be discharged from the army.

'Have to rain check that, too much to do. But I would like to go over those distances you mentioned. How about after supper?' he asked.

'Yes, okay. Now it's time I got breakfast and some shut-eye. See you later then.' As he turned and entered the billet, he sensed Bill Howie was slightly suspicious of him.

Bill watched him go, wondering if he was the man, he said he was.

CHAPTER 19

Ed had not slept. She lay on her bed, watching the clock, waiting for the house to sleep. So much had happened to her in the past weeks, and while she watched the clock tick round towards twelve thirty, her journey back from France was central in her mind.

When she boarded the boat in Boulogne, she was unsure what was actually happening to her. Then she met Frank in the cabin, where he had been so incredibly sweet as he told her of the sacrifice her brother, Edward, had made. Hardened by a year at war, she hadn't found it in herself to cry as she was devoid of any emotions just then. His immense bravery had staggered her, and she knew that when she was alone, she would sob with all her might.

She remembered the choppy sea as they sailed back to England and her freedom. She sat in the back seat of a Rolls Royce and four long hours later they had arrived at a country estate, the likes of which she had never seen before. She was given a wonderful room, her own maid, the best food anyone could wish for and clothes for every occasion. She would soak in her bath for over an hour each day which seemed to invigorate her. Frank had started to make a home for them both and they would go for long walks across the fields and ride each day. She had grown stronger in every way and realised she was falling in love with a man she had previously only known as her friend. She knew she was to marry Frank and smiled to herself.

She recalled the day Lord Hardcastle had spoken to her in the library about General Davis's plight and remembered she hadn't reacted to his words, although she knew instantly she would have to avenge Edward's death. She remembered looking at Frank, who was nodding gently as if he knew what she was thinking. His loyalty towards her then showed he understood and she loved him for that.

She suddenly heard the great clock high on the tower of the Hall chime the half hour and her heart thumped in her chest. She rose off her bed and carefully opened her door. A single hall light glowed in the corner by the stairs. It was all very quiet. She checked the Webley Frank had given her before she left and took a deep breath. She was ready.

Going down the servants' spiral staircase was not easy as the old timbers creaked at each step. To avoid any noise, she followed the trick she'd used as a child, when she didn't want her parents to hear her, by walking on the inner part of the step, nearest the wall. This seemed to work.

Ed was aware that Stevens sometimes walked the upper floors, even at this late hour; however, she had listened at her door and heard nothing. Two floors down, she pulled the door gently and stepped out onto the general's landing, checking each way at every turn. She walked slowly towards the corner beside a huge pot plant and saw the narrow door. As she slipped the key into the lock, she was acutely aware that if she was seen now, it was all over. After a final look around, she turned the key and the lock clicked open. The door eased open and, without any fuss, she withdrew the key and quickly stepped in, leaving the door unlocked. She placed the key on the shelf next to the door to avoid any chance of misplacing it, and turned ready to face the man she hated most in the world.

It was stuffy in the room, and she could smell cigars. There was a faint glow creating shadows across the ceiling that, at first, she thought was from the fire. But they didn't move; it was definitely a lamp. She heard no movement and felt calm, never wanting anything in her life as much as this moment.

She walked forward, pulling the small Webley pistol out from under her jacket and eased the hammer backwards, listening carefully. She stopped by the large bookcase and peered around the corner. She could hear the gentle rhythm of a man snoring, but couldn't see him at first, then stepped further into the room and finally saw the back of his head in a leather armchair. The small table lamp next to him gave off the faint glow. Watching her footing and with her pistol pointing forwards, she approached him.

It was less than ten paces to his chair and suddenly she was standing before him. It would have been simpler to shoot him through the top of his head as he slept, but she wanted the pleasure of him recognising her before she took his life.

She stood slightly to one side of him to be sure he would not be able to launch himself at her and lifted her weapon, holding it firmly, at the ready. She then stepped forward and kicked out at his feet, once, then again, until he started to stir. As she stepped back, he smacked his mouth then lifted his hand to his face, itching his nose rapidly before opening his eyes.

He looked up and then jerked his head towards her. When he saw the gun, he physically jumped in his seat. Slowly he shuffled upright in his chair and coughed as if signalling someone, but no one would hear him, not this time. He stared at her, totally speechless, clearly trying to work out why a member of his junior staff would be there, in his room, with a gun. She removed her glasses and tossed them to one side before pulling out her false teeth and tucking them in her pocket. Only then did she remove her wig. He seemed bemused at first and frowned at her, not understanding what was happening, and then the penny dropped. His face suddenly contorted and he swallowed several times.

'But... but you are dead. You are a German spy. You were found guilty by a military court and shot by a firing squad. How can this be?' he said, his voice rising.

'No, I am not dead, General. You were tricked by some of your officers and the man you had killed was my brother. And now it is your turn to die.'

He physically cringed in his chair. Ed stepped back another pace to keep enough distance between them to avoid any surprise attack.

Although she had killed many times before, this was different. She had never seen the whites of a man's eyes before or been this close to her enemy. She had no feelings for this man, who had shown little humanity. Ed paused, the gun pointing at his face.

'Now, I am not a violent person by nature, but I have decided you must pay for killing an innocent man.'

The general then calmly placed his hands together on his lap and smiled, his attitude changing.

'Surely there must a way out of this for us both,' he said, opening his hands to her. 'I was just doing my duty, as the evidence came before me. You cannot blame me for that, surely? I am a very rich man and would like to put this right. I can offer you anything, anything you want,' he said with a wry smile. 'Name it, it's yours.'

Ed was insulted that he might think she could be bought, but then realised he was trying to distract her. She played his game.

'Anything?' she said, as if she was interested in his proposition, but all the while she gently tightened her finger on the trigger. Slowly he started to stand, facing her, just ten feet away. He held his hands out.

'Yes, anything,' he said, and started to turn to his left as if reaching for something on the table. But then, dropping his head and, moving his foot back as if turning around, he suddenly lunged at her, snarling as he moved forward, but he was always too far away.

She was ready and corrected her aim before squeezing the trigger. As if in slow motion, and before he had moved more than a few feet, the bullet smashed through his right eye, throwing him backwards. He hit the side of the chair and rolled off it sideways. He came to rest on his back, his one good eye looking upwards, while the other, filled with crimson fluid, was gone. She was never going to miss.

Ed stood motionless, feeling nothing, before closing in and aiming at his chest, ready to fire again. But she knew a dead man when she saw one. Her anger then rose and she wanted to empty the remaining shells into his body but, as a professional soldier, she knew better. Her eyes welled up, not for her prey, but for the loss of a loving brother. This was for him.

In the gloom, she could see blood pooling around the general's head, seeping into the ornate rug. She lowered her Webley, a slight smell of cordite still in the air. There was no remorse or time to ponder; it would be only minutes before someone came. She then sensed someone to her left. Instantly raising her pistol, she turned to face a man in the shadows.

'Come out now, or you will die too,' she said coldly. Slowly, a man appeared from behind the bookcase, his hands raised. She instantly recognised Dave Gibbs, who now stood quite still, his mouth open, and she lowered her weapon.

'Beat you to it, old man. Did you get all that?' she asked, and Dave nodded, frozen to the spot.

'But your brother? How was that possible?' he asked.

Ed looked at him for several seconds, as she tucked the weapon into her trousers.

'It's a long story, Dave. Someone arranged for the swap without my knowledge. All I knew at the time was I was suddenly free and being ushered through the rear gate of the chateau. I was then taken away by car to Boulogne. But listen, we don't have time for this now. We need to get going before the guard raises the alarm.'

'I've taken care of him,' Dave said.

'OK, put a stout chair under the door handle and then help me smash all the lights. We don't want to make it easy for them, do we? But leave this one for now,' she said, pointing to the lamp by the body.

While Ed ran around one way, Dave fixed the door and then worked the other half of the room. Glass soon littered the carpet, and when all was done, she headed to the general's bathroom. Above the toilet, she saw the large double window and jumped up onto the toilet seat to unlock the catches. Ed pushed gently on the frame, but only the bottom half moved. Her heart raced as she tried to understand what was stopping it from opening.

Dave appeared. 'There's another lock at the top, Ed. But what are you doing that for?'

'False trail,' she said, and then released the final catch before stepping back down. Then, quite without warning, she suddenly felt sick. She lifted the lid and leant over the toilet, throwing up violently. This took Dave by surprise, as her reputation in the trenches was one of an ardent professional, a killing machine, but she was human after all.

Where did that come from, she thought, wiping her mouth on her sleeve before heading back into the bedroom to stand at the general's feet one last time. They both looked down at the man who had killed her brother. There was no feeling, it was just like killing a rabid dog: cold, meticulous efficiency. The only difference was that she hadn't seen the end result of her executions before. She looked around the room one last time, before smashing the final lamp. Then they heard voices. It was time they left.

The door they were about to exit from was a secret entrance built specially to allow the general to slip out unnoticed to visit his female guests during society weekends before the war. She'd been told he had also, on occasion, been known to take advantage of young servant girls on the top floor too. She would now use it to her advantage and told Dave to follow her.

She reached for the key on the shelf and the one still hanging on the hook, before opening the door. There was a loud thumping on the general's main door and several voices. She peered through the gap. All was clear. Dave followed her out before she locked the door once more.

'Ed, I have an exit route already planned and have help waiting in the grounds. Are you ready to leave?' he said in a whisper. She nodded as she discarded her maid's uniform.

'Yes, I have done what I came for. Let's go,' she said, as he led the way.

CHAPTER 20

The sentry was now conscious and Bill Howie, still in his pyjamas, was pulling him to his feet, shouting, assuming he had fallen asleep on watch. Then he saw blood on the carpet. At the same time, two men were shoving hard with their shoulders on the general's main door. One then dropped to the floor and looked through the keyhole, announcing the key was still in the lock on the inside.

'Right, is there any other way into the room?' he asked the men present. No one answered and he was about to yell when Bark appeared from the darkness, asking what all the commotion was about.

'We think the general's been shot,' replied one of the guards. Bark stopped dead in his tracks.

'So, what happened?' Howie asked the sentry.

'I was hit from behind, sir, and don't remember anything until just now. I think I heard a gunshot,' he said, rubbing his head.

'We don't know for sure, lads, but we need to get into his quarters. Is there another entrance, Bark, this one is blocked?' asked Howie.

'Well, yes, there is, umm, through the dressing room. It comes in behind the bookcase from the next corridor.'

Bill Howie took charge as he had done a thousand times in the trenches, and shouted for the men to follow him.

'Morgan, stay here and watch the door. Let me have your pistol.' He turned away down the short corridor and found a small door tucked just around the corner. He tried the handle, but that door was also locked. Stooping down to peer through the keyhole he could see only darkness. Harper, who had just arrived from his quarters on the ground floor, asked if he could help, but Howie ignored him.

'Right, men, be warned, the gunman might still be in the room. Have your weapons to hand. OK, lend your shoulders, men. Stand by, heave, and again, heave.' The door suddenly gave way, crashing open against the wall, rebounding so fast it almost flattened one of the chaps who had stepped in just at the wrong moment.

With the Webley in his hand, Howie led the way, with three men close behind him. He stepped gingerly into the darkened room, peering nervously around the bookcase.

'The lights, turn on the lights,' he shouted as the rear man reached for the switch by the door. But nothing happened. He tried again before informing Howie they didn't work. By this time, they realised why; glass crunched underfoot as they explored the darkened room. Bill Howie, always thinking on his feet, ran over to draw the curtains trying desperately to get some light from outside, into the room.

'Try the others, quickly, we need some light.' Suddenly, from behind the door, one of the men found a lamp still intact and as though the sun had suddenly come out, there was light. What met their eyes made one man instantly sick.

Bill Howie approached the body lying prone on the floor. He crouched down to inspect it but knew already that the general was dead.

'Docherty, run to the roof and alert Gibbs and Kemp. Check all arcs to see if you can see anything or anyone running away. Pay particular attention to the west and the main gate. If anyone is making a getaway, they will surely be heading in that direction. Now move.'

As he ran from the room, Howie was in full flow.

'Harper, go and call the gatehouse and tell them to secure the gate and then call the police. No one is to go in or out. Then unlock the rifle locker in your study and issue a rifle to each man with twenty rounds. Is that clear?'

Harper, in shock, nodded furiously before disappearing out of the room.

'Someone, get that chair removed from the main door,' Howie shouted, as he inspected the body. He saw the bullet entry point clearly, as there was just blood where an eye once was. He recognised this was an assassination if ever he'd seen one. A professional had done this, someone who knew how to kill. He was trying to work out how anyone had got into the house, but then it dawned on him that it may well have been an inside job. He looked around the room at the men surrounding him, wondering who he could trust. He tried to work out how the intruder had escaped, as both doors were locked. And then he saw the light from the bathroom. As he strode over to it, he felt something crunch underfoot. He looked down and saw a broken pair of spectacles, which he picked up and viewed with curiosity. Were they the general's, he thought, or the assailant's? He put them in his pocket and moved forward, gently kicking the door to the bathroom open, and instantly saw the window wide open. He stepped up onto the toilet and stuck his head out to see a flat roof some ten feet below and the roof of the kitchen. No one was in sight, but then he hadn't expected anyone to be. He stepped down and moved back into the main room.

'We have a murder here,' he said softly. 'Someone, find a sheet to cover the general's body. Smith, once everyone has a rifle, gather the men in the courtyard. I want patrols to go out immediately, in pairs, to cover the grounds in all directions. Check all the ground floor windows and doors for forced entry and all the outbuildings too. Time is important. I want a report within half an hour. Is that clear?'

Smith nodded and was gone.

The general's body was now covered. Bill Howie calmly walked over to the window and peered out into the darkness, but he could see nothing, only a faint light at the entrance to the west, some thousand yards away. Behind him, Docherty appeared and he turned from the window to see him standing in the doorway, looking rather perplexed.

'Docherty, what's wrong?' he said, walking towards him, just as another man came into the room carrying some rope. 'Kemp, what are you doing? Where's Gibbs?' The two men looked at each other.

'Sir, Gibbs knocked me unconscious, and when I woke, I was tied to the chimney stack and gagged. I have been up there for ages. What's going on, Mr Howie?'

Bill was stunned. 'Come into the light, laddie.' He checked the back of Kemp's head, seeing a blood-stained scalp, and then pointed down at the sheet beside the bed, a single foot protruding from one end.

Kemp stepped forward then stopped. 'Shit, is that the general, sir? Was it Gibbs?' he said, staring at his boss.

'Don't know yet who it was, but with luck, we will have the culprit before morning. Now, tell me exactly what happened.'

CHAPTER 21

Knowing all the house staff would be in their quarters on the top floor, Ed and Dave ran down the back staircase so they wouldn't be detected. At the bottom, Dave told Ed to wait as he had something he needed to do. She watched him disappear down the corridor and waited under the stairs. He returned in less than a minute.

'OK, all set?' he said, and they quickly went out of a side door, taking a moment to lock it and throw the key into the undergrowth. Dave immediately moved left into a recess and sank into the shadows, Ed dropping down beside him.

'So, what was so important?' she asked.

'Oh, just fixing the padlock for the rifles, that's all. I broke my key in the lock. They won't get them free in a hurry,' he said quietly. Dave was just about to flex his leg muscles to stand when several men suddenly appeared from the annexe, the door banging loudly against the wall as it was flung open. They quickly started running towards the house, one stopping momentarily after something dropped to the ground from his coat. When they realised the door to the house was locked, they banged repeatedly, shouting, but to no avail. After a few minutes, they moved off around to the left and out of sight.

Dave whispered into Ed's ear to move and the two figures slipped along the eastern side of the Hall in the darkness, stepping around each flower border and ducking under each window in turn. They reached the corner and stopped. Ed closed in behind Dave, covering their rear. With his heart pounding and his breathing raised, Dave slowly peered round the corner and scanned the garden ahead. The coast seemed clear.

He tapped Ed on the leg and they both ran across the gap towards the potting sheds, some fifty yards away, Ed now facing the rear as they dropped down into cover. They could hear a faint banging upstairs in the house, presumably as the guards tried to break into the general's apartment. Dave peered ahead, eyes wide, scanning their route, weapon poised. Ed then heard a noise above them and saw two heads pop out from behind a chimney stack, talking loudly. All hell then seemed to be breaking loose behind them, as lights sprang on all over the house.

'Time to go, Dave,' Ed said and they both got to their feet and started running along the hedgerow, away from the house and towards the trees. Even though they hadn't worked together in France, their training had been the same and their actions were quite automatic, honed by expert tuition and operating in No Man's Land. It was time they put some serious distance between them and the estate and Dave urged them on. They reached the trees within a minute where they dropped down almost together, settling on their haunches, just as a friendly voice spoke from the bushes opposite.

'Brought a friend?' asked Ricky. Dave quickly moved towards his voice, Ed following right behind him. Ricky watched the figures close in and felt ill at ease that someone else had now joined their discrete group.

'Where's the boss?' Dave asked, just as a figure rose to his right.

'I assume the job is done, Dave,' Corn said. 'We heard the shot. But who's this?' They were now huddled together in the darkness, close enough for their shoulders to be touching.

'Yes, the job is done, boss,' he said, with a nervous edge. 'The general is dead all right. But it wasn't me who fired the shot.' He could see Corn's head turn towards Ricky, then back to the strange figure to his left.

'What do you mean, it wasn't you?' Corn asked. Then a voice they all recognised spoke up.

'It was me, I killed him, sir, something I needed to do,' Ed said calmly.

'Look, this ain't the time, boss, we will explain later, but let me introduce you to the late Ed Mitchell,' Dave said, with a tremble in his voice.

'Is this some kind of a joke, Gibbs?' said Corn, a little too loudly for their surroundings.

'No, boss, I'm as shocked as you are. It's Ed, she has been working at the Hall as a maid and, well, before I could get to him tonight, she shot him in the head,' he said abruptly.

There was total silence amongst this small elite band. 'But I was there, I saw her shot!' Corn said. It was Ed who broke the spell.

'Boss, I will explain, but we can either sit here and have a conversation or get the hell out of here. Which is it to be?' she said sarcastically.

Corn, a man who always liked to be in the know on any operation, didn't understand what was happening, but whomever this was, they were quite correct. They had to go.

'I don't quite know what to say, Ed, but I look forward to hearing your story. Right, we need to change plans, so I'll brief you as we go. Dave, behind me, then Ed and Ricky as tail-end Charlie. Keep your weapons handy, but let's hope we don't have to use them.'

They got to their feet as distant voices rang out behind them. Dave knew the standard of the security team and that the only other professional amongst them was Howie, who had clearly taken charge. He must know by now that Dave was involved but might not have realised that he had someone else with him. So, for now, he was sure they would only be looking for one man. If he knew his drills, patrols would be the next stage so they must move.

They ran off, reaching the wall before turning west. Within a few minutes, Dave saw the large tree that he had used for several days as a marker. They headed for the low point in the wall and, without hesitation, Corn quickly clambered over followed by the others, reaching the hide totally unscathed.

Quickly distributing the gear, they set off towards the north-west corner of the wall, a gap of just a few feet separating each shadowy figure. They stopped and listened for a few moments, and saw the Hall lit up like a Christmas tree off to the south-east. The good news seemed to be that no one was remotely close to them so far, although they could hear distant voices. Their first problem was to get past the main gate and the lodge which was always manned. They climbed over the wire fence next to the railway track, crossed over the track and headed straight up the steep bank opposite. Dave followed his boss closely, estimating it was less than fifteen minutes since he had witnessed the assassination.

As they reached the top of the bank, they circled left before going to ground. The gatekeeper was standing under a light by the cottage with a rifle in his hands, pulling on a cigarette. Suddenly, they heard a vehicle approaching and the man stubbed out his fag as a dark car pulled up. In the light from the lodge, they saw a policeman leaning from its window. They knew what he was there for, and as the gate was unlocked, they took advantage of the noise and scrambled up onto the track opposite, ready to run past as the car pulled through the gate. Just as they stepped from cover, another car suddenly turned the corner some two hundred yards to the south, the headlights arcing slowly round as it took the bend, before settling on the track, aimed directly at them.

They had only seconds to react and dropped back into cover, their weapons aimed directly at the headlights. The vehicle came straight towards them before turning right into the entrance and dropping through the gates, down the hill and out of sight. This was their chance. Corn stood up and the others quickly followed as they ran along the top hedgerow, reaching the corner in less than a minute, breathing heavily. They heard a clang behind them as the gate was shut and Corn took off again, running past the junction, before crossing over to the opposite verge. He then veered into the tree line to his left and, one by one, they followed until they were crouching down in a close circle next to the Norton motorcycle. Between breaths, Corn disclosed his plan.

'OK, listen in. We know they will be following us and so getting to Pickering is our priority. I only want to make two journeys. We will all walk down to the main road and only then will I start the engine. Dave, I will take you on the bike first, carrying most of the gear, and drop you short of the town, just past that first level crossing we saw in the dip. You can then start walking into town and stop in the lane on the right, just before the signal box. By the time you have got there, all being well I should be back with Ricky and Ed and, importantly, we should have put about six miles between us and the estate. Ricky, Ed, when we have gone, you start making your way towards Pickering. Run if you can as every hundred yards you gain will save us time. More police cars may well arrive, or perhaps estate vehicles coming this way. I don't need to tell you to keep your discipline, just do what you're best at. When we get there, you need to catch the milk train to York which departs at zero three thirty. Ricky has plenty of money for your ticket, Ed. I will then leave you to it and RV with you at the pub outside York station. Let's go.'

Within a few minutes, they reached the corner on the main road. Dave slung his leg over the rear seat of the bike and Ricky and Ed loaded him up until he could carry no more. With a single kick, the bike fired, Corn revving it gently before slipping it into gear. He felt Dave grip his sides, heavily laden with most of their gear, as he pulled away.

'Right, let's go,' Ricky said, and started running at a steady pace along the side of the road, Ed close beside him. She tried to stay in step to reduce any noise and soon they were running to a steady rhythm.

As she focussed her mind, it suddenly dawned on her that these men, her friends, had left the trenches at great risk to themselves to avenge her death. Were they AWOL, she wondered, or were they granted leave? Either way, it was an extraordinarily courageous act. But then she started to feel tired, her rhythm of earlier starting to desert her and she struggled to run.

CHAPTER 22

The police had arrived from Pickering and a sergeant in a long coat stood over the body of a once-powerful British army officer. The notebook in his hands remained blank as Harper and Bill Howie, now fully dressed, stood to one side awaiting his instructions. He suddenly scribbled something down, just as a young officer in uniform entered the room.

'Sir, there is a lady here asking for Mr Harper.' The estate manager looked around and then back to the inspector.

'You can go, Mr Harper, but I will want to speak to you later.'

Harper left the room to see the housekeeper standing next to Stevens, looking rather forlorn. They walked away, chatting, before climbing the back stairs to the servants' quarters.

'So, what are your thoughts, Sergeant?' asked Bill.

'I'm the one asking the questions, Mr Howie. But first, where is the telephone? I need to make a call to my superintendent.'

Howie, angry that this officer spoke to him that way, pointed towards the general's phone by the bed. The sergeant walked over to make the call and was heard mumbling into the mouthpiece for several minutes, before returning to the body.

'OK, sorry about that, but had to report it up the line as the chief constable will need to know about the general's death. So, can you tell me how is it that you had a guard on duty, right outside this apartment, and yet someone was able to get in and kill General Davis?'

Bill was annoyed and was about to rebuff his officious manner when a knock came at the door.

'Yes, what is it?' said the officer. Smith stepped into the room and informed Howie that all the patrols were back apart from one and were gathered in the staff dining room. Bill, glad of an opportunity to leave, quickly dismissed himself and walked out.

'I will want to talk to you later, Mr Howie, and my inspector is on his way from York,' yelled the sergeant as Bill disappeared.

Howie arrived to see the guards sitting in the dining room, supping tea. A very young-looking policeman was present in the corner, his notebook to hand. Rather than ask each man for a patrol report, Bill came straight to the point.

'Does anyone have anything significant to report? Any signs at all?' he asked. To a man, they all shook their heads. Smith then stated that a key had been broken off inside the padlock for the .303 rifles, so the patrols were conducted just with handguns. This confirmed to Howie that this was a well-planned act, done by a professional. He thrust his hands into his pockets and shrugged.

'So, we have a murdered man upstairs, your employer, and the weapons were tampered with and now the killer disappears? That's not good enough, chaps,' he said sternly.

'Mr Howie, may I suggest we might be talking about killers. Dave Gibbs knocked Kemp out and then tied him up against the chimney stack. He has now gone missing. Plus, the two men who arrived two days ago, Collins and Blain, have also not returned, so perhaps they might be the culprits?' said Smith.

'What do you mean, these men have not returned?' he asked as he looked around the room.

'Well, sir, Gibbs has definitely gone and no one has seen those other men since they were sent out on patrol, with orders to be back in thirty minutes. I should also report that the rear door is locked and the key is missing.'

Howie screwed up his eyes as he peered across at him.

'Which patrol route did you send them on?'

Smith took out his notebook.

'I sent them to the south to circle round to the main entrance and back up the drive. Have they been killed too?'

Howie stayed completely calm, seeking a logical answer. He tried to work out in his mind what had happened, as eight faces stared at him blankly.

'OK, have you sent a follow-up patrol out to check they haven't been shot themselves?' he asked.

'Well, no, sir, I haven't.'

'Bennett, Franks, set out now and reverse that same route and report back to me. I want you back in ten minutes. Now go.'

Mr Harper appeared in the doorway. Bill noticed him and sighed.

'I'm rather busy, Mr Harper, can it wait?'

'Well, no, it can't. I thought you might like to know that Edna, one of the house staff, is missing.'

'What do you mean, missing? Are you sure she isn't just hiding somewhere after the shooting?' he asked.

'I assure you, Bill, I have spoken to Mr Stevens and gathered all the staff. The housekeeper went back up to search the staff quarters and the stairs down to the basement. All they found was her black uniform dress. She has gone all right.'

Bill then reached into his pocket for the glasses he had found in the general's room. He pulled them out and studied them, and realised they didn't belong to General Davis: they were Edna's.

He turned back to face the men. He now had four people missing and one dead body.

'Smith, Barber, grab your gear and your weapons and come with me. We are going to York.'

CHAPTER 23

Colonel Ian Anderson, a man of huge experience within the SIS, was busy completing a report, late into the evening, when the old Bakelite phone receiver rattled in its cradle. Still writing, he reached out with his left hand, fumbling for the receiver before lifting it to his ear.

'Anderson,' he said. He stopped writing and looked up, listening for almost a minute. 'Yes, thank you, Hastings. Can you tell the brigadier's secretary I need five minutes? I'll go right up.'

He dropped the receiver onto its cradle and headed out, down the hallway towards the small stairwell. As he climbed the three flights of stairs, he was preparing in his mind the briefing he must now give to his boss. When he arrived at the outer office, Miss Ritchie was putting on her coat to leave. She smiled and directed him to a chair opposite her desk.

'Sorry, no tea today, I have to leave.'

Ian, having a bit of a soft spot for this lovely lady, nodded.

'That's OK, Jane. Going anywhere nice?' he asked with his usual flirtatious smile

'None of your business,' she said with a grin. 'You know, we could always grab a bite one evening if you're free?' So far, Jane had always avoided his attention and yet, he was a handsome and seemingly kind man, who she was definitely warming to. Ian grinned, thinking he had perhaps finally found an opening.

'Any biscuits?' he asked. She looked up at the clock and checked her watch before pulling open a drawer in her desk. She took out a small tin full of McVitie's digestives.

'Only one mind. I have to buy these myself.'

He reached across and cheekily took two. 'I will buy you a box tomorrow, I promise,' he said, putting a whole one into his mouth in one go. As Jane did up her coat, shaking her head, Ian stood up to peer at a golfing photograph he hadn't noticed before on the cabinet. Two men were wearing full tweeds; the ladies, one of them Jane, were in long dresses. Quite how she managed to play dressed like that, Ian could only guess.

'Still playing golf then, Jane?' he asked.

'Yes, I try and play every weekend, but my friends are not always available. My usual partner is my friend Veronica. We meet at her local course in Croydon. You should learn, Colonel, it's great fun and very healthy.'

Ian, clearing his teeth of biscuit with his tongue, huffed. Although the idea was appealing, he was practically married to the service and he knew trying to sneak off for a few hours to play golf was impossible.

'Well, maybe, when I am less busy. If I did take it up, perhaps you might teach me?' he said, flirting with her once again. But then his attempts were foiled as the door to the inner office suddenly opened.

Brigadier Cotton handed Jane a file and asked her to drop it at the registry on her way out, then beckoned Ian inside. As he stood up, she walked over to him and whispered, 'Dinner sounds good,' before closing the door behind him. He walked in, unaware he was smiling broadly.

'What is it, Ian, do we have trouble?' Cotton said, closing a secret file on his desk.

'We may well have, Kenneth, yes. I am referring to Operation Corkscrew with Butler and Thomas. I haven't heard from them since they entered Marshall Hall as part of the security team. As they are now under cover, of course, it may just be they simply cannot get to a phone.'

Ian was waved into a seat, while the brigadier reached for one of his cigars.

'Can we put someone else into the field, at this stage, or do you think that's somewhat premature?' he said, drawing on the cigar.

'Well, I do have another field agent taking some annual leave who lives in a small town north of Peterborough. He is less than three hours away, so thought I would place him on standby. Wicks has worked closely with Butler before and they know each other well. It would be the usual criteria of course and we might even get something back by the morning.'

Cotton was already nodding to his trusted field officer.

'It's not the first time we have held our breath during an operation, Ian. But let's get him up there. Better to be prepared, eh?'

Ian nodded and stood to leave.

'Keep me abreast of the situation, Ian. This is a big one, as you know, and we cannot make any mistakes.'

When he left the brigadier's office, Jane had gone, and he practically ran all the way back to his office. He tapped on Hastings' door as he walked past.

'Before you go, Hastings, can you dig out Wicks' file? That's Mark Wicks. I know he is on leave, but we need him. Also, I need a dispatch rider in my office in twenty minutes.'

Hastings was back in double quick time and handed him the buff personnel file. 'Rider will be here shortly, sir. Will that be all?'

Ian looked across his desk and then waved him off. 'Have a good evening,' he said as he opened the file.

Ian Anderson had known Mark Wicks for many years as he had been his regimental sergeant major five years earlier. He was an outstanding man who had fallen back into his life quite by accident when he literally bumped into him in the west end of London. They greeted each other like long-lost brothers which, in a way, they were. From that day onwards, their old relationship had grown considerably, and after Wicks joined the bureau, he became a highly trusted operator.

He scanned the front page for his contact details and then read his cover story, designed to protect the sensitive information he was about to discuss on an open phone line, before dialling the operator.

'Can you get me Bourne, Lincolnshire, 397 please,' he asked politely. After a short silence, a female voice spoke softly in his earpiece.

'Hello, can I help you?' she said.

'Could I speak to Mark, please, Mrs Wicks?' He waited for an answer, but it went silent. He thought he had been cut off, but then a voice he recognised spoke to him.

'Hello, Mark here, can I help?'

'It's Ian. I have a job for you.'

The line went quiet again and then he heard a door slam in the distance. 'What's up, boss?'

Ian told him he was needed to fix a power outage in Yorkshire and a dispatch rider would be with him inside three hours with all the details. 'Call me once you have read the file and again when you arrive,' he said, knowing full well Mark knew his drills.

'Happy to oblige, boss. I will get on the road as soon as details arrive.'

The phone then went dead and Ian set about writing his brief, before placing it in a buff envelope with Mark's home address on the front, sealing the envelope with a bureau stamp.

Thirty minutes passed before the dispatch rider entered his office. This small group of a dozen or so men, were all ex-army soldiers who ran urgent errands around London and across England. They played a key part in enabling secret documents to be transported and were, in many ways, the backbone of the service. Without their diligent sense of duty to drive in all weathers at any time of the day or night, life would be a great deal more difficult.

He handed over the document and the rider studied it briefly, then nodded, turned and was gone, never saying a word. It was now a little before ten o'clock. With luck, Wicks would be on-site sometime in the early hours. He had total confidence in his old RSM, more than any other.

The next morning, Anderson was in his office for seven o'clock. Hastings arrived fifteen minutes later and immediately entered his office.

'Sir, this message arrived zero three twenty-five today.' Colonel Anderson thanked him and reached for his paperknife.

He ripped open the envelope and told Hastings to wait. He read the message with interest.

Butler: 334192
Target neutralised.
In pursuit of unknown assassin, heading south.
Report to follow.
CB

He had little to go on but assumed Butler and Thomas did not make the kill and were now in hot pursuit of those who did. This was not part of the plan and clearly something unexpected had happened. Even though he trusted these men, they would need to pull out all the stops to finish this.

CHAPTER 24

Ed always knew running was going to be a test for her, as it was only four weeks since she had been lying on a surgeon's table with a bullet hole in her chest. Ricky was admirable in his endeavour to keep her focussed and ran alongside her, chatting, while weighed down with most of the kit. They had been doing the old 'Rifles' regimental tactic from the Peninsula wars, of walking and running, thirty paces about. It was Ricky's idea; his knowledge of the Napoleonic period had kept him and others alert during many a long night on duty back in the trenches. It was a very effective way to move, as the body stayed fresh but distance was covered quickly. In the twenty minutes they had been on the road, they had covered about a mile, but Ed had felt every yard. When her ears finally caught the drone of the motorbike engine, she was quite ready to be carried the rest of the way. Ricky grabbed her arm and told her to stop.

They knew Corn would not have the headlight on, so as the noise slowly increased, they stood out in the road, waiting for his arrival. When he was just a few hundred yards away, Ricky flashed his torch beam on, several times, pointing at the ground. The engine volume immediately subsided and Corn slowed, before swinging the bike round in the road, coming to a halt beside them.

'No time to lose,' he said as he shuffled forward, almost sitting on the fuel tank. Ricky quickly helped Ed onto the seat, nudging her forward as far as possible, before squeezing on the back. He reached around Ed with both arms, grabbing his boss's coat, before shouting for him to go. Corn slowly released the clutch and, shakily, the bike moved off and gradually picked up speed.

Within five minutes they entered the edge of the town and Corn eased the throttle back, coasting down the hill, pulling up just short of the station. Dave had heard their approach and stepped out from the shadows. As if rehearsed, Ed and Ricky jumped off and they quickly loaded Corn up with his holdall and rifle, before strapping his satchel on the seat behind him.

'Right, you're now on your own,' he said. 'I will see you at the pub opposite York station. Dave, did you dispose of the spare gear?'

'Boss, it's all taken care of and I have purchased the extra ticket for Ed. We are all set.'

Corn reached across to shake the hands of his men. 'Go steady, chaps, and thank you,' he said warmly.

He then turned to Ed. 'I am still shocked to see you, Ed, and rather confused too, but it's good to see you alive. You can tell us your story when we get to York.' He shook her hand, hanging on for a moment longer than normal before pulling down his goggles, just as the train could be heard pulling into the station. He revved his machine, waved his hand and was gone.

The others quickly ran to the entrance, climbing the few steps up to meet the train. With only two passenger carriages, Dave got into the first one and turned left, getting into the front compartment, while Ed and Ricky walked to the rear of the second and found seats at the back. They all kept their handguns close as they had no idea whether they had been followed. Within a minute, the guard blew his whistle and the train slipped out of the station into the darkness. They had only just made it!

Ed laid her head back against the seat cushion, peering at the reflection of the door as someone walked past. She was sure no one could have beaten them to the train as no vehicles had passed them on the road. She relaxed slightly, thinking of Frank, and smiled to herself, knowing it would soon all be over. She hoped her friends would get back safely to France, without mishap, and that they could all meet up again in happier times. The honour they had bestowed on her to avenge her death was immense. They had put their own lives at great risk; how could she ever repay them?

She thought back to her shock of seeing Dave Gibbs that first morning when he arrived at the Hall. She had made no connection at all to him being there for purposes other than work, and then to make matters worse, she heard Sergeant Major Howie's arrival was imminent. How was it possible that of all the grand houses in England, they had ended up at the same one? She remembered lying awake that first night, doubting her ability and wondering if she should leave. But her yearning to get revenge for her brother dominated her feelings and she'd pushed aside her doubts, certain she would see this through, no matter what faced her.

She tried hard to keep out of Dave's way after that, but it wasn't always easy and she hated not being able to converse with him. Oh, how she had wanted to tell him her story, but it was just too risky as she had no way of knowing whether his loyalties to her were uppermost in his mind. She assumed he must have been discharged from the army and found the only work he knew, but had no way of knowing his circumstances or his reasons for being there. Oh, how she wished she had trusted her instincts.

Meeting the others was a greater shock. To realise friends from her squadron had left the front to kill a man they didn't know, for her, had shocked her. She decided she owed them an explanation and would spend some time in the pub telling them what had happened and thanking them.

***

Dave sat alone in the front compartment, feeling relaxed for the first time in days. He did take the precaution of sitting next to the door, facing backwards, enabling him to react quickly if needed. As he peered through the window, he noticed vehicle lights on a road below and realised the road was shadowing the railway line. His lieutenant was out there somewhere, speeding south to meet them.

Just a short time later, the train began to slow. Dave wondered what lay ahead. He stood to gather his gear, and after checking the corridor, spun around the corner to the nearest door. He pulled down the sash window, relishing the cool morning air. York was waking up, but they had far to go.

As the train eased to a stop, he released the door handle, gathered his things and stepped out. He looked up at the clock to see it was just past four o'clock. Ed was already walking across to the underpass, Ricky some ten yards behind her. She was quickly down the steps and minutes later they had crossed the road and were entering the pub.

It was surprisingly busy for such an early hour, as people ate their morning meal. When Dave arrived, Ed and Ricky were already at the bar. He walked straight past them and found a table opposite the door at the back. With food ordered, they both wandered to the rear and plonked themselves down with their backs to the door.

Five minutes later the sound of a motorbike could be heard. Corn entered, wet from a morning shower, wrapped in his heavy waterproof coat. He glanced over, removing his goggles and gloves before joining them.

'Caught in the rain then? It was quite dry on the train, boss,' Dave said with a grin. Corn just smiled, dropping his coat onto a chair before sitting to face the door. All eyes then turned to Ed.

'So, come on, Mitchell, I need to hear this.' Corn said. 'I can't tell you how confused we all are at seeing you again.'

Ed was about to start when a young woman headed in their direction with a tray of sandwiches and their tea. When she had left, Ed took a swig from her mug.

She began by explaining the operation to kill the Joker, then getting shot on their return. How Frank saved her life and then got her to safety before her situation was discovered. Then being smuggled away from the hospital only to be hijacked on the road by the MPs under General Davis's orders. She went on to explain how on the morning of her execution she was extracted from the chateau by an MP corporal, not knowing what was happening.

'I was told to head to the end of the garden and a car would be waiting. I was nervous and thought it was a trap and I would be shot whilst trying to escape. But no, the car was there and the driver took me to Boulogne, where I met Frank's guardian on the quayside. He had arranged a passage back to England, and to my utter shock, Frank met me on board in a private cabin. After my brief moment of joy, he then explained that my twin brother had travelled to France, on the pretence of being a journalist, somehow making his way to the hospital at St Mahon, and just by sheer chance had met up with Frank coming out of the hospital. Together with Major Leigh-Smith, my doctor, they got him into the chateau and it was he who took my place at the execution.' She paused to take a sip of tea, the chaps sitting in silence.

'The authorities never realised it wasn't me, as Edward and I looked very much alike. That's it, really, but I knew I had to avenge his death, and with Frank's help, here I am.'

The boys sat staring at a remarkable woman, a bloody hero.

'You should have seen the general's face!' she said with a sly grin as she tried to lighten the mood. Ricky suddenly started to laugh; Corn stared at her in utter amazement.

'So, you came up here to kill him, but how were you going to get away?' asked Dave.

Ed, her mouth full of sausage sandwich, paused for a few seconds as she finished chewing.

'Oh, I was just going to walk back to Pickering during the night and then get a train here to York. No one would have recognised me as my disguise was gone. I have a bag across the road in the left luggage office with a change of clothing, some money and my return ticket. I am all set to go, all I need is a train timetable.' Ed then went quiet and dropped her head for a moment, as if emotions had gripped her. The boys looked at each other, concerned, before she raised her head again.

'There is something I want to say,' she said, meeting all their eyes. 'Seeing Dave at the Hall was a massive shock and I almost decided to pack my bag and go home. But then he didn't recognise me due to my disguise and I felt safe again, even though I still didn't know why he was there. I even thought of telling him everything but felt that was an unnecessary risk. I feel terribly humbled now I know you all chose to put your lives at risk, for me. I can't find the words to thank you.'

The boys looked at her, struggling to know quite what to say. It was Corn who broke the silence.

'When I spoke to Dave and Ricky in their basher, they almost took the words right out of my mouth. They jumped at the chance, even though they both knew it was a great personal risk. I simply arranged leave and we quietly went about our business, organising the kit we needed and our travel documents. We even got help from Sergeant Worrall, who I know would be more than delighted to learn that you are alive.'

Ed grinned at the thought of her old mentor, a man she so greatly admired and respected, offering to help. 'How typical,' she said smiling.

'We wanted this man dead as much as you, a man who was an insult to the British army. Your two friends have been professional throughout and I couldn't have done it without them. But in the end, good old private Mitchell, slayer of many a German soldier, managed it all on her own.' Corn then prepared himself to tell her something she just had to know.

'Ed, I need to tell you. I was present at the chateau on the morning your brother was shot.'

Ed stared at him. Her mouth opened, she wanted to speak, but the words wouldn't come. Instead, her eyes slowly filled, her bottom lip twitched and, as she blinked, tears ran down her cheeks. She shook her head, trying to cut the vision of him dying by bullets meant for her. She took a deep breath and wiped her face, to gain control of her emotions, then, speaking deliberately, she said, 'I'd like to know more, boss.'

Corn looked at her for a moment before taking a long swig from his mug of tea. 'It's not a good tale, only full of pain for you.'

Ed, now in full control of herself, leant forward. 'Edward did the most heroic thing anyone could ever do. I need to know what happened, second by second, so when you get your next leave, I implore you to come to Gloucestershire and stay with me and Frank. I need to hear this.'

Corn nodded, before reaching for his coat. He put his hand into an inside pocket then held out a clenched fist, across the table. She held out her hand, and when she looked down, she saw an empty .303 cylinder in her palm.

'I picked it up in the courtyard,' he said. 'I have carried it ever since, but I think you should have it.'

Ed held the small piece of brass in her fingers as the others looked at her in silence. She studied it momentarily, without reaction. Corn suddenly checked his watch.

'Blimey, we need to make a move, it's almost five o'clock,' he said, standing up. As Ed tucked the cylinder into her inside pocket, Dave's eyes were drawn to the door.

'Shit! Don't look up, but I think we have company.' Instinctively, those facing the door glanced across at two men looking around the bar, except they didn't look in their direction.

'Those are the chaps from the Hall, the two I told you about. I think they have just given themselves away,' Dave said quietly.

Corn turned to them. 'That's also the same chap I saw in the car by the station. I think they are British agents. We have to split up, right now.'

CHAPTER 25

Thomas and Butler had no intention of fulfilling the task set by young Smith as the chase was now on. They were sure Gibbs was the assassin and logic told them he would probably head south towards Pickering and then on to York. They now must move quickly as he had a twenty-minute start.

They decided they had nothing to lose and ran down the main driveway to the inner gate. They slipped through and crossed over the railway track, running left along the trackside until they could climb the fence and scramble up the bank opposite. They could see the light from the lodge, now off to their right, and a man sitting on a bench staring into the darkness, a rifle in his hand. The advantage was all theirs as his vision would be impaired by the porch light just above his head, tricking his senses and not allow him to see beyond the near distance. They quickly reached the gravel track, swung left and moments later they reached the corner.

Some distance away they could hear an engine, and listened for some time, trying to work out the direction. With their senses on alert, they decided it was coming from the main road but then the noise faded. Had they caught up with Gibbs already? They had to move, and quickly.

'Come on,' said Chris. 'The car.'

The two men ran along the road, not worrying about the noise their boots made on the gravel track and dived into the bushes to clear the car of undergrowth. DT opened the boot to change clothes, and as he did so he thought the car seemed low. Had it sunk in the mud, he wondered, before squatting down to see the rear wheel was flat.

'Damn, we have a flat tyre,' he said.

Chris walked around and noticed the other one was flat too. 'Wait a minute, they are both flat.' He moved to the front and peered down. 'He's done us, DT, they are all down.' A man of long-standing experience, he calmly went to the rear of the car and leant into the boot to retrieve a foot pump, before throwing it down next to the back wheel.

'Quick, get changed and then get to work on the tyres. I'm going to the corner to see if I can see anything. Be back in five.'

DT immediately got to work as Chris ran off into the darkness. Within minutes he was breathing heavily and his right thigh ached. He swapped legs several times as slowly the first tyre was inflated. Then he heard footsteps in the distance. A minute later, Chris returned, breathing hard.

'Can't see a thing. How are you getting on?' he asked.

'One down, three to go.'

Working in pairs, they stamped the pump as hard as their legs would go until, finally, some ten minutes later, they threw the pump into the boot and started the engine. Turning the car around, they headed towards Pickering.

'We need to find the police station to call this in,' Chris said. After a few minutes, DT applied the brakes and Chris dived from the car. He was back within a few minutes and DT stamped his foot back on the accelerator, the car taking off, sending gravel spewing out behind them. It was a scary ride and on one bend they were travelling so fast they almost collided with a milk lorry coming the other way and were forced over into the hedgerow, scraping the bodywork, before DT regained control. The time was three thirty. As they came down the hill, they heard a whistle.

'The train,' said Chris. 'Faster, DT, faster.'

The car, now at its maximum speed of fifty-five miles an hour, started to struggle. They could feel the off-side wheels lift on each corner. DT was in no mood for caution and kept his foot to the boards until they came around the final bend, the station dead ahead. But as they drove down the hill, they saw the level crossing gates across the road and the red light from the rear carriage of the train heading away. They had missed it. Gibbs was gone.

DT slowed and pulled up next to the gates. The signalman was already pushing the gates back across the tracks. They didn't speak. A minute later, his foot to the floor, they headed south to York.

CHAPTER 26

Bill Howie, knowing they were at least forty minutes behind the assailants, accelerated down the narrow driveway towards the main gate. Smith dashed out to open the gate and as they crossed the railway line with a bump, Bill started pressing the horn repeatedly. Just as they came up the rise, the gatekeeper was opening the top gate and jumped backwards as he sped through.

He pulled the wheel hard at the next corner, almost ending up in the hedge, gaining control at the very last second. Smith, sitting in the front, hanging on for dear life, asked where they might be heading.

'York, it has to be York,' shouted Bill over the revving engine.

'What's the plan, sir?' said Barber, sprawled in the back. Bill had been thinking about that for several minutes.

'Well, firstly, we need to get to the railway station as fast as we can. That will be their first port of call as they are bound to head south to London. If they are together, it will be hard for them to slip away unnoticed. When we arrive, we will split up and start searching the platforms, local cafés and pubs and rendezvous back outside the station. Remember the signs back at the Hall: the rifle padlock sabotaged, the rear door and the general's apartment locked, breaking the light bulbs and knocking out the sentries. All the signs of professionals, so have no doubts, lads, they will almost certainly kill us all to make their escape.'

Smith turned his head to peer back at his mate Ross Barber, who looked decidedly worried.

For the next few miles, no one spoke and once they were through Pickering, the miles quickly fell away. They could see the lights of York many miles before they got to the outskirts. Bill knew the station was the other side of the cathedral and he remembered crossing the river just days before. On instinct, he headed into the town centre until he could see the vast towers of the Minster dead ahead. It was Smith who saw a sign to the station at a junction and pointed off to the right. Within minutes, they had pulled into the car park at the rear, leaping from the car.

'Smith, you check the pub opposite and the cafés. Barber, go and check the far platforms and work your way back. I will check the main concourse and ticket areas. I will meet you on the concourse. Be back in five minutes, no later. If you see anyone we know, come and find me. Remember, we are looking for three men and possibly Edna, who is somehow mixed up in all this. All clear? Good. Now go.'

The station clock chimed five o'clock as Smith arrived at the pub. He stepped through the door, trying to hide his heavy breathing, his hand holding his pistol firmly, deep in his coat pocket, as he walked through the bar seeking familiar faces. There were none. He wandered into the rear bar, but the story was the same. They were not there.

Across the street, Barber had cleared platform 11, studying every face he saw. He worked his way back through each platform, through the underpass, until he reached platform 7. As he came up from below ground, his first glance across was to platform 6, where several young women were sitting on a line of benches, but none of them were Edna. As he ran, he thought of the quiet young girl he had seen several times but hadn't thought of as a threat. Maybe she was innocent and Gibbs had simply taken her hostage? Either way, she was in danger.

On the main concourse, Bill had covered all the toilets and searched everywhere he could think of and was now leaning against a stone pillar, seeking a face that he knew. He saw the next train for London was due to depart from platform 2 in just five minutes. That's it, he thought, and made his way to the underpass, turning first right up a long brick staircase. As he approached the top step, he tried to put himself in their shoes, wondering whether they would stand in amongst a crowd or find a quiet spot. He chose the latter and headed along the platform, pulling his cap down over his eyes, carefully scanning each person he passed. At the far end, he had seen nothing and had turned around to walk back down when, off to his left, he saw someone dip behind the wall of a brick outbuilding. He instinctively tightened his grip on his pistol, his palm sweating, and moved across towards the building. Then he saw the train approaching: his time was limited.

As the powerful engine drew alongside the platform, he knew this was the moment. If they were there, someone would make a move. He walked into the centre of the platform, watching, as the noise increased and the giant locomotive passed him, slowing gently, the brakes squeaking loudly. Suddenly, just forty yards away, a man ran out from behind the hut, straight towards the platform edge, and jumped down in front of the train, onto the track, the great engine narrowly missing him. Bill then lost sight of him momentarily and ran to the platform edge to peer through the carriage windows. His view was obscured, but he caught a glimpse as the man clambered up onto the other platform and ran off towards the underpass. It was Gibbs!

He had only moments to decide to follow him or stay put as he was sure the others would be on the same platform. He quickly searched the faces all around him but was unable to identify anyone he knew. He had one chance.

He ran towards the steps to try and head the man off but, as he ran past a group of people, he suddenly found he was falling heavily onto the concrete floor. He had been tripped, but he wasn't deterred and got to his feet and ran on, his knee bleeding from the fall. He ran hard down the stairwell, shouting to people to clear the way, but on reaching the bottom he was bundled over by someone, leaving him momentarily stunned. Lying on his back, with a heavy knee on his chest, he looked up into a pair of familiar eyes. Dave Gibbs held him by the throat.

'Don't, Bill, this is a private matter, leave it,' he said, tightening his grip. Bill's face went a deep red and he started to feel the life being squeezed out of him, but then suddenly Dave let go. Bill instinctively coughed and reached for his throat. As he turned slightly, his handgun dropped from his pocket onto the concrete floor. Dave picked it up before standing over him.

'That's the end of it, Bill. Don't follow me or things will be different next time.' He nodded once before running off towards the exit.

Back on the platform, Ricky, having seen Dave jump down onto the track, decided not to catch the train as his mate was in trouble. He had managed to stick his foot out at just the right time, but now he must follow him.

Walking quickly down the stairwell into the underpass, he saw a man at the bottom getting to his feet. He realised instantly it was the old sergeant major and he seemed in a little discomfort. He stepped past him to the left and quickened his pace towards the exit. When he arrived at the concourse, Dave was nowhere in sight. He wondered where his lieutenant might be and, as he turned around, he saw he was following him, some twenty paces back. Good, they were together again, strength in numbers, but where would they go?

When Dave reached the exit, he was alone and went to stand behind a pillar near the door. After a minute, he saw Ricky coming his way, and beyond him, Corn came into view. He noticed him twitch his head sideways to the left, so Dave headed outside and walked towards the bridge into town. Then he caught sight of Smith and Barber staring at him. He glared at them and shook his head, running his finger across his own throat, before heading away.

Ricky, now only twenty yards behind Dave, followed, giving the two men a wide berth. Dave, forever vigilant, kept an eye on his team and stopped after a hundred yards, before crossing the road. Corn was now closing in and, just before they crossed the bridge, they regrouped before stepping into an alleyway.

Ricky noticed a path that led down a slope to the right, where, at the bottom, a myriad of streets and alleyways went off in all directions. He shouted for them to follow. Within a few minutes, they were securely hidden in someone's backyard.

***

Smith and Barber now felt distinctly uncomfortable following Dave Gibbs' gesture at them. Had he killed Bill Howie perhaps, and was now threatening them too?

'We didn't sign up for this, Ross,' Smith said, and they looked at each other, wondering what to do next. 'If Bill doesn't return in five minutes, I think we should leg it.'

Barber nodded, but then a familiar face appeared, its owner looking bedraggled, holding his throat. Good, Howie wasn't dead after all.

'Did you see anything?' he asked.

'Yes, sir, three of them, I think, all left a few minutes ago and headed into town. Are you OK, sir?' Ross asked.

Bill coughed several times, before swallowing hard. 'Three of them you say. And the girl?' he asked.

'No, sir, didn't see her anywhere,' Barber said

'So, who did you recognise?'

'Dave Gibbs was there and two men followed him out.'

Bill was confused. 'But surely he was with Blain and Collins?'

Barber shook his head. 'No, sir, I've never clapped eyes on either of them before.'

As he was speaking, Bill noticed two men walking away, looking like undercover cops. They both wore the same dark coats and flat caps but he couldn't see their faces. He thought quickly.

'OK, our duty now is to track down those three men. We have some unfinished business. Which way did they go?' he asked, stepping towards the door. Smith looked at Barber nervously before taking the initiative and leading the way. The two agents watched them leave.

***

Mark Wicks turned into the gatehouse of his destination. He was ready to impersonate a police superintendent, something he had done many times before, with an appropriate false identity card. As he pulled in, a man from the gatehouse walked over. He flashed his card and the gate was opened, the man muttering something undistinguishable. As he drove down the slope, he knew he would need to be quick and thorough in the belief that if you act in a superior way and ask the right questions, people respond. But he didn't have long.

CHAPTER 27

When they stepped into the bar, Chris had noticed four men on the far side almost before he had fully opened the door. He was blessed with a photographic memory and instantly recognised Gibbs and one of the men sitting next to him. He was the chap on the motorbike he had seen a couple of days before at Pickering station.

Pushing the door fully open, he turned slightly as if helping his friend and whispered to him not to look up. He stepped in and they moved over to their left, sitting with their backs to the door. In front of them hung a large picture of a steam train, its glass reflecting what was going on behind them. Within a minute of arriving, they noticed the four men slink out of the bar and into the street. They looked at each other and counted to ten before leaving the pub. As they did so, the small group were just entering the station across the road, one man turning just as they stepped onto the path. It was Dave Gibbs; they had been rumbled.

Although still quite early, there were already lots of people going about their daily business. This would no doubt help them later, as they could mingle freely with the crowds. They had orders to ensure all loose ends were tidied up which they believed to mean that people had to die. They wanted to finish the job but needed to avoid a blood bath in a public place at all costs. Somehow, they had to get these men away from the station.

They had worked together for several years with a freedom seldom granted to men of their status within the SIS. But they were the best there was and they were fully trusted to finish a job without compromise. They were determined to carry out their instructions to the letter.

'So, what next, Chris?' DT asked.

As they crossed the street, Chris pondered his question before leading his friend over to a kiosk where he ordered two teas. 'OK, this is what we know. We have this Gibbs fellow who assassinated the general and now three others in tow, who, by all accounts, are his support team. This is clearly a professional killing by people unknown, otherwise, we wouldn't have been sent here to kill him ourselves. I think firstly we need to identify them and, one by one, take them down. I believe the man we saw at Pickering railway station is their leader, as he was the one who I saw in the pub. Then as we left, that Dave fellow looked back and pinged us too. They know we are after them all right.'

DT stopped sipping his tea and looked up. 'What do you mean, he saw us. When?'

Chris smiled at him. 'Just as we left the pub, Dave looked back across the street and clocked us,' he said, almost with pleasure. 'Don't worry, it's good for them to know we are on their tail. They may now make a mistake and we can then capitalise on it. You do have your US trench knife?'

'Yes, of course. You know I never go anywhere without it.'

Chris smiled, knowing how proud DT was of the knife he had acquired from an American officer they had worked with the previous year. With its unmistakable double-edged blade and brass-knuckled handle, it was an impressive item to own and was the envy of many in the bureau.

'It's imperative we dispatch them without alarming the good people of York. Have it ready; we need to get this job done and quietly.'

They finished their tea and Chris led them into the station. They started working their way through the platforms but didn't get far, as on platform 2 Chris recognised the leader of the group.

'OK, you stay here. Keep an eye on the chap in the overcoat to your right. I am going to see where the others are.'

He slipped away and DT reached for a discarded newspaper and leant against a wall, half looking at the news while peering carefully across to their target. Chris walked to the underpass, heading towards platform 3. He climbed up the steps and looked across the twin tracks, spotting a chap walking away, taking up a position behind a small brick hut. He then observed someone else studying every person on the platform, before realising it was the ex-sergeant major.

What's this, another wingman or is he on a different side? What is going on, he thought. How many sides are there?

Suddenly, over his shoulder, he heard the whistle of a train approaching and turned to see it entering the station. He was by now at the far end of the platform and quickly started walking towards the underpass. He was focussed on looking across the tracks and almost bumped into a couple of elderly gentlemen who got in his way. As the noise of the train increased, the platform opposite him filled with people and then the locomotive ran past him. His view was now blocked. Then suddenly a chap jumped down from the opposite platform, just yards in front of the train, before stepping across the tracks and clambering up onto platform 3 just forty feet away. It was Gibbs.

Within seconds he had dropped down into the underpass and Chris tried to follow but was held up by a porter with a large trolley turning around in front of him. When his route was clear, he set off towards the steps, running hard.

When he reached the bottom, he looked to his right but could see nothing, then turned left to see a man walking slowly away towards the exit, holding his neck. It was Howie. Had he been attacked? Chris followed him and stopped at the kiosk in the concourse, DT arriving a few moments later.

'OK, we are on the move. Where is the other man?' he asked.

'He just left with two others.'

He then saw Howie talking quietly and remonstrating with his hands with the two guards from the Hall before they all left together. They waited until they had got to the corner before following them.

'Let's keep our distance, DT, don't want to spook anyone.'

They were now following six men. Where would all this end? Behind them, just fifty yards away, Ed Mitchell was tracking them all. It wasn't over for her quite yet either.

***

Back at the Hall, "Superintendent" Wicks was leaving the scene of a murder. He had ascertained that four people were now missing: a chap called Gibbs, a woman called Edna and his friends Chris and DT. He was thinking fast. He felt the two assassins had probably had help, so maybe he was looking for others too. It was further complicated in that a Mr Howie, the head of house security, along with two house guards, had also now disappeared, making a total of at least seven people ahead of him.

CHAPTER 28

As they stood behind the wooden gate in the yard, daylight was fast approaching. Dave was peering through a tiny gap, looking down the alleyway, ready to make a bolt for it if they were rumbled.

'So, what's the plan, boss?' Ricky asked.

Corn hesitated as he realised their return to France was now a priority. They would soon be listed as AWOL and the MPs would then also be on their tail. The war was calling them back, so whatever they did next must happen quickly.

'OK, I think we must assume that all these men are out to kill us, for quite different reasons. The men from the Hall are clearly determined to get even for the death of the general and I have an opinion about the others. What is clear is we must be ready to take more lives as these men will clearly not back down, and now are very close. What do you think?'

Ricky looked across at Dave, who was still watching the alleyway. Dave turned around.

'Boss, when I escaped the platform, I pinned the ex-sergeant major to the floor, slowly squeezing the life from him before releasing my grip. I stared into his eyes and told him to back off as this was a private matter. He looked at me as if he understood. If he still follows us, I won't make the same mistake again.'

Corn stared at him, realising he was as capable of killing a man with his bare hands as he was with his Lee Enfield rifle.

'It sounds like you gave him a chance, Dave. But I think we have certain advantages here. Howie knows Dave is ex-army but doesn't know we are with him. The other two men, according to Dave's report from the other day, are inexperienced amateurs and probably not up to much. So, that leaves the two agents. Now, I believe they were sent up here to kill the general themselves which is why they arrived at the house in the first place and have followed us, and not returned to the Hall. There can be no other explanation. But I can't work out why the British Government decided they wanted Davis dead. Do governments kill off their retired generals? I don't know, but I expect the agents will now see it that they have some unfinished business.'

Dave was nodding through Corn's summation, while Ricky just absorbed the information blankly.

'So, I think we have one of two options. Firstly, circle back to the station, find a suitable hide and then you both rush the train just as it's pulling out of the station. Once you're away, I will collect the Norton and drive south. We can then meet in London later. The only other option is to set them up and kill them all, one by one.'

Dave looked up to see a young girl looking down at them from the upstairs window.

'Uh oh, we have company.' The others looked up just as a woman pulled the child from the window, then moments later a man's face appeared. He looked angry and started to pull the sash window open, but before he could slide it up, they were running down the alleyway.

Dave was now leading and as he turned the corner, he ran straight into Smith who was coming the other way. The boy was clearly taken by surprise but reached for something in his pocket. Dave grabbed him with both hands, turning him around, but Smith started to struggle and pulled his pistol from his pocket. Dave held him with his left arm and pulled his knife from inside his coat. Without hesitation he stabbed him once in the side of his neck, twisting the blade as he pulled it out, dropping him to the floor. He would be dead in seconds. Dave picked up his gun and wiped the blade on the chap's trousers and turned to see Corn watching him. He nodded his approval and then urged Dave to follow him around the opposite corner and along the road, seeking a route back towards the station. As they disappeared, Bill Howie turned the other corner to see his man on the floor, blood seeping from his neck across the ground like spilt paint. Behind him, Barber appeared, looked down and was promptly sick.

Ricky, forever the best tail-end Charlie of them all, watched carefully for a follow-up as they reached the next corner. The coast seemed clear and they worked their way back to the top road by the bridge and stopped under a small arch. Ricky then had an idea.

'Look, boss, no one knows what I look like so what if I head back to the station to find out the time for the next train to London. You can then wait here until a few minutes before it leaves and then adopt your plan. I can be back in just a few minutes.'

Corn looked at Dave Gibbs who nodded, then back to Ricky. 'Sounds good to me. OK, off with you then and be bloody careful,' he said, studying the alleyway behind them.

Ricky quickly took off his coat and hat, tucking his pistol into the back of his trousers and covering it with his jumper. His knife remained down the inside of his left boot. He walked up to street level, casually looked around before joining the many other people on the path heading across the bridge.

They could now only wait.

***

Bill Howie, realising they were not paid enough for the risks they were taking, looked at the now petrified Barber and thought of what Dave Gibbs had said to him when he was held to the ground. It was time to depart. He quickly searched Smith's body, withdrawing his notebook and a knife, but realised his pistol had gone. He then grabbed Ross by the arm and left the scene of Smith's murder, crossing over the bridge and heading to the pub opposite the station. Barber was now a jabbering heap and as they entered, Bill told him to go and sit in the corner. He bought two double whiskies.

'Here, get that down you.' Barber picked up the shot and downed it in one, closed his eyes and then put his head down into his hands and sobbed. Bill had seen this type of reaction in the trenches hundreds of times and reached out for this chap, trying to console him.

'I can't do this, sir,' he blubbed. 'He was my friend.'

Bill knew they were out of their depth before they even left the Hall, but had felt it was his duty to try to catch the murderers. He was quite wrong.

'OK, let's go.' He stood up to leave and pushed Barber through the bar door, back into the street, before crossing the road and following the track around to the left into the large shed where he had left the Wolseley.

Barber stopped by the door and peered across the car roof at Howie.

'What do we do now, sir?' he asked. 'I mean, do we tell the police about what happened to Smudge?' He then opened the door and got inside.

Bill remained standing, leaning on the top of the car. He was angry that his decision to chase the killers to York had meant the death of young Smith. He pondered the question, hardly noticing the car rock slightly from within, and after a few moments, he opened his door. He leant in to set the starter switch before walking round to turn the starting handle, the engine firing instantly. He jumped in, laying the bar down beside his seat before closing his door. He then looked across at Barber who was leaning over sideways. He noticed blood dripping from the side of his mouth and tried to pull him upright. As he lifted him, Barber's head dropped forward. What on earth is going on, he thought, just as an arm was wrapped tightly around his neck. He looked up to the rear-view mirror to see a pair of eyes, his last memory, as a long blade pierced his skin, sinking into his neck, killing him in seconds. The man behind his seat climbed out and then opened the driver's door, bending to switch off the engine. He casually wiped the blade on Bill's shoulder.

'Out of your depth, sergeant major,' he said scornfully, before placing the knife back into the sheath strapped to his calf. Just as he was standing back up, a gun was placed against the back of his head.

CHAPTER 29

Ed had been following the agents at a safe distance, and they themselves were some fifty yards behind the sergeant major and the other two guards from Marshall Hall. She had lost sight of her lieutenant, Dave and Ricky, but assumed each group had eyes on their own target. She paused on the bridge as the men had stopped just ahead, next to a butcher's shop, looking down an alleyway to their right. After a couple of minutes, she decided to chance her arm a little by walking past them to see for herself what was happening. The lane dropped away towards terraced houses, but she could see very little and she meandered past, not drawing attention to herself. She walked on a little further and turned to gaze into the first shop window she came to. Out of the corner of her eye, she saw the two men cross the street. She used the window as a mirror and watched them standing together, clearly waiting to locate the six men now somewhere in the backstreets. It was at least ten minutes later when she saw Howie, and another man she didn't recognise, come up from the street below and turn back towards the station.

The men opposite then shadowed their movements along the opposite path, following them back down the road. She crossed back over the bridge, mingling with the morning flurry of street people, keeping a watchful eye. Ed had a distinct advantage as no one knew her true appearance. Leaving her disguise behind at the house had been a masterstroke. Ahead, she saw Howie and the other man enter the pub and realised they were one man down. She stopped and sat on the wall next to the bus stop, waiting for their next move, but recognised the two other men in flat caps now chatting under a tree away to her left. When one pulled a knife from a sheath on his inner calf and placed it in his coat, she knew that they were up to something. She must be ready. They were chatting, looking quite casually towards the pub entrance. Then the one with the knife walked off, crossing the road and disappearing behind the station.

She decided she had to follow him. Just ahead, some ladies were heading across the road and she quickly joined them before slipping away on the far side. She wondered where the boss, Ricky and Dave might be and hoped they would surface again soon. As she turned the corner, she peered back to see the agent in the long coat still under the tree and then saw Bill Howie and the security guard exit the pub. They started to cross the road as she turned and carefully followed the agent to the rear of the parking area, but she lost him in the darkness. She stopped at the corner and waited to see what happened next.

Within minutes, Bill and the other guard came into view. They walked up to a vehicle and chatted briefly over the roof before the young chap opened the passenger door and climbed in. Howie stood outside momentarily, peering down at his feet, waiting for almost a minute before starting the car. When he finally climbed in, nothing happened and she wondered why they hadn't moved off. Then quite unexpectedly a third man clambered out from the rear of the car. She instantly recognised him and, pulling out her gun from her inside pocket, she moved closer, using another vehicle to mask her presence.

The man looked tentatively to the right before reaching for the driver's door handle. He pulled the door open, then spoke to the person sitting in the front seat. He bent down to do something out of Ed's view and she closed in quickly, placing her feet carefully until she stood by the rear bumper. She looked through the rear window to see two men slumped over, realising they were both dead. As the man in the dark coat straightened up, she took her chance and stepped forward, placing the barrel of the pistol against his head. She shot him, once. He fell awkwardly, hitting his head on the inside of the door, his face now gone. Ed looked quickly towards the main entrance, before peering inside the car to see Howie and the guard she had seen earlier. Keeping her pistol in her hand, she withdrew the man's notebook from his inside pocket and then saw a rather fancy knife protruding from the sheath on his calf. She bent down and withdrew it before disappearing around the rear of the building towards the platforms.

On the opposite side of the road, the man in the flat cap looked at his watch. He realised something must be wrong and walked straight across the road, pausing at the entrance to the parking shed. There was no noise and no sign of his partner. He reached inside his coat and pulled out his Webley before skirting down one side and moving swiftly across towards a car with its doors open. From some fifty feet, he could see a pair of legs protruding from below the open car door and blood-stained ground. As he got closer, he could see that his friend and long-time partner in the SIS had been shot. He peered inside to see two other men, also dead, one with his throat cut, the other slumped forward, his head squashed against the dashboard. He bobbed down to empty his friend's pockets of any weapons and his wallet, but his notebook and trench knife had gone.

Chris was now alone and quickly walked towards the station concourse, calculating in his mind who remained following the morning's blood bath. Although now on his own, he still had a job to complete. He stepped back into the throng of people, a little shocked that his partner was dead. He was determined to settle the score and went over to view the timings for the next train to London. He was sure the assassins would probably target the very next train and immediately went across to platform 2. He had less than ten minutes.

***

Dave and Ricky were in position on the platform, sitting tight behind some railway trollies stacked with woollen bales at the far end of the platform. They couldn't be sure the agents were not already present, somewhere, but their plan should catch them unawares.

From a distance, Corn saw one of the agents arrive and wondered where the other one was. Standing behind a group of people who were milling around in a jovial manner, Corn felt his position was secure; however, he searched the remaining areas of the platform, seeking the other man. The agent then skirted along the platform edge, looking back casually, probably checking faces, before stopping and looking up at the large clock. Corn checked his watch; there were still five minutes before he would have to get into position.

Ed, not willing to catch her train to Moreton and leave her friends, had collected her bag and withdrawn her money and ticket before dumping the bag in a rubbish bin. She circled back through the underpass to platform 2 and as she climbed to the top of the stairs, she cautiously looked over the low wall to survey the length of the platform. She saw Corn behind a group of people and he held out his hands as if asking 'What are you doing there?' She didn't acknowledge him; instead, she walked right up to the platform edge and stood next to a young family with two children who were clearly very excited about the train that now approached.

As the steam engine got closer, it belched plumes of smoke just outside the station and was now just a minute away. Corn casually moved back down the platform, watching every face and keeping one eye on the agent. He knew he must wait until the middle carriage of the train had passed the end of the platform before he could make his move. The boys must leave it until the very last second to give the agent no time to react. Their speed and agility now would be crucial.

As the train finally eased to a stop, Ed decided to help the young couple with their suitcases. While the lady took her children by the hand into the first compartment, the gentleman was most grateful for her help, clearly thinking she was a station porter, as when all the cases were safely aboard, he reached into his pocket and gave her some pennies. Not wishing to offend him, she accepted the money and smiled.

She then went along to the next carriage and opened the first door, climbing aboard. She shut the door and put her head through the sash window, watching the last of the passengers clamber on. The porters began slamming the remaining doors, but then she saw the agent, standing some forty yards away. He was looking pensively at the far end of the train and slowly walked forwards, scanning every carriage, taking no notice of her at all. Then a whistle sounded, and his head jerked around towards a rotund guard at the rear, waving his green flag. She could see him grimace as he searched repeatedly for any movement. The power of the vast engine as it pulled forward caused the carriages to shudder as the couplings took the load. They moved off and she could feel her heart pound in her chest as she saw the agent walk further down the platform, his hand by his side as if ready to grab a door handle. As the train slowly gathered speed, he started to drop back, unable to keep pace, then suddenly he started to run — he had seen something — and reached for the nearest door handle, fumbling several times.

Ed swung her head round to see her lieutenant rush the train at the far end of the platform, followed closely by Dave and Ricky. Corn reached a door and twisted the handle before flinging it open, running alongside. He was shouting at Dave as the train gathered speed, who ran hard for the opening and suddenly dived headlong through the open door. Ricky, very close behind, was now running alongside the train, hanging onto the door rail, throwing his large bag and rifle case into the opening. Corn watched, as the end of the platform was now just yards away. He urged Ricky on, who then grabbed the top of the open window and jumped onto the rim of the doorframe just as the platform disappeared from beneath his feet. As Corn thought all was lost, an arm reached out followed by the smiling face of Dave Gibbs as he pulled him in, the door slamming shut behind them. Ed sighed with relief as she watched Corn on the platform, before looking back to the rear of the train. The agent was nowhere to be seen.

**

Wicks finally reached York railway station and swung the car into the parking shed to the rear. He was surprised to see two police cars and three officers, all in uniform, standing chatting next to a car towards the back of the shed. He knew at once he had to investigate, so with his false warrant card in his hand, he walked over. As he approached, he could see a body lying by the side of the car and another sitting half upright in the driver's seat. One of the officers then stepped in his path.

'Sorry, sir, you will need to step away.' Mark confidently moved forward, presenting his false credentials before the officer apologised. He assessed the scene but was suddenly shocked as he recognised the coat on the prone body. He realised the dead man was one of their own, but with his face gone, he couldn't be sure who. Then he recognised the sheath strapped to the man's calf and bent down to look. Yes, it was his friend Dave Thomas.

'He was shot, sir,' said the constable, trying to be helpful. Mark Wicks ignored him and peered into the vehicle to see two other bodies. The young constable tried further to impress.

'A member of the public reported a body, sir, but when I got here, I found three bodies.'

Mark, using his wits, checked DT's pockets, but as expected they were empty apart from his handkerchief. He briefly looked inside the car again, then noticed an empty shell case by the rear tyre.

'Mark that shell,' he said, pointing down, before asking who was attending from the local station.

'Our inspector is on his way. Will you be taking over the investigation, sir?' asked the young constable.

'No, I am following a series of deaths in the area that may be linked. I will report to the chief constable this evening,' he said, before walking away back to his car.

He climbed in and sat thinking for a moment, pushing his mind to calculate what the gunman would probably do next. In his position, he would head south. He decided he should report in.

CHAPTER 30

Ricky laughed as he got up from the floor, thinking of himself as 'the flying sniper,' diving through an open door of a moving train. Dave was sitting in the corner, grinning, quite unscathed.

'That's one to tell the grandkids, Dave. I have seen some close shaves before, mate, but that takes the biscuit. Did we get everything on board?' he asked.

Dave looked around the floor, counted three bags and a rifle case. 'Yes, I think it's all here. Come on, let's find somewhere to sit, it's a long journey south.'

Ricky squeezed past him and walked down the carriage, passing several compartments with two or three people in each, before finding one empty. He pulled the door back, but it would only partially open. He leant on it with his shoulder, before he resorted to using his boot.

He put his large rucksack on the rack first and placed the rifle case behind it, out of sight, before dropping into the seat by the door. Dave sat on the opposite side, near the window, leaving the small bag by his feet. He pulled out his water flask, taking a drink before tossing it over to Ricky.

'I wonder if the boss got away OK?' Dave said, undoing his coat.

'Well, unless something happened, he should have a straight run south. Where are we meeting him again?'

Dave pulled a face. 'I thought he told you. If not, then I assume we all meet back at Folkestone. Do you remember where we caught the bus? Well, on the opposite side of the road was a pub. I think if he is not around when we arrive, we grab a few pints and then board the next boat back. What do you think?'

Dave peered out of the window then turned back. 'Sounds like a plan,' he said yawning. 'God, I'm knackered, I'll grab a few winks first, give me an hour or so.'

But just as he started pulling the door shades down, someone stopped outside the compartment. They looked up to see Ed Mitchell peering through the glass at them. She looked both ways before stepping inside.

'Don't get comfortable,' she said. 'We have company.'

Dave sprang to his feet and pulled out his pistol, checking his ammunition. Ricky reached for his knife but found it gone.

'Shit, my knife must have dropped out when I got on board.'

Ed looked at him before reaching for the knife she had taken from the agent. 'Here, have this one.'

'Thanks, Ed. Wow!' he said, looking at it carefully. 'Where did you get this? But hang on, I thought you were heading home. What are you doing here?'

Ed sat down to explain.

'Well, firstly I got that from one of the agents. And yes, I did too. But then I pinged one of the men from the Hall searching the platforms for you and presumed if they were here, the agents must be too. Turned out they all followed you around York for a time before doubling back to the station.'

'Yes, we bumped into the guards in a back street. Smith is dead. I had no option,' said Dave.

'Well, the numbers are falling fast,' she said. 'One of them killed Mr Howie and the young guard he was with in their car.'

Dave looked stunned. 'Killed Bill Howie, shit,' he said leaning through the open door and peering both ways down the corridor.

'Don't fret, I shot him in the head. That's where the knife came from. So, by my reckoning, the other agent is now on this train.'

The boys looked at each other, alarmed.

'We must split up then. Dave, you go as far forward as you can and sit tight,' said Ricky. But then Ed cut him off.

'Look, I know what he looks like, but he doesn't know me. It would probably be better if I scouted through the train, and when

I locate him, I will come back to brief you. Do you have anything I can wear, in case he clocked me getting on?' she asked.

Ricky dug into his rucksack and pulled out his old pullover and hat and a belt.

Ed looked down. 'Is that it?' she said smiling.

'Yes, we dumped most of our gear.'

Ed sniffed the jumper and frowned. 'It will have to do.' She removed her coat and pulled the jumper over her head. It came down way past her hips and she grabbed the belt and tied it round her waist. Placing her gun inside her jacket, she pulled it back on and grabbed the hat.

'I suggest you move to the front of the train and split up. I will work my way backwards and return as soon as I can.'

The boys grabbed their kit from the racks above their heads and Dave shot off down the corridor. Ricky followed behind with Ed now bringing up the rear. When she caught up with them, Dave was at the rear end of the first carriage, Ricky as far forward as he could get. If an attack came now, Dave was first in line. Now she knew where they were, she could walk back down the train.

Checking every compartment, she was able to look at each face in turn, and then, as she passed by, she would spin round to glance back to view the people on the opposite bench. As she turned into the second carriage, she noticed the family she had helped earlier; the children, with their noses pressed up against the glass, were a pleasant distraction. She moved quickly on, and after five minutes had cleared five carriages, arriving at the buffet car. As she was about to pull back the sliding door, she saw a man wearing a long brown coat past his knees and a flat cap, not unlike the one the agent was wearing by the tree in York. She couldn't see his face as he was slightly turned away from her, but he was talking to someone whose face was also obscured. She held her nerve and stayed put for a few moments, trying to confirm whether it was him. Then he turned and she saw a young man with a beard. It was not her man.

As she was about to enter the carriage, she wondered what the likelihood was of someone wearing the exact same coat as the

British agent. She studied it for a few seconds and was convinced it was one and the same. He had clearly disposed of it! She stepped through the door and entered the buffet car, walking up to the counter to buy a tea. As she turned, she deliberately bumped into the man, spilling her tea over his coat.

'I am so sorry,' she said, placing her cup back on the counter. 'It was the train; I just lost my footing.'

The young man wiped the dribbles of tea with his hand. 'It's OK, don't worry, I only just got it ten minutes ago, a chap in the next carriage gave it to me. Can you believe that? I've been wanting a coat like this for ages.'

Ed smiled and looked back towards the door. 'Well, I hope I haven't ruined it for you. So, which chap was this?'

The man looked at her a little strangely, wondering why she needed to know that. 'Tall chap in the next carriage, wearing a brown jumper,' he said, before turning back to his friend.

Ed now knew what he looked like and what he was wearing. She needed to brief the chaps.

CHAPTER 31

Corn was chuffed that they had managed to get aboard, even though it was causing quite a commotion amongst the porters on the platform. It was touch and go for a moment and he thought they had blown it until Dave successfully pulled Ricky to safety. Provided there were no more delays, they would soon meet up again back in Folkestone.

He felt relaxed for the first time in days and stood and watched the many faces pass him by in the last few carriages. As the final carriages went past, he was beginning to think of the long drive back south and heading back to France. But then he saw a man standing at the very last door, wearing a dark brown coat and a flat cap, staring at him. Corn instantly recognised him. It was the agent from the car. In a flash, he was running towards the Norton motorcycle that was still at the far end of the platform.

Donning the leather helmet and gloves and checking his holdall was secure, he pushed the bike down the ramp to the roadway before giving it one hard kick. The engine flashed into life and quickly selecting first gear he sped away, out into the morning traffic.

Within minutes, he was on the open road, hoping the road shadowed the train line. He was in luck, as after just a few minutes he crossed over a railway bridge and saw a train speeding underneath him, steam filling the air. He had no idea whether their train would stop en route to London but he needed to overtake it. He somehow had to alert his men as he had inadvertently put their lives in jeopardy again. He pulled hard on the throttle, tucking his head forward, eager to catch them. He thought back to the road map he had studied when he came north a week ago. He remembered Doncaster was almost directly south from York and if he was right in his assumption, that would be the next stop. He gambled everything, overtaking vehicles when he could, pushing to get there ahead of the train. He had no idea if he could make it in time, or, if he did, whether his men would still be alive.

As he passed over each rail bridge, he slowed, taking time to listen and peer into the coming dawn, but there was nothing. It was on the third bridge that he finally heard a train approaching, and suddenly the bridge shook and smoke quickly filled the air around him. He smiled as he accelerated down the hill, confident he now had a chance, opening the throttle fully, taking the little engine to its limits. Finally, just over an hour after leaving York, he approached the outskirts of Doncaster. He slowed at each junction, looking for directions to the station. As he approached a T-junction, the train whistled somewhere behind him, then on a lamp post, he saw a sign. He shot down an empty street and ahead of him, he saw the lights of the railway station forecourt. He drove towards the building and quickly dismounted, switching off the engine before pulling the bike onto its stand.

He ran towards the ticket office in the semi-darkness and saw the bright light of a steam engine approaching. He ran into the ticket office as an elderly lady was collecting her change from the counter, fumbling several times.

He took some money from his inner coat pocket and stepped forward, asking the man behind the counter for a single to London just as the locomotive passed the door. As the attendant looked up the cost on a sheet on a clip board, Corn looked over his shoulder and realised he had only minutes. But the man seemed in no hurry, finally taking a ticket and punching it in his machine before speaking for the first time.

'That will be two and eightpence,' he said, without looking at him. Corn only had a ten-shilling note and slapped it down on the counter. The man took the note and placed it on the till board before counting out his change into his hand. Corn heard several carriage doors slam shut and was now irritated at how long it took to get his change. Finally, the coins were put down on the counter and Corn scooped them up, dropping them into his coat pocket as he ran. He stepped out onto the platform just as the whistle went, signalling the train was about to depart. He ran to the nearest door and climbed aboard. He had only just made it. As he pulled down the sash window, the train lurched forward, slowly accelerating out of the station. Corn stood with his back to the engine, breathing deeply. He remembered the look the agent had given him from the rear carriage at York station and he would, no doubt, be utterly surprised to see him. But that was over an hour ago and anything could have happened.

He knew they would now be three against one, so the balance was in their favour and he set off, looking at each person in every compartment, briefly, in turn. After ten minutes, he reached for a window and pulled it down to see he was midway down the train.

Leaving the window open, he worked his way along the narrow corridors, seeing no one he knew. He had started to become concerned as he now had only four carriages left. Had he missed them? Were they still on the train? He felt a little uneasy as he turned into coach J and halfway down the corridor, he saw the ticket collector reaching into a compartment. He couldn't pass as the corridor was too narrow, and as he approached, the man spoke to him.

'Ticket please, sir.'

Corn, unsure where he had put it, started searching his pockets. 'It's here somewhere,' he said, a little embarrassed, until his fingertips dug it from his inside pocket. 'Ah, here it is,' handing it over.

The ticket collector briefly looked down, then back at Corn. 'Change at Lincoln, sir,' he said as he handed back his ticket.

Corn's heart almost missed a beat. 'What do you mean, change at Lincoln. Isn't this the train to London?' he asked.

'This train terminates at Lincoln, sir. You will have to change trains there.' Corn stood frozen to the spot, staring at the ticket. What a stupid mistake! The boys were on their own.

CHAPTER 32

Ed, now feeling they had an advantage, started walking back along the corridors towards the chaps, confident their man was behind her. They had time and numbers on their side and she hoped the boys had come up with a plan. She stepped through into the next corridor from the buffet car, the footplates rattling beneath her feet, and as she turned the corner, the toilet door behind her clicked open. She peered over her shoulder just as a familiar face appeared through the carriage door. She recognised the agent from the station.

What should she do? Let him pass her or stay in front? She had to think quickly. Her tactical brain told her they would have an advantage if he was in the middle, especially as he had no route of escape. Then she felt a presence behind her.

'Excuse me, can I get past?' he asked politely. Ed didn't look round, just pushed herself against the window allowing him to pass her, and as he did so, she turned back to face the way he had just come. After just a few seconds, she looked back casually to see him peering into every compartment and studying each face meticulously, before moving on. She stood watching him out of the corner of her eye until he reached the end of the carriage and turned the corner. There had to be a way to alert the boys. She walked down the carriage and at the corner, she found her answer.

Just above her head, a small emergency chain hanging in its recess caught her attention. She knew pulling it would apply the emergency brakes, but it was surely her only option to alert them. Ricky and Dave were bound to make the connection as they were quick thinkers. She looked behind her and took a deep breath before reaching up and grabbing the chain. She held onto a wall bar and pulled down, hard.

The train suddenly lurched forward as if falling off a cliff, the brakes biting into the wheels, causing loud screeching beneath her feet, like nothing she had ever heard before. She braced herself against the wall, hearing screams from the compartments just behind her. As the speed fell away, she was able to stand again and she rushed forward, through into the next carriage to see the agent hanging onto the bar beneath the window, peering back at her. She pulled her left arm into her ribs, feeling the pistol still in the position where she had placed it, watching him carefully for any sudden moves. She was momentarily distracted by a child crying inside the compartment directly to her right, taking her eyes from him for just a moment, but it was enough. He must have sensed something as he suddenly bolted down the corridor. Ed, in her calm calculating way, walked on quickly, but he was already into the next carriage, closing in on the boys.

She sped up, reaching the end of the carriage, her gun now in her hand. She leant cautiously around the corner but could see nothing. The train was now stopped, and people were starting to pull their doors open to see what was happening. She had to do something.

'Stay in your compartments!' she shouted, repeating it several times to keep the corridors clear. Heads quickly disappeared and doors slammed shut.

She walked on to where she thought Dave and Ricky were and stopped to listen. She moved further into the carriage and then suddenly, ten or twelve feet away, a body lurched out from a compartment. It was Dave and he was in trouble. An arm suddenly appeared and he punched at it several times, before a hand holding a knife swiped him across the face, blood instantly dripping down his cheek. He reached for the sliding door and pulled it across hard, trapping the offending arm, the knife dropping to the floor. As he kicked it away up the passage, the noise of a single gunshot filled the air, the bullet crashing through the glass door and into Dave's body, dropping him where he stood, his head twisted to one side. He didn't move.

Ed was already thinking of a follow-up, realising the agent was stuck and couldn't escape. She stood firm in the corridor, taking aim, waiting for the agent's head to appear, but her instincts were for caution and she decided to check her advance and stepped back into the toilet, holding the door slightly ajar with her fingers. She now had the perfect cover, with an arc right down the corridor. Her thoughts were of Ricky, who would clearly have heard the commotion and would probably be making his way back to protect his friend. She must be careful about crossfire as the corridor was narrow, and he would be all guns blazing when he saw Dave.

She flexed her hand around her pistol several times, blocking the door with the side of her right foot, holding the door handle on the inside, ready to yank it open and fire when needed. Then she heard the door handle to a compartment click and a door slide open.

She waited just a few seconds and saw a man step into the corridor. Her mind was ready, her finger on the trigger, and as she pulled the door open, she stepped forward, aiming for mid-height to take him in his chest. As he finally cleared the compartment, she fired and he fell on top of Dave, his face looking towards her. She then realised it was the wrong man. A moment later, the carriage lights went out.

She stepped back around the corner, holding her breath, as she realised this was the first mistake she had ever made in making a kill. She was angry with herself, taking a life so needlessly. But she mustn't dwell on it now or she too would die.

She realised the agent must have fused the lights in the compartment as it was too much of a coincidence for them to go out at that precise moment. He would now have to move, or he would be caught in a trap. She wanted to give him just enough time to step into the corridor to make his escape, then she would emerge and shoot all in one action. She counted to ten: it was time.

She swung around the corner, almost jumping out into the corridor, and in the dim early morning light, with her pistol cocked and ready, aiming at the door, she saw only Dave's prone body lying some twenty feet away, with the body of the man she had shot partially lying on top of him.

She was careful not to charge down the corridor in case it was a trap, and paced steadily, eyes wide, pistol at the ready. She avoided the faces staring at her from the first compartment and stepped cautiously on, leaning against the outer wall of the corridor and peered through the open door. The compartment was empty: he was gone.

She instinctively dropped down to feel for a pulse in Dave's neck, but there wasn't one. She closed his eyes with her fingers, all the time focussing her eyes down the corridor. She quickly checked the other man too, but it was the same story. Bastard, she thought, standing up, realising the agent was now on his way to find Ricky.

It was time to move on and she progressed down to the last few compartments, before reaching the corner at the end of a corridor. If she had counted correctly, there was only one carriage left.

CHAPTER 33

Ricky Miller was crouched down opposite the toilet door at the front of the very first carriage, when the train started to brake violently. He couldn't hold his stance and tumbled over, falling sideways against a waste bin opposite, blood instantly running down the side of his face from a deep cut. He struggled to get up as all the weight from the carriages behind him was pushed forward, keeping him pinned down. Finally, as the braking eased, he managed to get to his feet, instinctively wiping his left eye with the back of his hand. Blood covered his fist, but he would worry about that later. He tightened his fingers around his pistol grip.

Clearly, the train's emergency brakes had been applied, but by whom? Was it Ed, perhaps, or Dave providing some sort of warning? Or was it the agent? He thought quickly, wondering what he would gain by doing that. No, he was sure it was some sort of warning from Ed as she returned along the train. She must have run into difficulty and this meant the agent was close.

He checked the door behind him to ensure it opened in case he needed an escape route, and as he turned the handle and pushed it slightly ajar, he heard a gunshot. He let the door go, allowing it to fall open back against the side of the train, then the lights went out.

He quickly returned to his crouched position, peering around the corner. He froze in the darkness, as his eyes adjusted, then he heard another gun shot.

The gentle light of the sunrise was starting to filter through the carriage windows and, after a few moments, he could see the outline of the corridor.

Being in the dark suited him as, although he couldn't see much, he was hidden from view. As he paused for a few moments, he felt a draught from behind him and suddenly had a spark of an idea. He took one last look along the corridor to check it remained clear before dropping down on his side and peering out through the carriage door. He could hear voices from somewhere towards the engine, so slid out through the door and dropped gently onto the gravel below. He immediately crouched down and under the train saw two sets of legs on the other side, heading back along the track. Clearly the engine driver and his fireman.

He gently pushed the door until it was resting against the lock, but not letting it shut completely. Stepping on the sleepers, he was able to avoid any noise from the gravel and he crept silently below the windows until he reached the next carriage. He could see very little and rose to put his ear against the concertina gangway that joined the two carriages together. The only sound was the scream of a young child somewhere off to his left.

He estimated that Dave was probably somewhere in the next carriage but had little clue where Ed might be. He also assumed that the lights were probably fused deliberately and either of them could well be in trouble. He decided to stay outside and listen just as a door from the next carriage opened above his head.

He stepped backwards a few inches and dropped his large frame into a crouch, his head now touching the couplings joining the two carriages. He was well hidden in the darkness and breathing softly, he aimed his pistol towards the noise. Suddenly, a pair of feet appeared and, within seconds, someone dropped down onto the track. The person, whomever it was, knew what they were doing as they went straight to ground and moved under the train. He took aim, only seeing the outline of the body, then against the pale dawn light he recognised the profile of his friend, Ed Mitchell.

'Ed, it's me, Ricky.'

She sighed, then moved towards him. 'Shit, you made me jump.'

Then they heard voices and on the other side of the train, the engine driver and his fireman returned, one cursing the person who had pulled the emergency chain. Once they had gone, Ricky closed in to Ed's ear.

'How did you know I was here?'

'I didn't but never mind that now. Dave's dead,' she said in a whisper.

Ricky thought he had heard her wrong. 'What, who is dead?'

She put her mouth next to his ear. 'He was shot through the chest. just a few minutes ago. He didn't stand a chance and now I have lost sight of the agent.'

Ricky was stunned and wanted to find the bastard who had just killed his best friend. Ed held his arm, knowing how he might react, pulling him back tightly as he tried to stand.

'No, stay here. We have to be clever now or we will end up like Dave. This chap is a professional, a British Government assassin, probably from the SIS, so don't be impetuous, we need to think.'

Ricky felt emotional and wanted to charge through the train, guns blazing, killing anything that moved. But Ed was right and he momentarily dropped his head as if crying, but he was visualising taking this man's life. It was going to be his greatest pleasure.

'I have an idea,' said Ed.

'I thought you would. What do you have in mind?'

'Look, we know this chap is moving towards the front of the train, and when he gets there, he is going to wonder how he missed you. He is then going to look outside. I know I would. I reckon he must be nearly there by now, so we have to act fast. You move back along the train to the door you came from and sit directly underneath it on the track. When you are halfway back, I will set off across the field where he is bound to see me and exit the train, determined to follow me. When he steps down into the open, you ambush him and the matter is then finally over.' Ricky looked at her and nodded.

'OK, where shall we meet?' he asked.

Ed looked across the fields and saw the faint outline of a church spire silhouetted against the early morning sky.

'I will meet you at that church. As soon as the job is done, run.'

He licked his lips at the thought of finally finishing this extraordinary operation. But then he frowned.

'Shit, just had a thought. Once he is dead, I will have to retrieve the rifle case in the compartment. The serial numbers on the weapons would be traced back to us. It won't take me a minute. I know exactly where it is.' Ricky put his hand on Ed's shoulder. 'See you in a minute,' and he moved back along the track, staying close to the train.

Ed watched him scuttle along, keeping low, and after twenty seconds set off down the bank and over the low fence before charging off as fast as her tired legs would carry her.

The dawn was now almost upon them and she hoped the agent was following his nose and had seen her. When she had been running for about a minute, she heard a shot. She started to swing round but then heard another one, then two more. The job is done, she thought. And dismissing the rendezvous point, she started walking back towards the train.

CHAPTER 34

Chris Butler had been working for the SIS for six years and, with his friend who lay dead in the car park at York railway station, this was his sixtieth operation since the start of the war. He was good at what he did and knew how to kill with a gun, a knife or with his bare hands. He didn't mind which he used. His method of delivery was subject to the situation at the time and he didn't care if others were caught in the crossfire. All that mattered to him was to get the job done, but this one had got messy. Although the general had been killed, as planned, his brigadier wouldn't be too pleased by the number of bodies that now lay in York and on the train. He had to finish this but realised he was up against military men or, at the very least, recent retirees.

He knew they were somewhere near and by his calculation, he now had two men to find following his recent encounter. Quite where the second man had come from, he knew not, but he didn't care. He just wanted them dead.

He peered out from under the bench seat that he had slithered under after he fused the lights. Through a small crack in the bench, he had seen someone check the compartment, but in the darkness, they had not seen his hideaway. He slowly moved out of cover and, staying on his belly, he crawled forward to check the corridor. Apart from the two bodies by the door, it was empty. He got to his feet and checked his pistol, ready to shoot at anything that moved. He had plenty of ammunition in a small pouch under his jumper but had lost his knife.

He looked both ways, getting ready to move down the corridor. As he stepped out, he saw his knife partially visible under the passenger who lay across the soldier. He picked it up and stowed it back in the sheath just above his boot. He started walking cautiously, his arm outstretched, his weapon moving with his eyes, checking behind him every other step. As he came to the corner at the end of the corridor, he shuffled round it and gently pushed the toilet door open. It was empty. Then he saw two men walking outside, both wearing boiler suits and caps. He assumed they were heading back to the engine and dropped back from the window and watched them go before moving on.

The morning light was now increasing and he could, at last, see the faces of the people in the compartments. One young boy glared up at him and he put his finger to his mouth to indicate quiet. The boy copied his action and he smiled back at him. The boy's father then put a protective arm around him and pulled him close. Chris knew this was the last carriage and he was ready to fire at anyone that came at him. He stood over to the left of the narrow corridor to get a better angle to fire into a compartment, if needed, and gently pushed forward, checking each one in turn.

Suddenly, he heard a noise behind him and instantly turned around, swinging his arm up, ready to face his foe. A ticket collector dressed in black walked into his line of sight and stopped dead.

'Go back,' Chris said quietly. The man opened his mouth and lifted his hands in the air before turning and disappearing back the way he had come. Chris turned once again and carried on as before until finally, he was at the end of the train. He peered around the corner, checked the toilet and was puzzled: it was empty. He walked to the carriage door and noticed it was partially open. Stepping back, he kicked it hard and it flew open, crashing against the side of the train. He looked to his left and then when he turned to the right, he could see someone running across the field, probably two hundred yards away. He was carrying a gun in his right hand. It was him, he had to follow — no loose ends the brigadier had said — and he dropped down onto the tracks.

Almost before his feet had touched the ground, he heard a bang and felt a deep pain in his back. He swung round to see a dark face under the train. He lifted his weapon and fired, but his arm wouldn't work properly, and he knew he had fired low. His right arm then froze and he reached up to change hands, but as he brought the weapon up to fire again, he was shot a second time, the bullet this time catching him in his midriff. He crashed down the bank into a ditch at the bottom, face down. He twisted round to see the man approach him and tried in vain to lift his hand to fire again. But the last thing he saw was a small plume of smoke from the muzzle of a gun.

Ricky dropped to his knees just a few feet from the body, panting hard. It was finally over. The dead SIS agent looked pitiful, crumpled in a heap. He was relieved he had killed the man who had slain his friend.

'This is for you, Dave,' he said and stared at the twisted body for a few seconds. As he stood up, he turned to see faces looking at him from the windows of the train. He instinctively pointed his gun at them and they all ducked down. It was time he left.

As he stood to walk, his leg buckled beneath him and he fell onto his side. It was only then he realised he had been shot, but the bullet had clearly passed right through the muscle in his upper thigh. It was bleeding but he didn't think it had hit the bone, so tried to stand again. He managed to balance precariously for a moment before he crashed to the floor once more.

'Bollocks,' he said loudly and started to crawl as best he could towards the second carriage to retrieve the rifles. As he approached the door, Ed suddenly appeared from the field, panting hard.

'Where are they?' she asked. Ricky was amazed at how she was always one step ahead.

'Third compartment, right luggage rack,' he said, grimacing in pain. She ran to the open door and clambered up, turning right and into a long corridor where several people withdrew back to their families. She ran into the third compartment, looked up and reached for the rifle case before legging it back the way she had come. At the door, she launched herself out of the train and onto the gravel, rolling a few feet before she stopped. Ricky was tending to his wound and had wrapped the sleeve of his shirt around his leg. He pronounced himself ready to go. He stood up on his good leg and Ed slung the rifle case over her shoulder, grabbing him on the same side as the injury and wrapping her arm around his body. He clung on as they clambered down the bank, over the fence and away across the field towards the village. As they distanced themselves from the train, they looked back to see the engine drivers beside the track, one standing over the agent's body.

After ten minutes, they reached a small stream by a wall and Ed halted, easing her friend to the floor. It was now after six in the morning, the sun was up and people were bound to be stirring.

'Right, we need to tend to your leg as it will draw attention. Let's get that dressing off.'

Ricky untied his handy work and Ed plunged his shirt sleeve in the cool water. 'Take your trousers down,' she said as she rinsed it through, blood filtering away downstream. They both looked at the wound which started to bleed again. Ricky cringed and noticed Ed's blank face.

'What?' he said.

'You were lucky, an inch to the right and it would have shattered the bone. Well, it looks clean enough. Take off the other sleeve,' she said, and he tore it from the shoulder, handing it across to her. She ripped one sleeve into two pieces and made a pad for both sides of the wound. The other sleeve she used as a bandage to wrap it all tightly together.

'What up?' he asked. 'Is it OK?'

Ed looked at him. 'Yes, it's fine, I was just thinking of Dave, still on the train. What will become of him, I wonder?'

'Well, the lieutenant told us to take off our dog tags, so he should be clean. I feel awful about leaving him, Ed, but what can we do?'

Ed looked at him and frowned. 'Yes, but when I get back to Gloucestershire, I will speak to Frank's guardian, Lord Hardcastle. He'll know what to do.'

Ricky looked at her, astonished she always seemed to know what to do. As she rinsed her hands in the stream, he splashed water on his trousers to wash away the blood.

'OK, you can pull up your trousers now.' As he did so, she peered over the wall to view the way ahead.

'Look, we're now in the middle of nowhere with limited funds and you need to get south. What do you suggest?'

Ricky thought for a moment and realised they were probably still in Yorkshire.

'Well, I have a ten-bob note, so we have money for a ticket, but what about you?'

'I'm OK, I still have my ticket and some money in my shirt pocket. We just need to get to a station. Why don't we go into the village and see if we can scrounge a lift? Can you walk unaided, do you think?'

Ricky stood up and put weight on his injured leg.

'It's pretty stiff and hurts like hell, but I think I can. If we are questioned at all, I will just say I was shot in the trenches and have been on leave and I am now heading back to France. That should stop any enquiries dead in the water. You can be my sister if you like?' he said.

Ed smiled. 'That sounds like a plan,' she said as they walked into the village.

CHAPTER 35

The HQ tent for the Glorious Glosters was largely under water following the torrential rains that had been falling for several days. Corporal Martin Lock, the orderly NCO, was a fastidious man who always did a job to the best of his ability. However, the war, and in particular the rain, was wearing him down. Water was at least six inches deep and even though the engineers had dug a host of gullies to help the water run away, it was now backing up and he was struggling to keep the regimental records dry. God knows what it's like in the trenches, he thought.

As he worked through his duties that morning, rain dripped through the saturated canvas of the large green tent and he realised he was fighting a losing battle. He looked across at the admin officer.

'Sir, would it be possible to box up some of these records and ship them out of here to higher ground? I fear we might lose important records if we don't do something soon.'

The officer had only been half-listening, but then looked up from what he was doing. 'Sorry, corporal, what did you say?'

Lock repeated his question, but the officer shook his head.

'No, that won't be possible. There are no vehicle movements at present as the access roads are completely bogged down in mud. We will just have to do the best we can, won't we,' he said, standing up and donning his cap.

We, Lock thought. 'When did you ever lift a finger to help,' he mumbled to himself.

'OK, sir,' he said, 'how about we shut down several administration procedures until the rain stops? I can at least keep everything dry then.'

'Look, you are the orderly corporal, do what you think is necessary and don't keep bothering me.' The officer pulled on his trench coat, before lifting the flap on the tent. 'Be back in an hour,' he said and charged out into the deluge.

The hard-working corporal shook his head, knowing that whatever he did it wouldn't be appreciated.

He pulled the signal log box up, removed all logs dating back over the previous seven days and closed the lid. On top of it, he placed the range log and all catering admin apart from the last three days, along with the transport orders and logbooks. Finally, he delved into the box containing leave records and noticed it was almost full. He sifted through the most recent pages and saw there were some twenty-nine men away on leave, all due back in the next five days. He ran his eyes down the list of return dates and saw six men were due back the next day and three at twenty-two hundred that night. He considered informing the sergeant major but saw there were two men he knew, Dave Gibbs and Ricky Miller, both snipers. He realised that with all this crap weather, they were probably delayed due to transport problems from Boulogne. He decided to ignore the leave book for the time being and placed it in the last box to be closed and lifted it onto the table.

He pulled a small tarpaulin over the top, tucking each of the corners under the boxes to keep them secure. The cabinet adjoining his small desk was now quite empty, but at least if the tent fell down, he would not get a bollocking for losing paperwork. He left to grab a brew.

CHAPTER 36

As Ricky and Ed entered the village of Hambleton, they saw the village store ahead, almost directly opposite the church. It was still early, but there were several people milling around outside. As they approached, conversations stopped and all faces turned to look at them. They didn't want to look suspicious, but they were carrying a rifle case and Ricky was limping.

'Morning,' Ricky said. 'Can you tell us how we can get to the nearest train station, please? Is there a bus, perhaps?' he asked.

An elderly gentleman on a seat against the wall waved his stick and pointed almost over their heads.

'You want Selby, you'm do,' he said. 'But there's no bus, not till eleven.'

Ed looked at Ricky.

'Look, I need to get back to my battalion in France. My leave finishes tomorrow and we were dropped in the wrong place by a truck driver, several miles away. I even fell into the stream over there and got a soaking,' he said, trying to explain why he had wet trousers. 'This is my sister who is coming with me to London. How far is it to Selby?'

It was the old man who piped up again. 'There's the milk truck, coming through around twenty to seven. They go to Selby.'

A much younger man started looking Ricky up and down. 'You a soldier then?' he asked. 'But you'm limping. What's wrong with ee?'

Ricky loved to tell a yarn and was about to spin a big one. 'Yes, I am. I was shot in the leg several weeks ago when killing three German soldiers in No Man's Land. I was sent on leave to recover but have left it a little late to get back south.'

The man looked across at Ed, who didn't react except to stuff her hands into her trouser pockets.

'So, this is your sister, eh? Why is she carrying your rifle then?' he asked with a certain mistrust.

Ed had heard quite enough. 'Look, my brother needs a ride otherwise he will be listed as AWOL. That means he will be charged by the MPs for not getting back on time. So, can you help or not?'

The mood suddenly changed, but her outburst had given them the upper hand. A lady stepped forward from near the shop doorway.

'My hubby ull take ya. Come with me.' And she set off across the road, heading for a narrow lane, pulling a small white Westie after her.

'See you later, Jenny,' said a voice behind them. Ed turned to follow and Ricky smiled. They followed the lady down the street to the bottom of the lane, where she spoke to an older man in a flat cap. He looked up as they approached.

'This way,' he said and walked off to the barn. By the time they had thanked the woman, he was already driving a green van across the yard and pulled up next to them.

'One of you will have to get in the back,' he muttered. 'Mind the spuds though.'

Ed was already walking to the rear doors, knowing it would be difficult for Ricky to climb in.

It was an uneventful journey, taking a little over fifteen minutes. The man didn't speak all the way there, but when they got out, he shouted at them, 'Get them Jerries,' and grinned as he pulled away. Ricky smiled at Ed and they ambled over to the station building.

They asked for two tickets to London, but the chap behind the ticket kiosk advised them they could only catch a train to Doncaster. They would have to change trains there. They paid up and as they walked onto the platform, they heard a steam locomotive's whistle sound somewhere down the track. The first bit of luck today.

Thirty-five minutes later, they had arrived at Doncaster station and quickly walked over to the train timetables. Ed realised there were only three trains that day that reached London, all into Euston station. The next train was in forty minutes.

'Ricky, I think we should take advantage of the time we have to get a proper dressing for your leg and some ointment. It wouldn't be good to get an infection,' Ed said, stating the obvious.

Ricky nodded and as they passed the station exit, they asked a porter where the nearest chemist shop was. He pointed across the road, telling them to take the first turning left. They thanked him and wandered out. Ricky was then struck by the motorbike he saw parked to their right.

'Hey, that's just like the boss's bike. Let's take a quick look.' Ed was about to object when he suddenly put his arm out to one side.

'Oh my God, it is his bike,' he said, surprised. Ed looked around, puzzled.

'But how can it be. He should be halfway to London by now.'

Ricky shook his head. 'It's his, all right. I remember the number plate and the yellow tank. What's it doing here?'

Ed turned, half expecting to see the lieutenant somewhere in the car park, but shook her head.

'Look, we don't have time for this. Why don't you leave him a note and hand it to the porters' office, asking if they could give it to the person who comes to collect it? You can write explaining things. While you're doing that, I'll go and get you some dressings for your leg.'

She quickly took off the rifle case and handed it to him before striding off across the road. Ricky hobbled back to the porters' office and obtained a sheet of paper and an envelope. He spent a moment thinking carefully about what to say.

CHAPTER 37

Lieutenant Cavanagh had arrived in Lincoln rather frustrated that he hadn't checked the train before he boarded. He was very concerned for the welfare of his men, even though he knew their capabilities.

As the train pulled into the outskirts of the city, he saw the castle and medieval cathedral sitting high above him, all empowering. They were an impressive sight and on any other day, he might just have taken a walk to experience their splendour. But today his mind was on other things and his first action had to be to catch the next train back to Doncaster to collect the motorcycle.

He walked across to the ticket office and dug out the small change he had been given earlier before enquiring when the next train departed. He was a little surprised that the price differed for the same journey in reverse and questioned the man, who simply shrugged and took his money. He had an hour and ten minutes to wait and went to sit by the kiosk where he bought a newspaper and ordered some tea and a bun. He read with interest the lead story of the terrible weather that had been hampering progress at the front, so much so that both sides had settled into survival mode, rather than mutual obliteration.

The time passed very slowly until just after seven forty-five he wandered back to the platform and got into the rear carriage, away from everyone else. Ten minutes later the whistle blew and the train lurched forward, before settling into a gentle rhythm as they sped away north.

It was an uneventful journey back to Doncaster and even the ticket collector hadn't bothered him. Within an hour he was walking casually out of the station, and over to his motorcycle which he had left three hours earlier. He unclipped the leather helmet from the handlebars and was just placing it on his head when a man approached him from the station office.

'Are you Mr Cavanagh?' he asked. Rather shocked someone knew his name, he looked around slowly, before answering.

'Yes, can I help you?'

The man walked up to him and handed him a brown envelope. 'This was left for you, sir. They said give it to the man with the motorbike.' He nodded and left.

Corn wondered how anyone could know he would be at Doncaster station. He ripped open the envelope and saw a short note.

Boss
Sad to report, DG dead.
Vengeance now achieved.
I am with Ed.
Meet you at the coast, tomorrow.
RM

Seldom had he been a man to ponder over the death of a soldier, but these were unusual circumstances and he regretted ever getting Dave Gibbs involved. He read the note again and wondered why Ed was now with Ricky. The last he saw of her, she was heading over to her platform in York about to set off home. How on earth had she become embroiled in this? But then, how did they end up in Doncaster? They were supposed to be on the train for London. It didn't make any sense and he couldn't work out what had occurred and could only guess where they now might be. He decided he could do nothing more and that his best bet was to head south, to meet up with Ricky in Folkestone before catching the boat back to France.

In deep thought, he eased the bike into gear and headed away.

CHAPTER 38

When the gunshots sounded, Norman and his young fireman stopped in their tracks and Simon stared at the senior engine driver with frightened eyes. He had only been on the service for a few months and never expected such a shocking turn of events. One minute they were flying along, the next the emergency brakes were applied and now a gunman was on the loose. They dared not speak in case he was still lurking about, so stayed hidden by the carriage wheels, staring at each other. Then Norman decided it was his duty to find out what had happened and told Simon to follow him, staying close.

They walked along towards the engine until they reached the front of the first carriage. Norman dropped down and peered under the train at what looked like the soles of a man's shoes. With no one else in sight, Norman moved round slightly to sit just under the couplings and then he saw the legs of a man lying headfirst down the bank. Across the field, off to his right, he thought he saw two people, but by the time he had moved around to the other side of the train, they seemed to have gone. Simon, feeling frightened on his own, quickly moved round to join Norman, as he reached the corpse.

The man's face was contorted, his clothes soaked with blood, and Simon turned towards the train and retched. Norman knew he needed to give him something to do.

'OK, I want you to run back down the opposite side of the train to the guard's van. If he's not there, climb onto the train and walk through the carriages until you find him. Tell him he must walk back down the track to the nearest emergency telephone point to alert the authorities and then he should inform the passengers of a long delay.'

Simon thought he had done enough already, but as he was about to leave, he turned back.

'But the gunman might still be out there,' he said, shaking. 'What should I do if I see him?'

Norman reached for the lad's wrist. 'Look, I have just seen two people running across that field. They have gone, so stop worrying and do your job.'

Simon turned back and quickly legged it.

Norman moved down to the body and as he reached the man's feet, he heard someone banging on the window to his right. He looked up to see a young family watching him, but he waved them away. It looked as though the victim had been shot several times. His eyes were still open so Norman went around to his head and did the honourable thing, gently closing them. He saw a pistol lying in the long grass but left it where it was. Dropping down to check the man's pockets, he was surprised that they were all empty. This aroused his suspicions, as who has nothing in their pockets?

This was the worst thing he had seen in twenty-seven years of being on the railways. He pulled his cigarette tin from his overalls and lit up a ciggy he had rolled earlier. As he took several long drags, he looked across the empty fields, wondering who the two people might be. Did they come from the train, perhaps? Were they the gunmen? He shivered and then turned as he heard footsteps behind him. Simon's face appeared through the gap between the tender and the carriage.

'The guard has sent Tom, the ticket collector, to the phone, so we have a bit of a wait,' he said, rather out of breath. He then tucked his head down and crawled under the couplings until he was standing next to Norman.

'Should we search him?' he asked.

'Already done that and, guess what, he has nothing on him. Not a wallet, keys, notebook, nothing. Don't you think that's odd?' Norman said, pulling the last drag from his cigarette.'

Simon looked down at the man and nodded. 'So, what do you think happened here?'

'I've no idea, son, not my place to worry about that. Anyway, we should be getting on with our job of freeing all the brakes. Let's leave the investigating to the police, eh? Go and fetch that blanket from my seat in the cab, we should really cover the body.'

As Simon walked off, he shouted at him to bring the brake release tools. A few moments later, Simon returned, handing a grubby blanket to his driver. It was gently placed over the dead man as a sign of respect.

'You go down the far side, I will start this side. If any passengers ask you anything, simply say what you know, no more. I'll meet you at the guard's van.'

When he reached the second carriage he was beckoned from above by Albert, the guard.

'Norman, can you get up here? I have something to show you.'

He dropped the release bar and clambered up into the open door. 'What is it?' he asked.

But Albert just led him around the corner into the corridor, where he could see two more bodies, one lying across the other, both quite dead.

'What on earth is going on?' he asked as he walked down the carriage. Albert came up behind him and stopped as Norman bent down to feel the faces of the men lying awkwardly in the narrow corridor. He started going through the pockets of the younger man, as he had done with the body outside, but once again there were no documents of any kind. He looked up, puzzled.

'That's odd. This chap has nothing on him either, the same as the man outside. Now I can understand one man being clean, but not two, in such circumstances,' he said.

'What about the other man?' Albert asked. Norman opened his jacket pocket, found his wallet and stood up. He handed it to the guard.

'We now have three dead bodies and I would suggest two of them are connected. This third man, looking at this carriage, with his suitcase on the rack, is probably an ordinary passenger. I suggest you cover these bodies and then clear the carriage of people, moving this half to carriage C and the front half into carriage A. That way no one has to step over the bodies. Then lock both doors until the police arrive. I'll leave you to it and see you at the guard's van. I need to get on with releasing the brakes.'

It was almost an hour later before he reached the rear guard's van where Simon was already sitting, drinking tea. As he looked out of the window, he saw police walking across the fields from the direction of the nearby village. When they arrived, Norman and his crew had a tale to tell.

CHAPTER 39

Mark Wicks stood in a small office in the main police station in York, briefing his colonel on his visit to Marshall Hall and confirmed the death of General Davis. He also reported that he had found Thomas dead in a car park at York railway station. The colonel had not responded to this information and Wicks had not expected him to. He knew him too well. But the colonel's reply, when it came, was unexpected.

He advised that there had been a major incident on a York to London train in the early hours of the morning. He told Wicks to check it out as a matter of urgency as there were reports of three dead men on board. He was to tread carefully as soon the place would be swarming with police, and he should head straight to a village called Hambleton, near Selby. His instructions clear, Wicks jumped back into the car to head south.

When he arrived in the village just thirty-five minutes later, he saw a line of four police cars parked in the main street with a white ambulance opposite. A lone police officer was leaning against the door of one of the cars, smoking a cigarette, his helmet on the roof of the vehicle. As Mark drove up, he slowed and drew up next to him, winding down the window.

Outside the village shop, a small crowd were watching as the young copper suddenly stamped out his cigarette and hurriedly put his helmet back on.

'Eh up, bigwig's arrived,' said the shopkeeper. 'Looks like he just gave him a rollicking.'

Mark drove slowly up the street, and stopped some fifty feet past them. He had wanted a quiet arrival and was just asking the young policeman how to get to the train when he panicked at being caught smoking by a senior officer and jumped to replace his helmet. Mark didn't think it did him any harm and he obtained the information he needed.

He pulled his false identity card from his pocket and climbed out, walking back up the pavement to join the villagers, presenting his false credentials to all present.

'Good morning, I wonder if you might help me with my enquiries,' he said, pulling out his notebook. 'I am interested in anyone that might have got off the train this morning. Did anybody see anything?'

The old man at the back suddenly coughed and then spat onto the pavement.

'Yes, we did. Not sure them from the train though. A young soldier and his sister came into the village, heading to London. Said they got dropped off on the wrong road,' he said, coughing again.

'To London you say? What did the soldier look like? Was he in uniform?'

The old man decided to stand up and greet the police officer and waddled over the few steps to where he stood.

'No, not in uniform, just in normal clothes, with a dark jacket, but he was tall and had his rifle with him. Oh, and he had a limp. Said he got shot in France and was on leave.'

Mark had made a definite breakthrough. 'So, how long ago was this and do you know where they went?'

'Yes, Jenny's husband took them to Selby in his van to catch a train to Doncaster. Full of spuds it was.'

'What time?' Mark snapped.

'Oh, about an hour or so, hour and a half maybe.'

Mark had had enough. He was a long way behind them and as he replaced his notebook, he thanked them all and went back to his car.

He was closing in fast but realised they would probably be well on their way to London by now. He must call the colonel urgently so they could be intercepted upon their arrival. He hoped he would be in time.

CHAPTER 40

Ed and Ricky were standing at the far end of the station, under the footbridge, watching through the gaps in the steps. No one seemed remotely interested in what they were doing which enabled them both to relax a little. They still had twenty minutes to wait. Ed told her friend to sit down on a platform trolley and she would attend to his leg.

He released his belt and eased his trousers to half-mast allowing her to remove the old shirt dressing she had put on outside Hambleton. She noted both wounds were still seeping blood, which she thought a good sign, and realised the wash in the stream outside the village must have kept it clean. She quickly applied new pad dressings on both sides before wrapping his leg in a clean, dry bandage. After just a few minutes all was done and, while Ricky moved back to their previous position, Ed walked over towards a kiosk to dispose of the old shirt sleeves in a dustbin. Ricky saw her buying two teas and when she returned a paper bag smelling of hot food was sticking out from her pocket. She offered him a mug of tea then pulled out two meat pies.

'Thought you might be hungry,' she said, biting into the pastry.

'You, my friend, are a mind reader,' he said, reaching forward.

Some fifteen minutes later a great plume of grey smoke loomed in the distance. When the train finally came to a halt, dozens of people rushed to the doors, passing those leaving the train. They stood waiting. Once they were satisfied there was no threat they would climb aboard. If it all went bad, they were ready to run.

Just as the conductor started waving his green flag, Ed nodded to Ricky, and as the whistle blew, they ambled across, opened the first door they came to and stepped aboard.

They waited in the corridor until the train was underway, the door handle clenched in Ed's hand, ready to jump from the train if they had to. Soon the countryside was passing by so fast this means of escape was impossible. Ricky poked his head around the corner into the carriage and saw the first compartment was empty. He nodded sideways to Ed then walked further along the corridor, checking each compartment. Ed stepped onto the seat, placing the rifle case on the rack above before taking a seat by the window. Ricky, forever vigilant, sat by the open door, facing to the rear, allowing him reasonable vision along the corridor.

***

At the station, Mark Wicks swung his car into the station forecourt, knowing he was now close. He had driven hard from Hambleton and hoped he was in time. Running from the vehicle, he went straight to the ticket kiosk to ask for the train times to London. He was informed they were only two more that day and one had left ten minutes ago. He now knew he had no chance of finding the men who had killed his friends. It was time to make one last call to the colonel.

CHAPTER 41

Ian Anderson hung up the phone, before calling the brigadier's secretary.

'Jane, is he free?' he asked.

'You are in luck, sir; he has just come back in. I'll tell him you are on your way.'

Ian jumped up and hurried along the corridor to the stairwell. He started running up two steps at a time before his fitness let him down and his legs could only manage a steady walk. He staggered into the brigadier's outer office, quite out of breath.

'You can go in, Colonel,' Jane said. He strode across the office, trying to hide his laboured breathing, and knocked on the door, walking straight in. He pulled the door closed behind him.

'I can confirm Davis is dead,' he stated.

The brigadier looked up and smiled. 'What about the chaps?' he asked.

'That's the difficult bit. It would seem Thomas was killed by a single bullet to the head in a car park in York. Butler is yet to be accounted for. However, Wicks thinks he may be one of the three men found dead on the train near Selby. He tracked the assailants to a London-bound train from Doncaster where he lost them.'

Cotton was making notes and then looked up. 'Bullet to the head? Sounds like someone who knew what they were doing. Anything else?'

'Yes, it appears the man Wicks is chasing is likely to be a soldier as the man who fled the scene of the train murders was carrying a rifle. He also had a limp, suggesting he might have been shot, but curiously he was with a young woman. So, we are not sure whether she is part of this or just an unlucky bystander.'

Brigadier Cotton, a man well known for his direct approach to all things SIS, was on to it straight away.

'Firstly, we need to take action on Davis's murder. I will call the chief constable in Yorkshire to stress the line he must take. It is imperative the words murder or killed are not used in any context. Next, I assume Thomas's body had not been claimed yet. Can you chase that, Ian? No doubt by now he's in a mortuary somewhere. So, usual routine, locate, identify and return to base. Once you have found his body, send someone up to fetch him. Don't want the locals involved. Regarding Butler, we can assume if he was alive, he would have made contact by now. It sounds like Wicks has made good progress in such a short space of time. Can he assist us further?'

'I have asked him to sit tight and call me in an hour for further orders. The trains from Doncaster arrive into Euston. I suggest we send a welcoming party to meet them. They won't be expecting that. Do you want them arrested or taken care of?'

The brigadier stared at Ian and smiled.

'I think you are forgetting something, old man. No loose ends.'

Ian left the office, clear on his orders, and as he passed his aide's office, he called Hastings in.

'Shut the door.'

Hastings took a seat and opened up his daybook.

'Right, a great deal has happened in a short space of time. Sadly, though, we have lost Thomas at York railway station and we think Butler on a train near Selby. The police are all over it, but I need you to make the necessary calls to locate them both and arrange for their bodies to be brought back to London. Wicks will be calling in just over half an hour so get him to clear this up and arrange for these boys to come back home. Secondly, who do we have available at present for a London job?'

Hastings pondered his question.

'Well, we do have Main and Willets. Both men were stood down last week after the Embassy finished with them. Shall I get them in?'

Ian thought for a moment, knowing he had both a giant of a man in Main and a slight but skilful operator in Willets. He also remembered that Thomas and Willets had worked together many times which would give Willets an added incentive.

'Yes, get them in immediately. The train will be arriving at Euston station in an hour or so. Brief them fully on everything we know about this man, including the rifle case, the limp and the girl he seems to be with. Make special comment regarding the death of Dave Thomas as that should stir them up. Can I leave it with you?' he asked, already opening a box file.

'Yes, sir, of course,' Hastings said, standing.

'Oh, and make sure they take care of them. This has gone on quite long enough.'

CHAPTER 42

'What will you do now, Ed?' Ricky asked.

'Well, I will make sure you get away first and then catch the next train to Moreton. I must send Frank a telegram when we get to London as he must be worried sick.'

Ricky smiled at her, remembering when he had first met her in a field tent a mile from the front line. She was probably the most amazing person he had ever met, having not only managed to hide her sex from thousands of troops for over a year but then becoming the best sniper in her squadron. She had taken many German lives, and when she was finally rescued from certain death, rather than go home to a happy life, she had sought to avenge her brother. She had killed the very man who had signed the death warrant, but instead of heading back home, she had then turned around and helped her old comrades to escape, killing an agent who was out to get them. If she were a man, she would be receiving the highest honour.

'So, what is it with you and Frank and how did he manage to avoid going back to the front line?'

Ed looked at her old friend and wondered how much she should tell him.

'Well, Frank was adopted by Lord Hardcastle and he will one day inherit the estate in Gloucestershire. He and I have grown close and we will have to see what happens, I suppose. I am staying on the estate at the moment but will have to go home to visit my own farm soon. Not sure really after that,' she said, keeping her future private.

Ricky sensed she was being coy and turned to gaze out of the window instead.

The train was now rattling along at great speed, creating that typically settled feeling that drives people to sleep. Even though

Ed was absolutely exhausted, she needed to stay fully alert; both of them did, just in case they were confronted when they least expected it. She looked at Ricky, realising she knew very little about him and wondered why he had decided to come north to avenge her execution.

'I haven't thanked you for joining the boss and Dave to kill General Davis. It was a brave thing to do, Ricky, putting yourself at great risk.'

He smiled at her then looked out of the window, thinking of his mate lying dead on the train.

'We all followed your trial as best we could, from the reports we received from the sergeant major and, to be honest, it was just ridiculous and did great harm to the men in the company. I still can't believe a senior officer would do that, especially after what you did for the war effort. I remember the day we first met, Ed, at the briefing when the major handed out some cakes. You made a big impression on me that day. So, when Lieutenant Cavanagh specifically asked me to go with him, I didn't hesitate.'

Ed fully understood loyalty, and this was of the highest order.

'I am just sorry you lost your brother. What was he like?'

Ed sighed noisily.

'Edward was a complicated person who never really got over the loss of our parents. He hated working the farm and my dad kind of cast him aside, favouring me, cos I could keep up with all the hard graft. We, that's my dad and me, became very close and I used his example to develop my own work ethic and to form my own beliefs. I suppose I was the son he never really had! When my brother's papers came to join up, Edward completely lost it. I just knew it was my opportunity to at last compete with men, which I had wanted to do most of my life. So, for him to give up his life for me was beyond anything I thought he was capable of and I will miss him terribly.'

Ricky noticed her voice drop as she turned to stare from the window. For several minutes she sat in deep thought and Ricky decided to let it go.

'Where are you meeting the lieutenant?' Ed suddenly asked.

Ricky stood up, realising he was starting to doze off, and as he opened the narrow sliding window, they pulled into Nottingham station. He shrugged as he dropped back to his seat.

'I can't remember exactly, but I do know it's at Folkestone harbour. The trouble is, we are due back today, so unless we get back early tomorrow, we will all be in the shit. Being AWOL, as you well know, is a wholly unhealthy business.'

Ed grimaced as she knew from experience that when the MPs got hold of you, life got difficult.

'If all goes well, you should easily be in Folkestone sometime tonight, Ricky. Maybe you can catch a boat then?'

He looked down at his watch and nodded. 'Yes, I suppose that's possible,' he said, as his eyes fluttered. Then, without warning, he fell asleep.

Ed was about to speak but smiled instead.

At just after eleven fifteen, the train, having stopped many times en route, started to slow, passing long lines of terraced houses with narrow alleyways and washing lines with grey clothing hanging in every rear yard. Ed kicked Ricky's foot to wake him. He spluttered as he sprang upright, confused about where he was. Ed stood up and peered out of the window, stretching her arms. She had no baggage, just what she stood up in, and about ten shillings in her pocket. Ricky reached up to retrieve the rifles and they left the carriage. His leg had stiffened and he walked with difficulty as they headed along the platform towards the exit. It had been a hectic time and they were both glad to be back in London. As they reached the ticket area, Ed suggested they grabbed a quick bite to eat.

'Yes, what do you fancy?' Ricky said with a grin, and they headed over to a sandwich kiosk and tea shacks on the opposite side of the station.

'Look, you order for me. I just want to check my train time and send Frank a telegram. Be back in a minute.' She shot off, visiting the ticket office first.

'You will need to catch the Hereford train, miss. Just one this afternoon departing at twelve eighteen. Stops at Watford junction,

Aylesbury, Oxford, Charlbury and gets into Moreton-in-Marsh at one fifty-eight,' said the chap behind the counter. She then went around to the telegram office, taking a blank form from the rack. She sat down and started writing.

Frank
All is well, now back in London.
Arrive Moreton at one fifty-eight, today.
Perhaps you would like to collect me? Edwina x

After paying the telegram clerk she walked back across the station, feeling in a fine mood and smiling to herself as she felt closer to Frank at every step. As she approached the kiosk, she looked across to where she had left Ricky and saw two men standing next to him at the table. Although he looked calm, a large-framed man with his government-issue coat and hat was leaning forward, his face just inches from Ricky's. Another man, of much slighter build, stood over them both, looking around, but then he clocked her.

She turned quickly and started walking away, heading across the concourse, unsure what she should do next. She looked over her shoulder and saw he was heading her way. Just ahead, two elderly nuns were walking towards her, chatting to each other. In an instant, she went across but waited until they were just past her, before she spoke, making them turn around, their backs now facing the unknown man. She started babbling at first not being very coherent, but this chance encounter enabled her to gather her thoughts and look over their shoulders, to monitor what was happening with Ricky. The man had veered off when he saw her talking to the nuns and was now looking across at her from a newspaper stand. She now knew he had a definite interest in her, but she couldn't fathom out how they knew to find them at Euston station. Had they been followed all this time? It would be pretty bad luck to be compromised at the final hour. She had to think, and quickly.

CHAPTER 43

Corn had reached the outskirts of London early in the afternoon. During his journey, he had wondered if it might be possible to meet Ricky and Ed from the train, but his timing was all out, and with so many stations and routes he realised he had better stick with his plan and meet Ricky in Folkestone.

He decided to visit a small eatery he used to frequent when at the Royal Military Academy, Sandhurst, before the war. It was a little-known Italian restaurant called Nico's, set in a courtyard in Kingston-upon-Thames. He had remembered it was near the river, behind Turks Pier, and he searched the streets for a while before he found it and pulled up outside. As he turned the engine off, he stretched, realising he had been driving for over four hours. He was about to go in when he heard a newspaper seller shouting just up the street and walked over to buy an early afternoon copy of the *London Evening News*. He wandered back with the paper tucked under his arm and went into the restaurant, where he was escorted to a seat by the window.

He ordered a glass of Italian wine and a jug of water before he sat down, and only then removed his coat and helmet. The waiter placed a single-page menu on the table, but he knew what he was looking for. It was in this very place, in 1914, he had been introduced to linguini. He scanned down the page, finding it at the very bottom of the selections. Decision made, he looked out of the window, knowing this was his last chance to enjoy some free time, and to relax, as by this time tomorrow he would be ankle-deep in mud.

He sat pondering how to tackle the Gibbs issue, knowing that his body may never be identified. He would have to brief Miller about dealing with it during their journey back on the boat. But, for now, he sat back, first gazing at the young ladies passing by, then scanning the headlines of his newspaper reporting the terribly wet conditions in France. He read that all military progress had been halted and conditions were extremely bleak. The articles also reported terrible injuries from "trench foot" and that the medical posts were full of injured men with feet that just didn't function.

As he turned the pages, a headline suddenly jumped out at him:

"RETIRED GENERAL SHOT"

He scanned the story with a sense of urgency, his heart pounding as he read the portrayal of a so-called "war hero", a retired lieutenant general, who had been struck down in a shooting accident on his private estate in Yorkshire. He had never considered the general's death might be reported in the newspapers. But a shooting accident? Why would the police lie?

He read on quickly, but the article offered few details. It was then he realised that the report of the death as an accident must be something to do with the agents who were chasing them in York. But why? Was it to save their own skins or the skins of the men who ran the secret government service? Either way, he realised it served to clear them all of any involvement and any possible charge of murder. They, or rather Ed, had got away scot-free!

He looked around again like a guilty schoolboy and sipped his wine, smiling to himself. He wished the boys were with him.

In celebration and remorse, he raised his glass and under his breath toasted their success and Dave Gibbs. As he finished, the waiter arrived and placed a large bowl of linguini in front of him. He didn't look up as he had tears in his eyes, just thanked him quietly.

Twenty minutes later, he left the restaurant, wondering where Ricky and Ed might be now. He presumed they were somewhere in London but decided he had to stop worrying.

He paid the bill and walked across to the Norton, firing her up for one last journey. He planned to head to his family home to make another surprise visit, hoping his dear mother would forgive him.

CHAPTER 44

Ricky sat back in his seat, the gruff face of the agent hovering above him. He kicked back his chair a few inches, allowing him some room to manoeuvre if he needed to make a bolt for it. His mind was racing as he watched this brute of a man before him, but he felt at ease knowing he still had his Webley pistol inside his coat pocket. Following the second man's sudden disappearance he realised that Ed must have appeared. He turned his head and saw her between two nuns, chatting, across the concourse. Clever, he thought, they won't touch her now. But where was the other agent?

'There's nothing that concerns you over there. Your troubles are here, soldier boy, so let's go through it again,' said the man as he sat back down. 'I know who you are, and what you have done, so this I'm afraid is the end for you, old chap. You will never see the trenches of France again!'

Ricky didn't flinch but swallowed nervously as he realised this time he was in deep trouble. He started considering every option, but nothing was obvious. If he was able to reach the trench knife he'd been given by Ed earlier that day, he might be able to take the man by surprise from under the table. If he decided to shoot him, in cold blood, would he get away? Probably not, and if caught he would more than likely be charged with murder and be hanging from a noose in double quick time. No, he had to somehow create a diversion that might just offer him a route out of here. He would now have to let Ed fend for herself, which he knew, of course, she was very capable of doing. He could always try and talk his way out of this situation. Maybe he could convince this chap he was not the man he thought he was. It was worth a try.

'Look, I don't know who you are or what you think I have done, but I am Lieutenant Chapel and I'm returning from leave to re-join my regiment. I have ridden down from home on my brother's motorcycle and have just arrived to catch my train to Kent. I am due back tomorrow, so any hold-ups now will cause me a great deal of bother.'

Main screwed up his face, more than a little suspicious of the man's tale. Then he realised it was all bollocks and pulled his chair in a little closer to the table.

'Look, I don't really care what your name is because I have been reliably informed that you were seen in a small village in Yorkshire earlier today, carrying that rifle case,' he said pointing to the case hanging on Ricky's chair. 'You were also travelling with a young woman and were seen coming from a train where three men were killed. Now, don't insult my intelligence by offering a lame excuse about why you are here. I know you are a soldier, you told some villagers, or have you forgotten that? No, soldier boy, your war is over, as is your life, and not because you killed three men on a train, but because you killed one of my friends.'

Ricky's heart sank. How could he possibly know he had spoken about the army in the village in Yorkshire? He now realised he would somehow have to take this man on. He smiled at him, trying to put him off guard, and then had an idea. His father always told him that the bigger they are, the harder they fall, a theory he was about to test.

He knew he would not be assassinated in front of all these people, but would, at some stage, be escorted away to somewhere quiet and out of the way before perhaps being dumped in the River Thames. Was the agent now waiting for his mate to return, or would he risk walking him out alone? What if he just refused to leave, what then?

The man sat back, looking at him with a smug grin, not giving his intentions away. Ricky realised that while he was sitting in a public place, he was probably safe. He took the opportunity to peer across the crowded station at Ed, who was now walking obliquely across in front of him with the two nuns, heading, he thought, towards a platform. She was clearly thinking on her feet, but just twenty feet behind her the other agent was stalking her. She didn't look at him, but he knew she would be fully aware of the situation and was not only trying to get away herself but, in doing so, was also keeping the other agent busy. This allowed him a better chance to escape. He then lost sight of her as they got swallowed up in the crowd. He now focussed on his own dilemma, realising Ed's tactic had, by accident, created a better chance for both of them. He suddenly knew what he was going to do.

***

Across the concourse, Ed was chatting to the nuns who were heading over to platform 9 to catch a train to Southampton. One of them was elderly and walked with a stick. Ed offered to carry her suitcase which not only made her a saint for a few minutes but also allowed for certain possibilities. She wasn't proud of her plan, but her life was now in danger and, although she was about to commit a sin, she was sure the nuns would rather see her live than be shot like a dog on the tracks.

When they got to the train, she helped them find a compartment and dropped the suitcase in the corridor while she pulled back the sliding door. She helped the older nun to sit down, enabling her to look out through the window where she saw a familiar face. As she left the compartment, she overheard the sister say to her companion, 'What a lovely boy'. She smiled. If only she knew.

Ed saw the agent looking at her through the window from some twenty feet away and realised she couldn't leave the train the way she had entered. From the corridor, she peered through the window and noticed there was just one set of tracks between her and the other platform. She had no choice.

She picked up the nun's case and grabbed the handle of the carriage door on the side away from the platform. With one twist the door swung open and she dropped down onto the track. Stepping over the rails, she climbed up onto the other platform, unseen by her pursuer, and walked calmly towards the ticket barrier. With no train at the platform, the gate was empty and she stepped under the low barrier, heading over to the ladies' toilets. She didn't wish to look back, so was unsure if she had been spotted. She went straight into a cubicle, locked the door and sat down. She waited for any sounds of someone following her but heard nothing.

She sprang the locks on the suitcase and, with a silent prayer, opened it to find a nun's habit, neatly folded, with a veil and a belt. She took it from the case, quickly pulling it on, and wrapped the veil around her head before tying the belt around her waist. She placed her jumper in the case and left the toilet, watching carefully for the agent, before walking slowly across towards platform 7. She looked up at the station clock and saw she now had just four minutes to catch her train. As she crossed the concourse, she saw the table where Ricky had been sitting, tipped over on its side, with a chair lying on its back. Ricky and the agent were gone.

***

Willets had stood back, opposite the train door, waiting for her to come back onto the platform, when it dawned on him that she would not play his game. He stepped to his right to gaze through the carriage window and saw her climb up onto the adjacent platform. He couldn't see her face, but whomever it was, they still carried the small leather suitcase.

He rushed back along the platform towards the small barrier, but it was blocked by several passengers. He shouted but everyone seemed to freeze, and he struggled for a moment to get through. On the other side, he looked left and saw her running through the crowd towards the main concourse. Willets followed, trying to keep his eye on her as she weaved through the morning rush of people. He could see her head and then she would disappear for just a moment before he caught another glimpse. He closed in but then realised she was heading to the ladies' lavatories and she quickly disappeared. He had no option but to stop and wait by the entrance. He stepped away to lean against a wall, under an advertising board. She had to come back to the concourse at some point, and he would have her.

After a few minutes, he was becoming impatient, wondering if there was another exit, but then a group of women came up the steps together. Close behind them walked a nun carrying a small brown suitcase. His curiosity was aroused and he studied her through the crowd as she walked away to his right. Then she made her mistake; she turned her head. It was his target.

Keeping his distance, he carefully followed her over to platform 7 where she boarded the train. Now he had her.

CHAPTER 45

Ricky seized his opportunity.

As the agent turned his head, seeking his colleague's location, he suddenly thrust all his weight against the edge of the table and pushed it back against the agent's body, knocking him over onto the concrete floor. His head hit the hard surface and he was momentarily dazed. A lady with a young child at the next table pulled her daughter to her bosom before standing and walking away. A chap behind his newspaper dropped his hands briefly and gazed across, but seemed unruffled and turned his eyes back to the stories of the day.

With the table now tipped on its side, Ricky reached into his coat pocket and withdrew his knife, aware of the many eyes upon him. He needed to act fast.

Stepping across his foe, he grabbed his collar, pulling him up into the sitting position, and crouched down, placing his knife, partially hidden from view, across the man's throat. He deliberately nicked his skin in the process, so that he knew Ricky meant business. Against his right thigh, under the agent's coat, Ricky could feel a weapon pressing into his leg, and reached inside the coat to retrieve it, tucking it into his trousers. Watching the man carefully, he ran his hand across the rest of his body, searching for other weapons, the knife remaining tight against his Adam's apple. With their faces only inches apart, Ricky had full control.

'Now, you have two options,' he said. 'You can make your move, in which case it will be the last thing you ever do, or you can live to fight another day. What will it be?' he said calmly.

The agent, now fully alert, looked at Ricky, knowing he was beaten.

'You and I are both professionals, and on this occasion, you have me. But never stop looking over your shoulder as I will track you down, I promise you that.'

Ricky smiled at him in an attempt to ridicule his statement, before pulling the knife very slightly. A trickle of blood followed the blade across the agent's neck. He winced.

'Stand up,' Ricky said into his ear, pulling on his arm. The man rocked forward and got to his feet as Ricky reached around his body and grabbed a handful of his coat under his left arm, pulling him in tight.

'Come on, mate,' he shouted loudly. 'Let's get you home,' as if the man were drunk.

Ricky tucked the knife across his own midriff and pushed it gently into the agent's side, just enough for him to feel the point against his skin. He nudged him forward.

'If you shout, try to run or reach for me, I will push this ten-inch blade up into your chest. I kill for a living, so don't think for one minute I won't kill you.'

As he spoke, Ricky quickly slung the rifle case over his shoulder then gripped his coat again before moving off towards the exit. Behind them, a waiter appeared, picked up the table and chair and wiped the table top as if nothing had happened.

When they were halfway down the exit stairs, Ricky saw a narrow alleyway off to the right, with steep steps downwards. He steered down them, and as they neared the bottom, he tucked the knife into his coat and grabbed his Webley. As the agent reached the last step, Ricky crashed the pistol grip down hard onto the back of his head. The agent went down like an ox, hitting the ground hard. Ricky quickly removed the man's shoes and took his notebook from his inside pocket before climbing back up the stairs, dropping the footwear into a dustbin at the top.

As he came within sight of the train information board, he desperately sought the time of the next train to leave the station. He didn't care where it went, he just needed to get some distance between him and London.

'Platform 7, Hereford,' he said under his breath and checked the clock, seeing he had just two minutes to board. He searched for directions before running with all his might, dodging passengers at almost every step, narrowly avoiding crashing into a flower seller who was pushing his trolley through the crowd. Finally, he saw the platform number high above the ground, just fifty yards ahead. He had seconds to reach it and shouted as he approached the barrier.

'Coming through,' he yelled to the ticket collector, who stepped aside as he rushed past. He was only twenty yards away when the train started to move.

He ran faster, heading towards the guard's van, where the door was open and an astonished guard, his green flag still in his hand, stood in the doorway, pulling on a cigarette. Ricky, now focussed on a carriage door just ten feet away, ran harder, finally coming up alongside the door. He yanked at the handle, flinging it open and, hanging onto the door rim, he steadied himself before lunging across the gap, landing in the corridor, the platform sweeping away behind him. As he closed the door, he breathed a sigh of relief and turned around to see the ticket collector staring down at him.

'Ticket please, sir,' he said.

***

After spending a few hours with his family, Corn changed back into his officer's uniform and his brother drove him down to Folkestone. He dropped him just before ten in the evening amongst hundreds of soldiers who were milling about, awaiting approval to board their ship back to France. His nervousness surprised him; he couldn't settle following Dave Gibbs' death and Miller's absence. As each man passed him, he studied his features, hoping to see a face he recognised.

He went to the transit office, seeking the times for all the boats sailing that night, and was advised by a rather obnoxious corporal that they departed at ten minutes past each alternate hour from twenty-one ten to zero five ten each night. He stood for a moment, before giving him a suitable bollocking for his rather bullish outburst at an officer. The man pulled himself upright, aware he had overstepped the mark, and stood abashed, with his feet together.

Corn walked over towards the embarkation point, feeling it was a stark reminder to him to snap back into being a British officer. He must cut the familiarity with the men that he had got so used to.

As he reached the gate, he continued to study the hundreds of soldiers who passed him, but Miller wasn't amongst them.

When the gangway was raised, he turned and walked back over to the kiosk, as a light rain started to fall. He looked at his watch and calculated the timings from York to London by train and realised something was clearly amiss. He felt more pangs of guilt at leaving his men fighting for their lives. He decided he would wait another two hours until the zero one ten sailing, and if he didn't appear then, he would board without him. With luck and a good sea, he should be back at HQ for an army breakfast.

CHAPTER 46

Even though Ed was confident she was finally clear of the SIS agents, she chose to sit in the buffet car in the middle of the train amongst other passengers. She had retained her disguise, even though she knew it was sacrilege to have stolen the suitcase from a lady of the church. At the time, her freedom and survival were the most important things and she dearly wanted her life back.

She felt relaxed for the first time in over a week as she watched the countryside go by and slowly the stations fell away, the train passing through Oxford just on the hour. She thought of Frank, who would soon be heading to Moreton to meet her, and she longed for their reunion.

The life that awaited her after her remarkable year in France was going to be extraordinary, especially living at Hardcastle Hall. It was a magnificent home and, if the feelings that simmered within her were honest and true, she might one day be the lady of the estate. She had done enough killing and wanted peace and normality. Nothing could surely get in the way of that now.

The train hurtled along at speed, the carriage rocking, the wheels clattering on tracks beneath her feet. She closed her eyes, catching a few minutes' sleep, before waking to see green fields full of crops as the train pulled into Charlbury. Just thirty minutes to go.

Her mind drifted back to her life in the trenches, her trial and then the miraculous escape, before heading north to kill the general. The mayhem that had followed since she pulled the trigger was quite unexpected and meeting the boys was more than a surprise. Then the killings continued, through the streets of York and at the railway station before Dave copped it on the train. With another agent killed and a passenger, the death toll had risen to seven. All because a man wouldn't let go and had murdered her brother!

If she had been left alone to kill Davis, she would be back in Gloucestershire by now, back with her beloved Frank. But then she had a thought: why were SIS agents in Yorkshire anyway? Were they sent to kill Davis too, or to protect him? If death was their mission, that meant the British Government had sanctioned his assassination!

She tried to fathom out how the agents in London had got wind of their arrival at Euston station. With the killing of the two agents in the north, how would the SIS know where they were? How did they know what they looked like? Her head couldn't grasp this fine detail, and with the gentle rhythm of the train, she closed her eyes, momentarily, thinking that other agents must have been on their tail all along.

A sudden jolt shook the carriage, and as she lifted her head her eyes landed on the face of a man entering the buffet car at the far end. He looked straight at her. She didn't react, but her heart started pounding. The agent who had followed her in the station was now just forty feet away.

Ed gathered her thoughts, knowing that for the moment, he wouldn't attack her, not in such a public place. But she realised the killing wasn't yet over.

She reached down between her knees for the small suitcase and stood up, heading towards the door. In the reflection in the window, she saw the agent move forward and, just as she was about to open the door, she saw a face appear in the window. It was Ricky Miller. He grinned at her, holding his finger to his lips. She was staggered. How had he ended up on the train? The last time she saw him, he was under the cosh, in difficulties with the large SIS man, back at the station. Then a voice shook her back to reality.

'Let me help you, sister,' said a middle-aged man. Edwina thanked him before she stepped through the open door. Willets waited just long enough for the door to close before he moved to follow her, but as he approached, the same man stood up in the aisle, reaching up to the overhead rack to grab his tatty brown suitcase. This delayed him momentarily, but then he stepped into the semi-darkness of the corridor connector, where the steel footplates rattled noisily beneath his feet. As he stepped around the corner, she was gone.

Ed tried hard to keep up with Ricky who practically ran through each carriage towards the rear of the train. When finally the connecting door opened into the guard's van, he spun round to meet her.

'This is where we finish it, Ed,' he said, gripping her by the shoulders.

She, too, knew it had to end.

'But what are you doing here and how did you know he was on the train?' she asked.

'I didn't. I had to find a quick exit and this was the first train to depart. Then I saw him in a compartment and realised you must be on board too. As I was about to enter the buffet carriage, your face loomed up in front of me. But look, we have no time now, he will be on us any second.'

Ed was a little confused, but he was right.

'You hide in the lav, with the door slightly ajar, and I will go into the area between the carriages. He won't see me coming from there.'

Ed gripped his arm, momentarily.

'You should be able to see everything from here if you hold the door open slightly. When an opportunity appears, you can step out, and we finish him.'

Once again, Ed found herself in a toilet, the door pulled against her foot, her pistol ready.

Ricky quickly opened the sash window in the connecting door at the end of the carriage, creating a strong draught to confuse his opponent. He went through the door, shut it and crouched down in readiness in the area between the carriages. He didn't have long to wait.

Willets, who had slowly worked his way through the train, checking every compartment, was worried his quarry might somehow slip from his grasp. He knew the carriages would end soon and was ready to kill her or throw her from the train, whatever was necessary.

As he came to the end of yet another carriage with no sign of her, the wind from an open window whistled around his head. He reached for the handle and pulled the door back slowly, just as the train entered a tunnel. The noise increased five-fold and it disorientated him. He paused, just for a second or two, waiting for his eyes to adjust and for the light to return. That was his mistake.

Ricky, taking full advantage, sprang from his crouched position just a few feet away, lunging upwards with all his strength, catching the man heavily in the chest, taking him backwards through the partly open doorway. They hit the carriage wall six feet away with an almighty thump. Willets had no idea what had hit him. His body hurt immensely and he had spasms of pain across his head and shoulders as he fell to the floor. He knew he would be in trouble if he didn't react, and from somewhere deep within he gathered the strength to push his assailant off him and try to get to his feet. Ricky rolled away. In the darkness, he sensed the agent's position and thrust forward, hitting him in the side of his body, sending him to the floor once again. This time, the agent clung to his attacker, and with clenched fists, was hitting out hard.

Ricky was taking a pounding, receiving several blows to his face, his nose suddenly exploding in blood with one direct punch. With a huge effort, he managed to pull away and stepped back before charging at Willets once more, crashing him against the carriage door.

Willets was amazed at the ferocity of the attack as he felt his ribs crack. The woman he had been following was clearly a formidable opponent and he dug in deep, determined to finish her, as more punches rained in. The noise from the tunnel through the open window spooked him, but as he spat blood, he regained his energy and knew this was a fight to the death.

Ricky continued to hit him with another volley of punches, sensing he had his man. But as he did so, Willets grabbed him by the cuff and then twisted him around, throwing him to the floor. Ricky lunged for him again and tried to get his hands around his throat, but the agent defended himself by forcing his knees up into Ricky's chest, stopping him thrusting his full weight downwards. The two men were fighting ghosts in the dark corridor as they struggled for supremacy.

Ed heard the thumping and opened the door of the toilet, but all she could see were two shadows fighting on the floor. She had no idea who was who. All she could hear were muffled voices and constant gasps, the sounds of men trying to kill each other with their bare hands. She watched helplessly from just feet away, as the crunch of fists on skin echoed through the corridor. For several minutes, they battered each other, yelling as punches landed, trying to end it.

Suddenly, Ricky yelled out, bringing Ed back to reality. She was ready to help her friend.

Ricky, battered by the powerful fists of his aggressor, had partially let go of him, just for a second and, with both feet kicked out at him, sending his body flying across the corridor. Ed shouted at Ricky, who yelled back.

'To your left,' he shouted, before trying to get back to his feet, knowing the agent was against the far side of the carriage. Willets suddenly realised there were two of them and all along he had been fighting a man! He knew he was now outnumbered and, in the darkness, drew his weapon. As Ricky recovered, he suddenly heard two shots in quick succession, but although he dived to the floor when he heard the first shot, he was too late and felt a bullet rip through the side of his buttock. Ed, now alerted to the agent's exact position, drove her body into him, then punched the side of his head and he fell down, his weapon falling to the floor. She dropped onto his prone body, trying to reach for his neck, but he twisted around and she found herself underneath him.

'Ed,' Ricky yelled, but she couldn't answer as Willets had her in a stranglehold. He assumed she was in trouble and dived in headlong towards the noise, hitting the agent with full force in his back.

Ed then yelled out as Willets let go and she wriggled free.

Ricky placed his foot on the door behind him to give him a lunge point for his next attack and thrust forward again, hitting the man in the chest, their bodies crashing into the wall across the corridor.

Willets, taking a beating from two people in quick succession, was now feeling overwhelmed, but knew he had to find some strength or he would die.

He responded by punching upwards several times, the second swing connecting with Ricky's chin, sending him sprawling backwards. Dazed, Ricky felt blood pouring from his nose and mouth, running down his throat forcing him to swallow it. He dug deep and turned again, grabbing the body of his assailant tightly and charging forward across the short passageway, forcing the air from Willets' lungs. He knew he was almost finished, but was not giving up, not after all he had been through. This was a fight to the death.

He sucked air into his lungs knowing he had to find the last of his strength from somewhere. Using every ounce of effort, Ricky pulled his arm around his assailant's neck trying to choke him from behind. Willets felt the pressure in his head start to grow and brought his arm up, inside Ricky's grip, dropping suddenly to the floor, breaking the lock. Ricky was forced to release him or have his arm broken, and panted for breath.

Somehow, Ricky found another surge of energy and pulling his trench knife from its scabbard he ran again at the agent, plunging the knife into his body. Willets yelled and ripped Ricky's hand away, the knife being flung across the corridor, blood now pouring from the agent's shoulder. Willets reached down for his own knife that was strapped to his shin but fell backwards slightly, putting him off balance. He scrambled back to his feet and thrust the knife forward several times, but the darkness denied him any contact. He yelled loudly, 'Go down, you bastard.'

Ricky smiled, knowing that was the cry of a dying man. He had got him. Running a few steps forward he hit Willets in the midriff once more, forcing the knife out of his hand. They both hit the far door with a mighty crash, and without warning the lock disintegrated, the door gave way, and the noise of the tunnel exploded around them. They both flew from the train into the cool air of the tunnel, hitting the side wall a foot or so away. At sixty miles an hour, they never stood a chance as they rebounded back towards the train, both still entwined, falling into the wheels of the train. Their legs crushed, their bodies dragged along at great speed, their yells of death going unheard.

As the train exited the tunnel just a few moments later, Ed was lying on her back, blood running down her face, panting. The door was stuck open with the force of the wind and she looked out through the doorway, the wind stinging her cheeks as she tasted the acrid smoke that billowed into the carriage. She peered back down the track, about to call out for Ricky, but then stopped. She knew he was gone.

Ed knew she had to accept the death of yet another friend. She slowly got to her feet and spat blood from her mouth. Exhausted, she leant against the side of the carriage, breathing rapidly, staring at the blood-stained floor and a discarded Webley. She momentarily had a terrible feeling of guilt that she was responsible for so many deaths. She had killed three people in the last twelve hours and in the last month had lost most of those closest to her: Edward, Dave Gibbs, and now Ricky Miller. And what of her lieutenant? She had no idea where he might be.

Ed kicked the gun out of the open door, followed by a knife. Then she saw the knife she had given to Ricky, with an engraving on the blade. It was the American trench knife, originally awarded to a Michael J Wiseman. She held it in her hands and was about to throw it from the train, but at the last minute decided to keep it.

She slid down to the floor and sat with her head in her hands and cried. Her battle to get even was finally over.

POSTSCRIPT

The Rolls Royce was sluggish on the corners; however, it did have a good turn of speed when at full tilt. Frank didn't spare the horses and arrived at Moreton-in-Marsh railway station fifteen minutes before the train was due. He was fidgety and pranced around, checking his watch before ordering a drink in the tea room on the platform. He sipped his tea, staring up the track, and then he heard the whistle. His heart pounded; it had been a long week without her. He stood up to see the train come around the bend and enter the station, the powerful engine gently slowing as it passed him. He watched each passenger walk down the platform towards him, but to his sadness, Edwina was not there. He sat back down with his head in his hands but then sensed someone standing next to him. He looked up to see Edwina smiling at him, but wearing a nun's habit. He jumped to his feet in utter shock, seeing blood on her face before throwing his arms around her. They walked arm in arm towards the car and they sat in the back seat. Frank offered her a small box.

Practically the first thing Edwina did when she arrived home was to arrange to post the nun's suitcase back to the address inside, with an apology, and plucking up some courage she asked Frank if she could have twenty pounds sterling for the Catholic Church.

Several weeks later, Lord Hardcastle received a letter from the War Office. It stated that due to a national security matter, it was necessary for Edwina to attend a meeting with Colonel Anderson from the SIS. Frank was particularly concerned and insisted that he and the family lawyer attend the meeting where certain details were revealed of 'the Marshall Hall incident', and the trail of death across Yorkshire. Edwina could only guess how Anderson had made the connection to her as he presented selected facts that only two people knew. Although at first, she thought she was to be arrested, he soon made it clear that he was aware of her military career, the incident at Marshall Hall and the deaths of his agents. He told her he wasn't there to arrest her; on the contrary, he wanted to offer her a job.

Edwina Mitchell, once a farmer, a soldier, a sniper and assassin, married her best friend in the spring of 1918. A hundred people attended the ceremony, including several British officers from the front line. The special guest was Captain Cornelius Cavanagh.

Over the years that followed, Edwina and Frank lived at Hardcastle Hall, raising four children. Throughout the 1920s she fulfilled her promise to the SIS but also became a force for women's rights. She was instrumental in promoting the Produce Guild, through which, with government funding, the Women's Institute encouraged people across Britain to produce more homegrown food, right up to and throughout the Second World War. She named her first son Edward and he joined the army and fought in that war. He returned home in 1945 as a captain and within a year he married a nurse called Hazel he had met during the war. On 3 August 1973, he became the thirteenth Lord Hardcastle when, sadly, Frank died. Edwina lived the rest of her life at the Hall, making sure fresh flowers adorned Frank's and her brother's graves under the oak tree every Sunday. She died peacefully in her bed at the age of eighty-eight. After she died, her son, Edward, found an empty .303 rifle cylinder in her bedside drawer.

***

Lieutenant Cavanagh returned to the front, and within weeks was promoted to captain. He survived the war and in 1920, bought land in Scotland, running shooting parties for the rich and powerful. He was never held responsible for the disappearance of Privates Gibbs and Miller, but he did ensure they received appropriate military funerals at the state's expense. He became a godfather in 1921 to Edward, the first son of Edwina and Frank Hardcastle.

***

The death of General Davis was reported as an unfortunate accident that occurred when he was cleaning his handgun. The Yorkshire police never publicly made any connection between the general's death and the deaths that occurred at York railway station or on the train near Selby. The coroner was ordered to pronounce the causes of death for the unknown men as misadventure. The following year, the Chief Constable of the Yorkshire Constabulary was offered retirement and honoured with a peerage for services to the British Government.

General Davis's last will and testament left his estate and possessions to his regimental association. They ran the estate as an officers' retreat for over twenty years. It was handed to the War Office in 1939 to be used as a rehabilitation centre throughout the Second World War. In 1949, it burnt down and was later flattened and the land used as a military training area.

Printed in Great Britain
by Amazon

66011761R00154